Deadfall

Deadfall

Crime Stories by New England Writers

Edited by

Kate Flora

Ruth McCarty

Susan Oleksiw

Level Best Books
Prides Crossing, Massachusetts 01965

Level Best Books
P.O. Box 161
Prides Crossing, Massachusetts 01965
www.levelbestbooks.com

text composition/design by Susan Oleksiw
Printed in the USA

ISBN 978-0-9700984-5-0

Library of Congress Catalog Card Data available.
First Edition
10 9 8 7 6 5 4 3 2 1

Deadfall

Contents

Introduction

As we look over the entries in our sixth anthology, the one consistent feature over the last years is the variety of voices and stories they tell. In case anyone should ask, the short story is alive and well in the world of crime fiction.

Robin Winks, the well-known historian and critic of crime fiction, was an eclectic reader but he once complained that the short-story format was too limited to allow the development that a crime story required—detectives remained ciphers and plots were abbreviated. Because of his stature, many writers—and readers, unfortunately—believed him, and focused strictly on the novel. Short-story fans know Winks was wrong. Readers offered a short-story collection are often surprised at the depth of character development and subtlety of plot found there.

The short story has its own charms—the opportunity to focus on a single incident and its effect on one or two characters, a woman recalling a close friend who has died, or on a single setting that then becomes as vital as the man walking on the ice through the cold. In this genre writers can explore ideas and characters new to them, take the kinds of risks less likely to be attractive in the longer genre of the novel. The short story is capable of an intensity of focus and emotion not available in the same way in a novel. The form draws and challenges many different kinds of writers, and brings its own distinct rewards. This collection underscores these truths.

Crime fiction has at its heart a vile deed and the kind of person who could do such a horrid thing, and we meet these villains in Woody Hanstein's "Rat," about a convict who has figured out a way to shorten his sentence, in "Bagging the Trophy," by Vaughn Hardacker, about letting a man's words convict him, and in Libby Mussman's "The Name Game," where we listen to a man working his way through his lifetime crime plan. Janice Law's "Therapy" takes us into the mind of a teenager who slowly reveals her true self.

On the other side are those faced with a crime and trying to counter it in some way, the ones who provide some counterbalance to the weight of evil. The father in Stephen Allan's "Some Things Can Never Be the Same" is memorable and sad, as is the young helper in "Susie Cue" by Steve Liskow. Stephen D. Rogers's "Tail" reminds us of how complicated fair play can be, and how hard it may be to achieve justice. The old woman in Kat Fast's "The List" takes control of her life, giving the reader great satisfaction. In John Clark's "Just Passing Through," a driver is kidnapped in an unforgettable encounter.

Several stories explore the concept of betrayal in its complexity and nuances. C. M. Falcone's "Justice" takes us into the hard life of a storekeeper and her husband. Joe Ricker's "Ice Shack" manages to provide as many surprises as a novel, right up to the end. "Circulation" by Pat Remick gives us a dark and cynical view inside the newspaper business. Leslie Wheeler's character in "Twenty-one Days" goes beyond the obvious betrayal to question her own motives in a disturbing assessment of the climax.

Despite its basic premises, crime fiction seems made for humor as well, and numerous stories in this collection play on the hapless, the inept, the cleverness of human behavior. Norma Burrows brings us to the brink in "Self Help," and A. J. Pompano's housewife finally gets her own back in "Promises to Keep." We cringe along with the cop in her disguise in J. E. Seymour's "Big Bash," and congratulate a con man in Mo Walsh's "Double Dare." Clea Simon keeps it light and plausible in "Dumb Beasts," and the police get a surprise in Kathleen Chencharik's "Shot by Mistake." Anyone who has ever lived in a small town, with its petty squabbles, will appreciate Mike Wiecek's "Vacationland."

We watch crimes being committed and wonder if they can be prevented in Judith Green's "Dark" and John Urban's "Courtesy Call."

Once again we are proud to publish the winner of the Al Blanchard Short Crime Fiction Award. Margaret Press provides another installment in the life of a single mother determined to make a better life for her son despite scheming, irresponsible relatives.

Crime fiction has been called formula fiction, but as we look over the variety of stories contained in this volume, it is hard to imagine a formula that defines them all. There is something here for every taste, and a few surprises for everyone.

Kate Flora
Ruth McCarty
Susan Oleksiw

Family Plot
Or, A Wolf in Sheep's Clothing

Margaret Press

FOR SALE: 4 burial plots side by side in Harmony Grove Cemetery, Salem, Mass. Asking $5200 each (valued at $5500).

Shortly before I discovered one cousin too many in the family, I happened to be cradling a cup of rewarmed coffee at my kitchen table, taking stock of my good deeds. I had recently buried both my grandfather and my brother. Before that I had spent countless hours by Granddad's side as he lay dying, and had run no end of errands for my useless, ungrateful brother. The world was a better place now that our overgrown, noxious family tree had sustained a bit of pruning. For which I like to take some credit.

Now I was executor of their estates. I was a single mom scratching out a life for myself and my seven-year-old son. Running out of heating oil in the middle of February, trying to find a job, and waiting for the estates to go through probate so I could finally afford to rent in a neighborhood with a little less crime. My neighbor's place had been broken into twice already. Apparently it was obvious to the rest of the world that I had nothing worth stealing. But I figured it was only a matter of time. My turn would surely come.

Meanwhile, I had devised this plan to rustle up a little cash to get us out of there. Although both my grandfather and brother's bank accounts were frozen, I had one marketable asset: four family plots in Harmony Grove Cemetery—very expensive plots.

Now when I say I buried my kin, I meant figuratively. Actually the chunky plastic boxes of their "cremains" were still in my kitchen holding up cookbooks. I intended to scatter them in the spring under a couple of rhododendrons in the back yard. I was sure they would have wanted to be together, and nearer to me, their only living relative. Well, probably not. But the rhododendrons would love the sweetened soil.

I had been a little mystified when I came across the deed to the burial plots among my grandfather's papers. He had never mentioned them to me. Perhaps Granddad had been a bit optimistic when he purchased them back in 1974. Thinking someday he'd be laid to rest in Harmony Grove beside his parents and his wife. With time a couple of his children would happily follow and keep them company. But my grandmother had been lost at sea. And as one after another of their offspring entered the sweet hereafter, none made it into the family plot. My own parents made sure their remains would be on the other side of town. In my family we have a bit of an aversion to each other.

So I composed an enticing ad and posted it on the Internet. Then I made a trip out to Harmony Grove, where I wrote down the family names on the neighboring headstones. I thought I could target those consumers most likely to be interested. My great-grandparents happened to be on one side—Joseph and Marietta Wolfe. In the same row on the right were two headstones belonging to distant relatives, Bertha and Frank Foley. Perhaps the Foley children would pay a good price for a chance to be together with their parents in the afterlife.

I looked up the only Foley on the North Shore I knew to be

a relative: Emma Foley, who was some sort of cousin of my dad's. As I said, we were never close with family. I had never so much as sent them a Christmas card. But now I stuffed a copy of my ad into an envelope addressed to dear cousin Emma with a cover letter describing the convenient proximity of these plots to her kin and saying I was notifying her personally because—family is everything.

I didn't bother looking for Wolfes. That was the psychopathic branch of my family tree. Genetically attached earlobes, detached consciences. My great-grandparents were probably the last two members who'd want to lie in the ground together.

Six days passed with no reply. I beefed up my ad:

> *FOR SALE: 4 burial plots side by side in the Perpetual Grace section of Harmony Grove Cemetery, Salem, Mass. Asking $5200 each (valued at $5500). Good neighbors, lovely shady area, quiet, near amenities. Great view of duck pond (from above ground). Seller to handle transfer fees.*

On the seventh day I got a response—not quite what I expected. "Cousin" Owen Foley showed up at my door on a chilly Friday night, just after I had tucked my son, Asa, into bed.

"Greetings! You must be Rhode! I'm Emma's son! Emma Wolfe Foley—she was your father's cousin!" His smile was broad and his face familiar. I recognized my ad in his hand. Cautiously—if you knew my family you'd understand—I invited him in.

"You sent this letter to Mother, who gave it to me. Your plots are next to my grandparents—Grandpa and Grandma Foley."

I led him into the kitchen and offered him a drink.

"Gosh, thanks! Sure, anything—as long as it's Scotch!"

I had a half bottle of a reasonably decent Scotch someone had left behind long ago. I poured him a shot and helped myself to a glass of red wine. Things were looking up, I dared to hope.

"By the way," I said over my shoulder, "did you lock your car? This is a really bad neighborhood."

He assured me he had. I joined him at my tiny kitchen table and studied him a moment. I didn't have a lot of experience with relatives. Owen had a soft, puffy body. But I could see some of Granddad in him—the shock of pale hair, the nondangly earlobes. Granddad's brother—Emma's father—clearly had passed on the same genes.

"So you think you'd be interested in buying them? It is a nice section, don't you agree? You've seen them?"

"Well, Rhode." He took a sip, then another. "I think my mother is considering it. But I'm actually here for a different reason. A related matter. No pun intended."

Disappointment crept in. I waited for him to continue. He sucked down some more of his Scotch as though the welcome mat would shortly be snatched away.

"I'm an amateur genealogist. My passion is family history. I even took early retirement last year to devote more time to my—well, I admit it—my obsession. Chasing down old census rolls is much more fun than installing heating systems!" Owen explained he had looked into DNA testing, trying to piece together his deep roots back through each of his four grandparents. Nowadays for a hundred bucks and a cotton swab you could identify pieces of DNA inherited pretty much unchanged from father to son, and from mother to daughter. Those pieces could tell the story of your family's prehistoric wanderings. What trees they came down out of. Where herds led them. Which Ice Ages deflected their paths.

As far as I was concerned, the less I knew about my family the better. Any DNA that Asa had inherited from the Wolfe line I considered to be a curse. True, his father had been no prize either, until you compared the guy to my line. The Wolfes should have stayed in their trees.

Owen droned on about ice ages, forces of nature, mutating genes, and ancient tribes. "Speaking of ice, could I have a bit more Scotch?" He waved his glass, clinking the naked cubes. He was sounding more and more like family all right.

What I remember of my own tribe: My mother. She used to beat the living hell out of me when I was young. For no fathomable reason. A rage would take over her body and I'd tear through the house to escape her flying fists. The forces of nature in our household herded me into the bathroom, where I'd slam and lock the door. I'd wait in there for hours, until she calmed down or my father came home.

I got up and fished out the bottle of Glenfiddich. As I was pouring, Owen pointed to a slender silver hip flask tucked among my wine bottles on the shelf.

"Whoa! Where'd you get that fabulous flask? Check out all that fancy engraving!"

I brought it down to let him take a look. "This was my granddad's. I just cleared out his apartment last week. This was his little secret—he carried it with him all the time. Not that anyone gave a poop."

Owen turned it over in his hands. In the center of the engraved face was a monogram: JPW. He puzzled for a moment. "This must have been our *great*-grandfather's—*Joseph* Wolfe, I'll bet."

I shrugged. It was mine, now. Not going to be Owen's, for all his admiring and coveting. "He must have given it to Granddad. Your family undoubtedly got something else of equal value."

He handed it over. I shoved it back behind the wine bottles.

"Great-grandpa Joseph Wolfe is the one I'm trying to find out about. He's our shared ancestor. I want to know where his tribe came from. His son, my Grandpa Seymour, died long ago, and had no male children. Just my mother. So the only way I can find out about Seymour's—my mother's father's—DNA is to locate a male relative. A descendent of Joseph Wolfe from an unbroken male line. I hadn't tracked any down until Mother showed me your letter. What serendipity! So Rhode, here I am! Now, do you have any male relatives with the last name Wolfe? Your grandfather—I gather he's passed on? He would have been my grandpa Seymour's brother."

I nodded and drained my wine glass. "Dead."

"How about your father, or cousins, uncles, brothers? I know Grandpa Seymour and your grandfather were the only boys in that generation."

"What about you? You're . . . male."

"Ah. Yes. Well, I carry Y-chromosome DNA from my father, Mickey Foley. It's my *mother's* father I'm trying to research. Like I just said."

I twisted my empty glass. "My father and my brother, Sheridan, are both dead, too. And my father had a sister, but no brothers." I thought for a moment. "I don't know of any more Wolfes. Don't think I can be of any help. Unless I were tested." And I wasn't so sure I would consent to that.

"No, no, you're a female. We could only get information on your mother's DNA."

A distant gunshot interrupted him. Somewhere on my street a life was probably ending. But Owen's interminable lecture, unfortunately, was not.

"Anyway, I did have the Y-DNA test done on myself. But—this is strange—a Foley cousin on my father's side had tests done too, and his results don't match. They should have. That can only mean somewhere in the Foley family there was a little something on the side. We call it a 'nonpaternal event.' " He gave a bit of a leer, but then frowned. "The real shame for me is all the time I've spent tracking down my father's family tree. I may have to throw it all out and start over."

I was listening for sirens. Usually took awhile to come, in

our neck of the woods.

My second cousin went on to explain that he was faced with a hole and a mystery at this point. I couldn't help him with the mystery of why his Y-DNA test wasn't matching up on his father's side. But the hole in his chart—deep roots information on his mother's grandfather, Joseph Wolfe—that's what he had come to me for.

"Sorry," I said with a shrug.

He frowned. "Hmm, do you still have anything of your father's, brother's, or grandfather's that might have any DNA? Toothbrushes, hairbrushes? Teeth?"

This was sounding ghoulish. I shuddered. "No, I didn't keep any of that stuff. How about a remote control? Or noise-canceling earphones?"

"Cigarette butts? Letters! Do you have envelopes, when they sent you letters?"

"Why would they ever have sent me letters?"

Owen had one last request before he took his leave. He wondered if I had any old family photographs he could borrow to copy. To oblige him I tiptoed into Asa's room where I kept a half-hearted family album somewhere at the bottom of his closet. I had one old shot of Granddad and his brother playing in snow back in the thirties. I carefully peeled it from the sticky, yellowed page and brought it out to the kitchen.

In the distance I could finally make out the sirens.

□ □ □

I didn't hear from any of the Foleys for nearly a month. Or anyone, regarding my ad. Cemetery plots don't move quickly, it seems. Meanwhile I was selling off my brother's, Sheridan's, electronic toys on eBay. Even that was slow going.

The court had informed me that since Granddad and my brother had both died without wills, as the next of kin I stood to inherit their estates after any known relatives could be tracked down and given a chance to contest. I didn't know of any other descendants of Granddad's. But it was an agonizing, slow process.

Then one day late in April second cousin Owen showed up at my door again. He sheepishly held out my photo and—Granddad's silver flask. "I'm *so* sorry it took so long to get back here with your photo. And I have to confess to 'borrowing' your flask. I really wanted to show it to Mother. She just loved seeing it! But now I am returning it. So, no hard feelings, I hope?" Again that grin, and that unnerving, familiar manner. This time I didn't invite him in. I reached my hand out for the flask and photo.

"I do have news," he said, relinquishing my stuff. "I was able to swab the neck of your grandfather's flask, and I sent it in. Cost a bit more, but, hey, eureka! I was able to fill that gap in my family tree. And you know what?"

I was getting tired of families and tribes and especially of Owen.

"I solved the mystery of my father's Y-DNA! Turns out he wasn't a Foley after all! Your granddad's deep roots matched my dad's! So, I remembered an old family rumor about my grandmother Foley and Seymour Wolfe's brother. You see, the Wolfe brothers were friends of the Foleys, which is how my parents met. *Their* parents had known each other."

I was so, so confused. Where was this going?

"The rumor was they had an affair."

"Who?" I stepped out onto the stoop.

"My grandma Foley and your granddad! I sent in for an upgrade on the DNA test. I paid for a full paternity test this time. And guess what?"

I saw it coming. I didn't want to hear any more. Where was our friendly neighborhood shooter when we needed him?

"So, my two real grandfathers were brothers! *Cousin* Rhode? Did *our* granddad leave an estate by any chance?" Again the smile. That dreadful, dreadful smile. So Owen's father had been a bastard. So was Owen, in my book. Why, oh why did he have to be my grandfather's bastard?

I retreated into my little house clutching my flask and photo, and firmly closed the door.

□ □ □

It was clear that my new first cousin Owen Foley was going to be a problem. This evil man was now in danger of getting half of Granddad's estate—money that Asa and I deserved and that I had worked hard for. It also occurred to me that Owen Foley should be put out of his nonpaternal misery. What a thing to have to live with! The shame of it all! And his own parents were first cousins. Was that even legal?

I read in a book once that females of many species are driven to "corner the world for their children." I had always had to be the protector. When I was Asa's age I had to take care of myself. I remember keeping a plastic bag of soda crackers at the bottom of the clothes hamper in that bathroom, in case I had to hole up past a mealtime. Well, I took care of that little girl back then, and I was going to take care of my little son now. No more gunshots at night. Or bars on his bedroom window slicing up the dawn's early light.

I still had a small ziplock of white powder my brother, Sheridan, had sent me a couple months ago to take care of another family matter. A magical white powder that took Granddad gently to eternal peace with no pain, no odor, no taste, and a nice convenient bit of delayed reaction. It could work its magic again. I fished it out of its hiding place, and brought out the rest of the Glenfiddich. There were still a good couple of inches left in the bottle.

The next day I called the number Owen had left with me on his first visit. "Hey, Owen. I'm sorry. I was in shock. I've recovered, and want to welcome you into the family. And I found some more photographs. Why don't you come by tonight for a drink?" I wondered, did that sound too obvious?

□ □ □

It was nearly nine that night when Owen showed up at my door, his jacket folded neatly over his arm. In the other hand was a blue gym bag. Asa was fast asleep. I let my cousin in and headed down toward the kitchen. I fetched out the Glenfiddich and placed it on the kitchen table.

Owen wasn't following me. When I turned back he still stood in the hallway, looking around.

"Owen, are you okay?"

"I'm fine. I'm very fine. You know, I think it's time to meet that son of yours."

"He's already . . ." I started to say. Then I noticed the big gun in his hand.

"I've been thinking, you know. I've been thinking that whatever Grandfather Wolfe left us probably won't go far with such a crowd."

"So you're *thinking* you're going to . . . *shoot* us?"

"Let's not bleed until we're cut. Shall we get the boy to join the party now?"

I protested, resisted, and delayed. But in the end he gave me no choice. I went into Asa's bedroom and gathered him up in my arms, trying as hard as I could not to wake him in the process.

Owen had settled on the hall closet as our prison. He jerked open the door, pulled the cord and flooded the interior with light. The space was crammed with boots and Christmas tree ornament boxes, a bag of recyclables, sports equipment, stained canvas bags. And a leash for a dog long gone. Owen ushered us in with a wave of his big gun. Asa was starting to wake up, his face morphing from dream to confusion. I knelt and placed him on the floor.

My cousin was a compulsive talker. He was rattling on about his HVAC job, and his experience with heating systems. "This will be quick and painless. You'll never know what hit you. You two will be blown to kingdom come. To Perpetual Grace! And best of all, it will just look like an accident—a malfunctioning boiler, how unfortunate. I've got it on a timer, but no one will know it's a timer! Hah! It's so fiendishly clever! It'll delay just long enough for me to go get an alibi." By then I had noticed the gym bag he had brought along, under his jacket. "And there won't be enough of this house left to tell that you were in the closet!"

The door was slammed shut. I could hear one of the kitchen chairs scraping, the knob banging, then the door quivered. I rattled the knob and shoved with all my might. It wouldn't budge. There was no lock—Owen had jammed it shut with the chair.

A moment later I could hear Owen directly below us in the basement. Putting together his ingenious timed fuse, no doubt, that would leave no hint that Asa and I had died in anything other than a tragic, accidental boiler explosion. Several very long minutes passed, then I heard Owen let himself out the back door in the kitchen.

Frantically I searched for implements I could poke under the door. I found a hockey stick, but it was too thick. I yanked a wire hanger from among the jackets and struggled to untwist it. When I finally managed to straighten it out, I fished it through the crack along the floor and felt for the legs of the chair. The hanger hit something, and I swept and jabbed. But the chair was jammed tight and the wire only bent helplessly against the wooden legs.

I started yelling. I always thought of our rented house as being tiny, with an even tinier yard. But when you're screaming at the top of your lungs in a closet, the yard is remarkably expansive. Neighbors were too far away, or they thought nothing of screams in the night on this street.

Asa was crying. I stopped and looked into the worried face of my son. My tribe. My flesh and blood. How long a fuse had Owen devised? How much time did we have? I grabbed the doorknob again and shook it violently. Then I dropped to my knees and whipped the hanger back and forth under the door again. Jab jab jab. Frustrated and panicked, I sat back on my heels, clasped my knees to my chest and buried my face. This cannot be happening. I imagined the timer. Tick-tick-tick.

So this was the world I had cornered for my son? No soda crackers in here. I rubbed my face, then gathered my resolve. I needed to reassure Asa. Lifting my head, I said in as steady a voice as I could muster, "Asa, let's pretend we're playing hide and seek, okay? I'm not sure who's 'it' right now, but I'll bet they'll find us soon."

Asa wiped his tears. He pushed himself further into the corner and covered his face with the bottom of one of my coats. I slid in beside him and he snuggled against me. He'd been doing that less often now that he was seven and a big schoolboy.

Tick-tick-tick.

Lately I'd been crying myself to sleep each night. Why did Granddad love Sheridan and not me? Sheridan was such a shit. Was it because Sheridan so clearly carried his Y-DNA markers? His blond hair, his earlobes, his psychopathy? Cousin Owen clearly did. He carried them in spades. Which gene mutation had hardened all our hearts?

I got up and tried body-slamming the door. All my chairs were cheap and rickety—legs and dowels were always loosening when we sat on them in the kitchen. But this one was apparently the exception. I slammed again, until my shoulder started to throb. All my doors were thin hollow Luan—coat hooks fell out of them and sound amplified through them. Except obviously the door to the hall closet. Six-panel, solid oak. Lord, why have you forsaken us?

Tick-tick-tick.

I started remembering all those years of hiding crackers in the bathroom hamper, and a realization came over me. All that time my mother had been doing the family laundry every week—fifty-two weeks a year—how likely was it that she never noticed my pathetic little stash at the bottom of the hamper? She would certainly have found them, and she would have understood their meaning. But she never disturbed them. I guess that passes for redemption in the Wolfe family.

Tick-tick-tick. Any minute now redemption wouldn't amount to a hill of beans. Enough with the epiphanies. I felt through more boxes for good stiff objects to poke with.

Then we heard him. Starting with a soft tinkle of breaking glass from the direction of the kitchen. Then the sound of the back door unlocking. Someone began walking around. I strained to listen.

Whoever it was, I wanted them to find us. I pounded on the door and began to yell again.

The visitor paused a long, long number of seconds, then came to the closet door and answered. "Um, where ya keep your cash?" He didn't seem at all bothered by the fact that I was trapped in my own closet. Maybe this was normal in his household.

I composed myself. If I told him the place was about to blow up he'd bolt and leave us there, or not believe me and we'd all go to Perpetual Grace together. Please dear God don't let me scare him off. "My purse is on the couch. But there's only about six dollars. Let me out and I'll take you to my ATM."

"Where's that?" He sounded interested. I prayed he wouldn't just ask for my PIN.

"BankNorthShore. We should leave right now." I willed my voice to be calm.

"How far away is it?" he asked, moving off. He was rummaging. I could hear drawers squeaking open. My purse falling to the floor.

"We should leave right now," I repeated, a bit more loudly.

From the living room: "What's the big fucking rush?"

I had to come up with something. He didn't seem too bright,

so I shouldn't have to think too hard.

"My husband will be home in a few minutes. He has a gun."

No response. More rattling sounds.

"He's six-foot-eight," I added. I considered explaining that this mythical husband had been the one who locked us in the closet, in case he started wondering about that. But I decided that would be needless complication and only waste time. This intruder sounded easily confused. I didn't want him to pause for any thoughts.

"He's a state trooper. . . ."

Tick-tick-tick. "He's got a temper. He's on steroids. . . ."

After an interminable length of time I heard the chair scrape and the door was finally flung wide. Even though the closet light had been on, I blinked my eyes.

He was a big guy waving a gun not unlike Owen's. He now pointed it at Asa. "Who the fuck's that?"

"He's my son. Let's get going."

The man started to argue. The kid could slow us down. He could get in the way. But I insisted. "Then shoot us both right here. I don't go if he doesn't go. Is that a car coming? That may be my husband's car. Cruiser."

The visitor nudged us into the kitchen. He had his gun in one hand and my ATM card in the other. Nothing else in my house had been worth taking apparently. We filed quickly toward the back door, which was still ajar.

I took one last glance—this dingy kitchen and the refrigerator feathered out with coupons, phone numbers, to-do lists, Post-its, and snapshots of Asa's life. The stove with one nonworking burner, yet we had managed with three. And where I had looked for jobs, and put food on the table, and raised my son, where I had listened to sirens and watched the weather reports, and the sunsets, and sipped my nightly glasses of wine, and taken stock.

Pushing Asa in front of me, I only hoped we'd make it out

the door before the fuse did its job. But the last sweep of my beloved kitchen turned up one notable fact: The bottle of Scotch was gone.

□ □ □

We barely made it to the curb when my house blew up, knocking all of us down onto our faces. When I lifted my head to check on Asa, I was happier than I had ever been in my life to see him look up at me in return. He started to whimper, but seemed—thank God—unscathed. I reached over to shield him from falling shingles. And the big guy with the big gun—the unwitting, serendipitous, good Samaritan—was hotfooting it down my street.

□ □ □

It was drizzling the following Wednesday, a soft and warm rain. We were staying in Granddad's empty apartment in the Sunset Senior Housing Center until I could find us a new place. A place that was safe. And where I could plant a few rhododendrons.

I had briefly considered reporting Owen to the police. But my best witness had vanished. And anyway I was holding out hope for a greater, more certain justice.

So Wednesday I was pulling on my slicker and preparing to pick Asa up from school when my cell phone sounded out the tinny first bar of Chopin's Funeral March in B-flat minor. To my hello a woman identifying herself as Emma Wolfe Foley asked if my family plots were still available.. I assured her they most certainly were.

"How soon could we arrange the transfer? I'm going to need one of them right away." She halted, then added, "I just lost my son. I think you met recently. He was your second-cousin Owen."

First cousin, second cousin, who's counting? "Oh my gosh! I'm so sorry to hear that! He was so young!"

Owen had apparently suffered heart failure. No warning, no prior signs. Took them all by surprise.

Out of respect, I didn't bring up the theft of my Glenfiddich. Instead I murmured, "You know, my grandfather died of the same thing. Golly, it must run in the family."

"Could we talk about those plots, please?"

Luckily I had kept all the paper work at Granddad's, so the title had not gone up in smoke with my little house. I succumbed to one last good deed. "Tell you what, Mrs. Foley. I'll give them to you for twenty thousand even." They were family, after all. And blood is thicker than Scotch.

The List

Kat Fast

They always call when I'm on the pot. Maude gripped her walking stick and aimed herself toward the telephone. She couldn't help noticing that the aluminum stick with its three balancing claws resembled her own emaciated arm and fingers. *How the hell did I get this old?*

Nevertheless, she welcomed the interruption. There were days she would string along market researchers, claiming to be in the 45-50 age demographic with household income in the middle bracket. She'd swear she'd purchased kitty litter, canned peas, facial masks or whatever, just to keep them on the line. There were very few callers she didn't welcome. Only one, actually—her stepdaughter, Dot. There weren't that many others still alive who knew her number.

Unfortunately, the caller was Dot, for the second time this evening.

"Could you hold on a moment? I need to put my ears in and turn a few things down." *Give me strength.* Maude needed fortification. She shuffled to the kitchen and poured herself a glass of wine. She wasn't supposed to combine alcohol with her pain pills, but what was the worst that could happen? Maude topped off her glass before setting out on the return journey to the living room. With a deep sigh, she eased her old bones into the reclining chair.

"Sorry to keep you waiting." Deeply ingrained manners forced the false words from Maude's mouth. She frowned. Hell, she was old enough, she could say whatever she wanted. But at the moment she couldn't come up with anything suitably churlish. Instead, she dropped the receiver and watched it crash to the floor. She took a leisurely sip of wine and then picked up the phone.

"Oops. Guess I'm a little tired." Hint, hint. Maude listened with half an ear to her stepdaughter's complaints about how horribly expensive wedding dresses were these days and how bridesmaids expected to receive expensive gifts from the bride.

In Maude's opinion, Dot's daughter, Claudette, shouldn't even be thinking about a fancy church wedding. She was re-marrying her ex-husband with her three-year-old daughter serving as the flower girl.

But Maude knew any suggestion she made would be WRONG, as were most of her solutions to Dot's real or imagined problems. Maude reached for a pen and opened the paper to the crossword puzzle while Dot moaned about the expectations of the younger generation and the state of the world in general.

Maude frowned. She didn't expect to be stymied by Monday's crossword, the easiest of the week. She didn't know if the seven-letter answer to 23 Down was "Correct" or "Genteel." She'd have to work around it. Certainly Ditty-Dot would be the last person to know a synonym for "Proper."

"Mom? Are you still there?"

"Yes, Dorothy." Maude hated it when Dot called her "Mom," first, because she couldn't imagine being a blood relation of that brassy, unctuous, walking *TV Guide*; second, because it was presumptuous; but mostly because it invariably led to a request for money or a favor.

"Actually, we bought the wedding gown last week. The dress really isn't why I called."

Maude already knew about the dress, because it had been charged to her MasterCard, but she noted that Dot omitted that detail. She filled in 30 Across and waited for the request.

"I thought we might go to the bank. When I met with my financial advisor this afternoon, he suggested that I should be a co-signer on your accounts. That way anything left in the bank won't have to go through probate. Besides, I could help you write the monthly checks and such."

"I'm still fit to conduct my finances, Dorothy."

"Mom, wouldn't it be easier if others could help with the details? Your estate is complex."

"I've never talked with you about my financial matters."

"Oh, but Mom . . . you have. You may have just forgotten about it." Dot pushed on. "I also thought while we had some time together, you might want to visit with your lawyer—he's close by the bank."

You want to hear the terms of the will, and find out how much of a pile you'll inherit.

"Mom, I'm just trying to help in any way that I can."

Maude let the silence hang before she responded. Why argue? "Okay. I'll make the appointments."

"Super. I knew you'd understand."

Maude hung up and leaned back in her chair. She was tired but she should probably make a list of things to do before she retired. She reached for a notepad and pencil.

No. Screw it. Her late husband had told her to lighten up, "screw at least one 'should' every day," and replace it with something she *wanted* to do. For proper Maude, it had been an uphill battle to overcome the "shoulds." She still worried about doing the right thing. Dot had cured her. Maude could safely say that she no longer felt any "shoulds" for Dot.

Maude had had a long and rewarding life. Too bad she hadn't been able to bear children, but otherwise, she had few regrets. She'd already done most everything she *should* do. What was left that she *wanted* to do? She couldn't hear, see, taste, feel, or even walk very well. She thought awhile and then, in a scratchy hand, wrote out her list:

To Do:

Abrams
Box
Bag
Back Door
Cards
Front Door
List

Why do they assume we're such fools? Maude swore as a split nail caught on her sweater. She reached into a drawer and withdrew a small container of Super Glue. *Because we* are *such fools.* Dot was right about one thing. Everything was getting harder. Even the mind games with Dot were tiresome.

Maude twisted off the cap and applied a few drops of glue to the offending nail. As she held out her hand to let it dry, she could see through the thin membrane of skin on the back of her hand to the veins and bones beneath. So fragile. Like trust, she thought. One little tear could destroy it forever.

A year ago Maude had been reading *Town & Country* in the oncologist's waiting room when she came across a set of pictures of Dot with some other "beautiful people" at a gala event. She couldn't remember what the party was about, because her eyes had been fixed on the antique emerald necklace around Dot's neck. It looked just like the family heirloom Maude's father had given Maude on her twenty-first birthday.

When Maude asked Dot about the necklace, Dot claimed Maude had loaned it to her for the event, and must have just forgotten.

"So where is the necklace now?"

"Oh, um, it's in my safe-deposit box along with the earrings you gave Claudette."

"Earrings?"

"Yes. You remember. You gave her diamond earrings for her birthday last year."

I did? Oh, no. Maude searched but couldn't retrieve the memory. "I'm sorry, Dorothy. Guess I'm getting old."

" 'Ninety-six-years young.' That's what I tell my friends."

And they say, "Well, bless her heart, the old dear."

Maybe this was dementia. You didn't know you were losing it until someone told you. *But I could have sworn that I gave her pearls. Didn't I? Or was that the year before?* Maude had unlocked the file cabinet in her study and withdrawn a manila folder. Inside was a list of valuables that she had prepared for insurance purposes. She scanned the list.

There it was. In black and white. Next to "Pearls" she had written, "to Claudette, 10-15-07." Phew! She wasn't losing her mind. But she had lost something else she could never recover. She no longer trusted Dot.

Such a shame. Maude remembered how sweet Dot had been when Maude had married her father, and how famously they got on. After all, Maude was a rich, childless widow. What was not to like? For the first ten years. Then Daddy died, and Maude began to outlive her welcome.

Maude had tried hard to be the good stepmother, always there to comfort and lend a hand as well as a lot of money over the years. Maude had purchased a condo and a car for Dot after her disastrous divorce. She'd sent Dot's daughter through prep school and college, although the girl was such a miserable student she hadn't managed to graduate.

Dot took whatever she wanted, usually without asking. She had no respect for privacy. Last week was a case in point. Dot had sailed in unannounced, interrupting Maude's dinner, unaware of how unwelcome she was. She stood too close and talked too loud. When Maude had shushed her, Dot bridled. "I'll talk as loud as I want in my house!"

"Not quite your house yet, missy. Trumpet your woes to the heavens after I'm gone, but until that blessed date, I'll thank you to keep your voice down in *my* house."

Dot pouted and spoke a few decibels lower. "I only talk loud so you can hear me."

"Don't be dull, child. I hear what I want to hear." With that, Maude had taken out her hearing aids and was rewarded by blissful silence.

□ □ □

Tuesday morning, Maude heard a light tap on the door and a polite, "Morning, Mum." Consuela waddled into the room, extended belly first. She looked as if she would have her baby momentarily.

"How are you two this morning?" Maude asked.

"The baby, he moves. See?" Consuela giggled and walked to Maude. She guided Maude's hand to her belly.

Maude felt a tiny foot kicking against Consuela's stomach. "He's strong!" Consuela was scheduled to have a Caesarian section Thursday. She was a petite young woman who had married a bruiser of a football player. There was no question about a normal delivery. The baby was way too big. "Have you decided on a name for the little fellow yet?"

"Oh, yes, Mum. Mauricio, for his father."

"That's a fine name. Sit a minute and have some tea." For the last two months of pregnancy, Maude hadn't let Consuela do any heavy cleaning, but she had asked her to come in and help with minor errands. The real reason was that Maude enjoyed her company. They chatted and laughed and talked about the baby and about nothing in particular.

"Anything special today?" Consuela asked in a soft Jamaican lilt.

"I think we should keep it simple, just tidy up a bit and check the tapes." After the incident with the emerald necklace, Maude had installed two tiny, motion-sensitive cameras. One was strategically positioned in a hanging plant in the corner of the living room, and a second in the bedroom.

"And then I'd like to do a few errands in town if we have time."

While Consuela hummed and puttered about, Maude brought up the MasterCard account details on the computer to see if there were any new charges she hadn't made. She was curious to see how much the bridesmaids' gifts cost.

Dot had suggested that the MasterCard account be billed electronically and paid automatically from an investment account, ostensibly to "save a few trees." Of course, the real reason was that she didn't want Maude to see the charge detail. Dot assumed that Maude's eyesight was too poor to read the numbers on the computer monitor.

Even with the large letters and numbers that Consuela pasted on the keyboard, Maude had to don her magnifier to read. It was a contraption used by jewelers that looked like a miner's headlamp but fit nicely over her bifocals. She typed in the passwords slowly, but otherwise she could navigate.

"Anything good today?" she asked Consuela, who was viewing the recordings from the past two weeks.

"Yes, Mum. The pictures, they are very clear."

"That's it then. We have more than enough."

□ □ □

When Consuela dropped her off after their outing, Maude said good-bye with a hug and kiss and gave Consuela an envelope with her last paycheck and a fat bonus. Then Maude sank into her chair and reached for the puzzle and her list. 23 Down was "Genteel." She wrote in the answer and then crossed "Abrams" and "Box" off her list.

To Do:

~~Abrams~~
~~Box~~
Bag
Back Door
Cards
Front Door
List

Enough. More than enough for one day. Time for a magic pill. The pains got sharper as the day wore on, and it was too early for wine. *Shouldn't mix.* "Should, should, should, shouldn't, shouldn't, shouldn't," Maude intoned. "Screw a 'should' every day." She took her pill with a glass of Merlot and finished off the puzzle before turning in. Just a few more things to arrange, and then Consuela had to do her part and have that baby. Consuela had to be in the hospital for the last act of Maude's little play, otherwise she would be the first person suspected of wrongdoing. Unfair, but true.

□ □ □

Dot called Wednesday morning. "How are we feeling today? Did you sleep well?" It took four or five minutes before Dot got around to asking if Maude had made arrangements to meet with the banker and lawyer. Maude assured her that she had booked appointments for a week from Friday.

"Oh. I'd hoped we could wrap things up this week."

Maude smiled at the disappointment in Dot's voice, but it was not a happy smile. "You know how busy they are. That was the only day I could arrange for back-to-back appointments. I only have the strength for one outing a day."

When Dot launched into the day's litany of woes, Maude put her on speakerphone. After a spell, Maude realized that the other end of the conversation had gone quiet. "I'm sorry, I missed that last bit."

"Don't mind me. I'm just feeling a little bored today."

"Why don't you get out and about? Find yourself a part-time job. Or sign up for some volunteer work. That's rewarding, and you'll meet new people."

"Oh, I couldn't possibly do that. I have a list of things to do that's a mile long. Shopping, errands. The hairdresser, the doctor. It's endless."

"Well, then, look at it this way. Be thankful that you have a full list."

"Huh?"

"When you finish everything on your list, it's time to shuffle off."

"Oh, Mom, I wish you wouldn't talk that way. You'll live to be 105."

'Twould serve you right.

After they said goodbye, Maude jammed her purse into a plastic bag with used Depends, double bagged the lot and placed it by the front door. Exhausted, she checked off "Bag," reclined the chair and instantly fell asleep.

To Do:

~~Abrams~~

~~Box~~

~~Bag~~
Back Door
Cards
Front Door
List

Later that evening, she rose unsteadily from her chair, holding onto the sides until she got her balance and could reach her claw. She inched to the sliding back door, unlocked it and pulled it sideways with effort. Outside, she closed the door and took in a deep breath of salty air. As she watched, a cloudbank moved in from the ocean, dousing the stars in its path.

This was the hard part. Maude leaned against the outside wall and raised the walking stick over her head. With all of her strength, she smashed the stick against the glass door. It bounced off. *Phooey.*

Try another angle. She backed up, took aim, and swung the stick like a bat sideways into the glass. Boink. *Damn.* Shouldn't swear. *Fucking goddamn piss shit mother-fucking phooey!* She couldn't break the flippin' glass, but she was rewarded by a sudden, no nonsense pain in her side. She leaned against the wall to catch her breath. Another stabbing pain tore through her. Tears streamed down the gullies in her cheeks.

Get over it, old woman. This last part of the plan wasn't really necessary, but it would have been a nice touch.

She shivered. The prongs on her walking stick were bent. Only one prong would be of any use—she would have to spike it into the carpet like a ski pole. She entered the house and yanked on the door. *Doubledamn*, she didn't even have the strength to close the door. Leaving it ajar, she poled her way inside. *Screw it.* An open door would work. It just wouldn't be as dramatic. Besides, she needed to get to her pain pills.

□ □ □

Thursday morning, Consuela's husband called to say that Consuela had just given birth to a nine-pound, six-ounce baby boy, and both were doing well.

Wonderful. Maude smiled and sighed and then called the heating company. "Would you please come check on the furnace? I don't seem to have any heat." She hung up and pulled on a second sweater and waited for the doorbell.

After looking around, the man joined her in the living room. "The heat's fine, missus, but you left the back door open."

"I certainly did not! I never use that door."

"Well," the man adopted the slow, apologetic tone people use for the feeble, "It's closed now. I'll turn up the heat until you're comfortable."

"But, I didn't open that door. I'm old, not senile."

"Afraid someone did, though."

Maude cobbled her way to the front hall. "Let me give you a little something for your trouble."

"Oh, you needn't—"

"My purse! My purse is gone!"

"Are you sure?"

"Dammit, man, you're not listening! I didn't open the back door, and now my purse is missing. I always leave it right here on the table so I know where to find it. Someone must have broken in during the night."

"But wouldn't you have heard something?"

"No. When I go to bed, I close the bedroom door and take out my hearing aids. Nothing short of an earthquake would wake me."

Maude entered the kitchen and took a ten-dollar bill out of a cookie jar. She handed it to the man and asked him if he'd mind taking her bag of trash out for pickup.

Before calling the police Maude crossed "Back Door" off her list and reviewed her plan, to make sure that she hadn't forgotten anything.

To Do:

~~Abrams~~
~~Box~~
~~Bag~~
~~Back Door~~
Cards
Front Door
List

□ □ □

At Abrams & Abrams she'd had her new will witnessed and left a copy along with the tapes. At the bank she'd emptied the contents of her safe-deposit box, leaving only the old, now defunct, will. Then she signed for a new safe-deposit box and placed the new will inside. She put the key in an envelope and asked Consuela to mail the key to the lawyer, the new executor of her will.

In Maude's new will, she set up an educational trust for Claudette on the off-chance she might get off her lazy butt and finish college. She created a similar trust for Consuela's little boy, Mauricio. The rest of the estate would be split between the Nature Conservancy and the World Wildlife Fund, Maude's favorite charities.

In the will she stated explicitly that she was not leaving anything to Dot because of gifts of real estate, money, and jewelry Maude had made to Dot in her lifetime. If Dot challenged the will, the lawyer was to threaten her with incontrovertible evidence that showed Dot stealing.

□ □ □

By late afternoon, the police had come and gone and Maude had canceled her credit cards just as if her purse had really been stolen. Her head ached from all the fuss and flurry, and it wasn't helped by the noise the handyman was making changing the locks on the front door. Maude wanted to make sure that Dot and her spawn wouldn't be able to pillage the remaining treasures in the house before the estate was settled.

After the handyman left, she crossed "Cards" and "Front Door" off the list.

To Do:

~~Abrams~~
~~Box~~
~~Bag~~
~~Back Door~~
~~Cards~~
~~Front Door~~
List

Only one item left. She shuffled to the study and fed her "To Do" list into the shredder. As she watched the machine's voracious metal teeth eat the record of her plans, a thunderbolt of pain ripped through her side.

When the pain abated, she struggled to the kitchen, poured a stiff nightcap and walked slowly to her bedroom, being ever so careful not to spill. Her list was finished. Only one more thing she wanted do. She donned her favorite flannel nightgown, washed two handfuls of pain pills down with wine, and crawled under the comforter.

Some Things Can Never Be the Same

Stephen Allan

Hank found the stale cigarettes next to a rusting coffee can underneath the sink. He examined the hard box for any evidence of mice chewing on the packaging, but didn't see any. He sniffed a bent one; it had a weak tobacco smell. They were a cheap brand to begin with, something generic that only satisfied the cravings rather than giving any pleasure. He struck a kitchen match and inhaled the disappointing smoke.

The Red Sox game had finished three hours before and the radio station had switched to some all-night call-in show with a couple of flakes talking about UFOs and secret government conspiracies. Hank wasn't paying the radio any mind, since the station wouldn't broadcast any local news until the morning; he just stared at the clouds of smoke as they clung to the yellow glow of the overhead kitchen light.

Hank pulled out the state trooper's card from his shirt pocket and read the contact information again. Andrews from the Ellsworth barracks. The officer had come the thirty miles from

Ellsworth to Penobscot a few hours after the bank robbery looking for Hank's son. He left instructions that Hank was to call him if he heard from John. Hank put the card next to the game of solitaire that was laid out in front of him. The game was unfinished and long forgotten. Without the distraction of the ball game or the cards, he was left with just the lonely guilt of failure.

He didn't sit for long before he was back at the sink, this time rinsing out his coffee mug. He bent down and sipped at the faucet water, swishing it around in his mouth before spitting it out. When he straightened he saw car lights coming down the road toward the trailer. He couldn't tell the model, but he knew it would either be his son or a state trooper. Hank walked across the curled linoleum and turned on the outside light for whoever it was and sat back down. He lit another cigarette so he would have something to do.

The vehicle's muffler sounded too loud for an official car. Hank looked up into the living room at his gun cabinet and wished he had taken out his .22 pistol.

John had a heavy knock, but he didn't wait for Hank. The man opened the door and came in like a strong windstorm looking to knock down trees. He was unshaven, perhaps three days away from a razor, wearing some rock band T-shirt. His tight black jeans were frayed at the knees and the soles of his boots were cracked. He didn't look much different from the last time Hank had seen him, in court before his last incarceration.

"Hey there, old man," John said as he stood in the doorway. "I was wondering if you could give me a hand with Ronnie." John went back outside and Hank followed him. He had heard that Ronnie Proulx was involved from the eleven o'clock news.

Hank looked into the Monte Carlo but Ronnie wasn't in the passenger seat. Instead, he was laid out in the back, writhing about. Ronnie opened the door revealing massive blood stains smeared all over the backseat.

"He's in pretty bad shape," John said. "The bastards got him in the gut, I think. He needs to lay down somewhere."

From the television, Hank knew that either John or Ronnie had killed a sheriff's deputy, probably the same guy who had put a bullet in Ronnie's stomach. John took Ronnie by the ankles and slid him out the door, handing Hank Ronnie's legs to carry while he lifted his friend under the shoulders. Ronnie yelled out in pain. No one else would hear him as Hank's nearest neighbor was two miles down the road.

"Let's take him into the bedroom," Hank said as they brought Ronnie inside. He led the way down the hall and eased Ronnie onto the unmade bed. As soon as Ronnie was down, Hank realized he would need to replace the bedding and mattress.

"Here, buddy," John said as he took a pint bottle of whiskey out of his jacket pocket. "Get some of this down." John unscrewed the cap and lifted Ronnie's head so he could drink the alcohol. "You have anything else to give him? Pain pills or some shit?"

Hank nodded and went to the bathroom. In the medicine cabinet was some old Oxycodone left over from when he had a bad back the summer before. He shook the last three tablets out of the amber pill bottle and took them back to John.

"Swallow these," John said and dumped the pills into Ronnie's mouth. He put the whiskey back to Ronnie's lips. A lot of the alcohol spilled onto his chest, but he drank enough to get the pills down. "Those are only gonna take a few minutes," John said.

Hank went to his closet and took out a ratty towel to put on Ronnie's wound.

"Ronnie, I want you to hold this to your stomach," Hank said. "We need to stop that bleeding."

"You're alright," John said. "You're alright. We'll just get this healed up and we can move on."

Ronnie reached for the towel and held it to his belly. He

nodded his head. His lips were pulled back showing his teeth closed together. The muscles in his jaw were taut and desperate grunts came from his throat.

"Why don't you head back out to the kitchen," Hank said to John. "There's some rum in the freezer. Go ahead and have a drink." John agreed, leaving Hank alone with Ronnie.

"I think we hit the guy who shot me," Ronnie said through his gritted teeth. "Do you know?"

"Yeah, you did," Hank said. "He's dead."

"We didn't mean to. He just came in shooting. It was a reflex."

"Just keep quiet," Hank said.

"Who was he?"

"A sheriff's deputy."

"Did he have a name?"

"I'm sure he did," Hank said and stood up to leave.

Ronnie reached out and grabbed Hank's arm. "Am I gonna make it?" he asked.

"I don't know," Hank said. "Just take it easy as best you can and I'll be back."

John was at the kitchen table with the open rum bottle in front of him. He had one of Hank's stale cigarettes lit in his hand.

"These the only ones you have?" John asked, indicating the generic cigarette box on the table.

"Sorry, that's it."

"We're gonna need some stuff anyway, so we can get us some real cigarettes," John said. "You'll have to get it for us."

"Ronnie's losing too much blood, he's gonna go into shock soon," Hank said. "What do you want to do about it? Bangor's forty minutes from here."

"No," John said. "No hospitals. He goes to the ER, the cops will get him."

"He doesn't go, he dies."

"So he dies."

Hank hesitated before taking a magnetized notepad off the fridge. It held up an aged photo of John in a Little League uniform. He was down on one knee with his glove and bat in front of him. It was the only picture Hank had of John. He put the photo facedown on top of the fridge and sat at the table opposite John.

"There's the all-night store on the way to Ellsworth. I can go down there and get just about most things," Hank said. "Tell me what you need."

John listed off some items: bandages, whiskey, beer, candy bars, jerky, three cartons of cigarettes. Hank wrote everything down. "And if you got a couple of gas cans, fill them up so I can put it in the car."

"Don't have any cans, but I'll fill up the truck and you can siphon the gas."

John reached into his jeans and pulled out a mess of cash. He counted off ten twenty-dollar bills and offered them to Hank.

"I'll get this for you," Hank said.

"Jesus, we got enough money," John said and smiled. "Just took out a withdrawal from the bank."

"You may need all that later on," Hank said and left the trailer.

It was a fifteen-minute drive to the Mobil station off Route 1. Even though he played his George Jones tape at high volume, Hank ignored it. Instead he thought about John's mother. She had died young and never knew what her son would become. Would she have been able to detect where John had gone wrong? Was there a point that she could have straightened him out? Hank didn't know when his boy had become trouble. All he knew was by that time it was too late. There was something he missed and he still didn't know what that was.

The Mobil station lot was empty, except for the clerk's car parked next to the dumpster. Hank pulled up to the gas pump and walked inside. He picked up everything John had told him to get, making a few trips up to the counter as his hands got full. He went to look for the bandages, but didn't see any.

"You got Band-Aids and that type of stuff?" Hank asked.

The clerk pointed to the end of the third aisle. "Should be some down there."

Hank followed where the clerk had pointed, but saw only bandages that were too small to help Ronnie. Hank looked around for some kind of alternative and saw a few beach towels left over from the summer and duct tape. He grabbed a couple rolls of the tape and all the towels and brought them to the counter.

"You need anything else?" the clerk asked.

Hank looked around. "Yeah, I need forty in gas out there," he said. He stopped scanning the store when he saw the package of sleeping pills. "Hold up a minute."

Hank took the box of sleeping pills off the shelf and read the back. Do not exceed recommended dosage. Without any medical help, Ronnie's suffering would continue until his last breath and there wasn't anything more Hank could do for him. Hank grabbed all five boxes on the shelf and brought them to the counter.

"This is everything," Hank said. The clerk rang him up.

George Jones sang "A Good Year for the Roses" as Hank pulled away from the gas station. He found himself absently singing along, low, under his breath, somewhere between forming the words and uttering a melodic mumble.

John was in the bedroom with Ronnie when Hank returned. John had brought in a kitchen chair and was sitting in the far corner, drinking straight from the rum bottle, which was nearly empty. His eyelids had turned to slits from the booze. On the bed, Ronnie was still awake, fighting the pain. He was covered in sweat. John had put a blanket over him. Blood had already soaked through.

"We're gonna have to change that dressing," Hank said. He had brought the summer towels and duct tape in with him. "They didn't have any bandages big enough so I had to improvise." Hank pulled the blanket off Ronnie.

"No," Ronnie said, "it's too cold."

"I have to do it, son," Hank said. "John, you should head back out to the kitchen. All your stuff is on the table. There's a fresh bottle of Canadian whiskey, too." John agreed, swigging the last of the rum on his way out of the bedroom. He stumbled a bit and smacked his shoulder against the doorframe as he left the room.

Hank threw the blanket to the side and took off the soiled towel. The wound was a mess. Hank put one of the beach towels down and taped it in place by adhering the gray duct tape to Ronnie's skin. He reached into his jacket pocket and retrieved a bottle of beer. He opened the bottle and set it next to Ronnie, and then took the sleeping pills. He opened each packet and placed the pills next to the open bottle of beer. He pocketed two of the pills.

"I don't think there's anyway you're gonna make it out of this," Hank said, looking down at the dying man. "These here will take care of you. Drink all them down with the beer."

"I don't want them. I'm not ready to die," Ronnie said.

"There ain't any shame in dying," Hank said. "Better men than you have done it."

"I didn't mean for any of this," Ronnie said.

"Nobody ever means it when things turn wrong. Take the pills."

Hank left and closed the bedroom door behind him. He could hear Ronnie crying as he walked down the hall.

John was at the table with the whiskey bottle at his lips. The robbery money was stacked in front of him. He must have retrieved it from the car while Hank was gone. The pile was smaller than

Hank thought it would have been.

"How's he doing?" John asked.

"There's nothing no one can do for him," Hank said. "I'm afraid nothing could've been done for him for awhile now."

"I gotta get out of here before long," John said. His words were slurred.

"What you gotta do is sleep off that drunk."

"I'm fine."

Hank walked to the radio and turned it off. The station had started to rebroadcast the Red Sox game from earlier. Hank couldn't understand why someone would want to listen to a game when they already knew the Sox had lost. He reached into his pocket and took out the sleeping pills and looked at John. He hesitated and then held the pills out for his son.

"You're gonna have quite a headache when you sober up if you don't take something," Hank said. "Take this here aspirin."

John took the pills and washed them down with the whiskey. Two should put him to sleep with the help of the alcohol.

"Why?" Hank asked.

"Why what?" John said looking up at his father.

"Why did you do it? Why rob a bank? You got probably a couple or three thousand dollars there, but for what? Cops chasing you and your friend dead in the other room. I don't understand."

"Oh Christ, you never did," John said. "And Ronnie ain't dead."

"He will be by sun up."

"Says you."

"Says that bullet hole in his stomach."

John looked away from Hank.

"Why'd you turn off the game?"

"Sox already lost."

"Well, I didn't hear anything about it."

Hank turned the radio back on and they listened as Oakland scored six runs over the course of two innings. By the eighth, John was nearly out.

"Go lie on the recliner," Hank said. John did as he was told. He flipped the footrest up and fell asleep. Hank switched the radio off and went to put the beer in the fridge. John's baseball photo fell and Hank picked it up. He looked at the eleven-year-old boy in the picture and then at the twenty-six-year-old man asleep in his living room. Somewhere in the past fifteen years his son had slipped away from being a kid who dreamed of playing left field at Fenway. Hank didn't know if he should be guilty somehow. How much blame was on him for John's failures?

Hank lit another cigarette and sat on his couch. John began snoring. The clock over the stove read four o'clock. Hank waited an hour, watching over John, before he went into his bedroom.

Ronnie's eyes were closed, but he wasn't breathing. Only one pill remained on the night table.

"Mercy on your soul," Hank said. He wasn't a religious man but thought something should be said for Ronnie just in case there was a god out there.

The duct tape was on the floor. Hank picked up the roll and walked back to the living room.

John didn't move as Hank wrapped the tape around his ankles. When he was satisfied the legs were secured, Hank pulled John's wrists together and bound them. As an extra precaution, Hank wrapped the tape around John's chest and the back of the recliner. John woke as Hank bit the tape off the roll.

"What's this?" John asked in a faint voice. "I can't move." He struggled, but the tape held. "What the fuck? What the fuck are you doing? Get me out of this."

"I'm sorry," Hank said and walked into the kitchen.

"I'm gonna get out of this. I'm gonna get out and I'm gonna

bash your head in." John's volume increased. "Are you taking the money, you piece of shit? That's mine and Ronnie's, you hear me? You touch it and I will make sure you die. Let me loose, you prick."

Hank picked up the handset of his yellow rotary phone and took the state trooper's card out of his pocket. He dialed the Ellsworth barracks. The dispatcher answered.

"This is Hank Burgess. My son is wanted for that burglary down in the southern part of the state. I got him here. Send someone out."

Hank gave the dispatcher his address and hung up.

"Why did you do that?" John asked. "Why did you call the cops?"

"There was nothing else I could do and live with it."

Hank went outside and sat down on the open tailgate of his truck and smoked one cigarette after the other until he saw flashes of blue and white light up the dark sky.

"Oh Christ. Untie me right now, Hank. I'm gonna kill you. I'll goddamn strangle you if you don't let me go. I'll . . . I'll . . . Okay. Okay. Listen, forget what I said. What do you want? The money? Take it. Just untie me. Jesus, they're going to fry me. Dad, let me go. You have to let me go. Dad? Daddy?"

Hank sucked in one last draw of smoke and flung the still-lit cigarette to the gravel.

Justice

C. M. Falcone

When the police come I'll tell them what happened. So much crime these days. Just read the headlines: this one killed, that one beaten and robbed. *I* don't even have to read the newspapers. I see what goes on, I hear people talk. Two blocks down, a building burned. Somebody had it in for the owner. A couple of months ago old lady Poulter took a hit on the head that made her go to the hospital for three days, or maybe a week, I forget. The whores, excuse my language, hanging out right in front of this store. They don't even bother to cover themselves up or what they're doing either. I see how they slip into the alley sometimes. I hear them, too. Filthy, dirty men using good money that's supposed to support a family, a wife who's stuck by them a lot of years. Bad, real bad.

He was so quiet coming in, just a little rattle against a crate in the back room. Probably the sauerkraut, I told Manny he overbought. You can't move that kraut in this neighborhood; not no more. This store is all we got now to keep us going; I'll do all the ordering from now on. Manny bought me the gun. A Smith and Wesson .38. The best, he says, for what we need it for. In this neighborhood everybody talks about their guns like they were favorite children. Guns used to scare me. I never wanted to learn to shoot. I changed my mind because the crime scared me, too, and not all of it was by outsiders. The cleaners was robbed, and McClusky's Liquor store—somebody is covering up there. I see the shifty look in Mrs. McClusky's eyes. I don't blame a mother for protecting her son, but if he's done wrong he's got to pay. There's such a thing as justice. I told Manny maybe a hundred times that those who do wrong got to pay. He knows I believe this.

So much blood all over. I don't suppose I should touch anything, clean up. I can hardly stand to look, but he does have such a surprised look on his face, almost comical. Good thing we don't usually get many customers this time of night. It gets dark early this time of year. Nobody is out except the criminals and the dirty whores and the perverts who go off with them. I wonder should I lock the door until the cops come? Like I said, not much fazes anybody around here anymore; crime's as common and bland as popcorn. But still . . . all that blood.

I'm a good shot. An excellent shot. I learned my lessons well. Manny took me to the firing range; he picked out the best instructor.

When the police come, I'll tell them just what happened. I was all alone here in the store, in this neighborhood where we lived fifty-one years, all our married life until now. Look at me, I'll say. Still working at my age, an old woman. Who can retire these days? I been missing some of the cash from the register, a thief, a dirty cheat, been sneaking in and taking it. I saw a dark figure coming slowly from the back, coming right at me. I had the gun Manny bought and registered, kept here in the drawer for when one of us was alone and somebody was where they shouldn't be, somebody was doing something they had no business doing.

Manny saw how I was with the gun. He should have known better. Why was he sneaking in from the alley like that, the whore's laughter following him, into his own store where his wife was waiting, working all alone? I won't tell them *I* know why. They'll see the horror on my face, the pain. What is in my heart I'll keep to myself. They won't be the ones to judge me. Accidents happen all the time.

Promises to Keep

A. J. Pompano

Harold was my uncle but he was no Lazzaro. He married my mother's sister, Marion, when I was a baby and even though they lived right in Sachem Creek, we had little contact with him over the years due to a falling out between him and my father. As far as I knew, neither one of them could remember why they fought, but they both remembered that it was the other one's fault.

My father earned good money for the long hours he put in at the Sachem Creek Quarry. He spent most of it providing for the family and blew the rest in the camaraderie of the village tavern trying to forget that his muscles ached.

Harold also worked hard, suffering the pains that come with farming the rocky clay of the Connecticut shoreline. He never wasted money in the tavern or anywhere else. He had my aunt Marion treat his aches with potions she whipped up from herbs, rather than spending money on booze or doctors.

Harold and Marion lived in a small clapboard house, scaled and mildewed from overgrown forsythia that smothered it on three sides. However, between the mismatched windows that closed in the front porch and a broken mailbox on a cedar post by the street,

Marion planted a wildflower garden bursting with yellow heads of yarrow, purple foxglove bells, blue globes of thistle, and orange clusters of butterfly weed. This tiny patch put a happy face on the sad little cottage, but it had a practical purpose as well. It served as her pharmacy, the source of the plants for her concoctions.

Although Harold didn't associate with our family, Aunt Marion occasionally sneaked by to see us, bringing something she baked, and flowers for my mother. When I was younger, she always had a special gift for me, such as an arrowhead or box turtle she had found.

They had a daughter, Lucy, whom Harold never allowed to go anywhere but to school. My cousin was a few years older than I was, so we never were close. Occasionally, I'd ride by on my bike and catch a glimpse of my aunt in her garden, but Lucy was always inside. If I didn't see Uncle Harold I'd stop, but if he caught me, he'd bellow for Marion. Then she'd kiss me on the cheek and tell me to come back another day, so she could run in to wait on the old bastard.

When I got older, I started to check up on my aunt more frequently, especially after Lucy left in the middle of the night. Recently, I hiked by after not seeing her for a few weeks. When I didn't find her in her garden, I dared to walk up to the front porch. I didn't see anyone, so I went around to the side and, sheltered by the overgrown forsythia, peeked into the open living room window. I caught a glimpse of Harold reading a newspaper as my aunt fidgeted with some knitting needles. Satisfied she was all right, I started to leave just as Aunt Marion spoke up in a nervous voice.

"Harold, it's going to be here in less than two months."

He hardly looked up from his paper. "What is, Woman? Say what you mean."

"You know perfectly well what I mean, Harold. Lucy's wedding. . ."

Harold kept on reading as if she had never spoken a word.

I ducked down to listen.

"Harold Day! How can you be so heartless and unforgiving when it comes to our own daughter?"

"I don't have a daughter. If I did, she'd be here helping us get by, not in New York City doing God knows what."

"Well, I do have a daughter, and I'm going to her wedding."

"Do as you wish, Woman. Just leave me out of it."

"And I'm—" she took a moment to regroup her thoughts. "And I'm going to buy a new dress for the wedding."

The bravery of that statement made me get up to look in the window again. I saw Harold look up.

"You will not waste my money to buy a dress for one day."

"I am, Harold. I sold some bulbs from the garden today and I'm going to set the cash aside. I'll use my own money to get a beautiful dress for the wedding."

Harold was quiet. I don't think Marion ever saw his fist coming. She slumped in front of the fireplace, blood trickling from her ear.

He spoke in a depraved voice. "You'll get a new dress over my dead body!"

As Harold turned to walk to the kitchen, Aunt Marion reached for the fireplace poker. Slowly and with a great deal of difficulty, she used the sturdy metal rod to get to her unsteady feet.

I ran around the side of the house and flung open the porch door with fire in my eye, ready to defend her. She spotted me from the living room and whispered for me to go, assuring me she'd be okay. I left, not to make matters worse for her, intending revenge for another day.

They say that everyone gets their due, and it wasn't long before Harold started feeling under the weather. Marion, ever the faithful wife, tended to his needs.

He had his good days and his bad days, but never a pleasant day. Marion, when I saw her, never complained. It was on one of his better days, just after dinner, that I rapped at my aunt's porch door.

I could hear Harold bark at her. "Get it. It must be that damned Quincy."

"Harold, what's going on? I don't want trouble."

"Just get the door, and mind your business."

I could see the anguish on Aunt Marion's face when I entered the house. I gave her a quick kiss on the cheek. "It's okay, Aunt Marion; no trouble. I promise."

Her voice was low and nervous. "I don't have any doubt on your part, Quincy." She led me toward the kitchen.

Harold put a piece into the puzzle he was working on before he looked up. "So it is you."

Already, I was sorry that I'd let my curiosity get the best of me when he sent a neighbor kid saying there was something I had to do for my aunt. "Yeah, I'm happy to see you too, Uncle Harold. Make it short and sweet. I'm supposed to be in a dart match at the tavern right now."

Harold picked up another puzzle piece, examined it, and then threw it aside. "I'm dying."

"Everyone's dying. If that's why you sent for me, I'll be going."

"It's his heart," Marion broke in. "He won't go to the doctor. He's making me treat him with the herbs."

It wasn't that Harold couldn't afford a doctor. In Sachem Creek, gossip is the sport of choice and people speculated that Harold had at least a quarter of a million dollars hidden in his shack.

I helped myself to the last cookie from a dish on the table. "For once he may be right. You're a better doctor than he deserves,

Aunt Marion."

Aunt Marion picked up the dish. "I'll get you more."

Harold glared at her. "Wait a minute, Woman. I didn't have your precious nephew come here for no damned tea party. There's something I need from him what's got to be done."

All I wanted to do was get out of there. "What do you want?"

"I told you, I think I may be dying soon."

I glanced toward the door. "There's nothing I can do to help you along, as much as I'd like to!"

"Damn you, I'm serious. I want you to be a witness that the woman here promises to bury my money with me, and then make sure that she does it."

"Harold!" Marion nearly fell in a faint and I helped her to a chair. Then I turned to Harold.

"What you do with your money is your business. Why involve me?"

"Because as much as I hate you, I know you're trustworthy."

"Thanks for the compliment, but no thanks."

"That's what I thought you would say. But if you want your aunt to go to your cousin's wedding, you'll do it."

"You'll let me go, Harold?"

"You can, if he assures me my wishes will be carried out. No new dress, but you can go."

When I saw the hopeful look on Aunt Marion's face, I knew I had to go along with Harold's ploy to cheat my aunt out of her inheritance.

"I guess I don't have a choice."

A smile, memorable for its rarity, crept across Harold's face.

"Okay, then. Now do you promise to put my money in the

coffin with me, woman?"

Marion hesitated.

"I said, do you promise, Woman?"

Aunt Marion's voice was just about audible. "Yes."

□ □ □

I stopped by the house a few days later and surprised Marion in her peaceful garden. Before she noticed me, she picked a pinkish-purple flower from the spike of a foxglove plant and held it to her face.

"My sweet little flowers."

When she realized I was there, she slipped the tubular little bloom into the pocket of her worn-out apron.

"Is everything all right, Aunt Marion?"

"Quincy, you startled me. My hearing isn't so good since . . . I injured my ear."

"Where is he, Aunt Marion?"

She bent over and pulled some weeds, throwing them into a wagon. "Inside. I have to weed around the foxglove before it rains." I picked up a few of the weeds that fell off the wagon.

"I'm going to talk to Harold about not holding you to his crazy demand."

"Harold is dead." No emotion. No tears. Just a flat statement. Three words.

I headed for the porch. "Are you sure?"

"I shook him and he didn't move. That's as sure as I can get."

□ □ □

Aunt Marion had Harold laid out on the closed-in porch with the mismatched windows, his casket vying for space with the divan, the broom, and the dustpan. She decorated with bouquets of wildflowers from her garden. If it weren't for the casket and Harold's dour face, the room would have been quite cheerful.

My aunt caught me eyeing the spray of foxglove on top of

the casket.

"Harold insisted that I treat his heart problem with it. It works the same as digitalis. Of course one must be very careful not to overmedicate." She lowered her eyes.

I looked away, and then went to the coffin to examine it, not even attempting to pay my last respects. I was surprised, but not disappointed at what I didn't find.

"Aunt Marion? Where's the money? We promised him."

"Now calm down, Quincy. I followed every one of Harold's wishes down to the letter. The day he died, I stood over his dead body and said, 'Harold, I'm going to buy a dress.' "

She twirled like a model in front of the casket.

"Do you like it, Quincy? I love this shade of red, and I think Harold will be happy to know that I'll get double duty out of it by wearing it to Lucy's wedding."

I took her gently by the arm to stop her from twirling. "But the money, Aunt Marion."

"I'm burying it with him, just as I promised." She reached into Harold's breast pocket and pulled out a slip of paper. "You never know who might be planning to rob a grave these days. Knowing how Harold wanted to protect his money, I deposited all of it into a checking account in my name and gave him this check for $235,334.82. So you see I kept every promise."

Dark

Judith Green

Black dark. The moment the door shut. She whimpered in fear. She had to get out—even if they found her, she had to get out! Her hands slid along the metal panel that covered the door, searching for the handle.

There was no handle.

She sobbed now, gagged, heaved with sobs. She thumped against the metal panel, but even on the inside her tiny fists made little noise. "Billy! Ted! Help me!" She hammered the door with her bare heels. "Help me!" At last Margie lay exhausted, her head curled tight against her knees. The sobs subsided to deep, shuddering hiccups, then sniffles.

The icebox had always sat there, tipped slightly, in a heap of old window frames and other trash out back of the barn. Only Ted, her oldest brother, could remember the icebox in the kitchen. It dripped a lot, he said. Their mother had done a little dance on the kitchen floor the day the new refrigerator arrived.

She'd thought it would be a great hiding place, the old icebox half-hidden in the weeds. Billy and Ted would never find her. They'd all been told never to go near the trash heap. Rusty nails, broken glass. Too dangerous.

Her brothers probably weren't even looking for her. They probably sent her to hide, then ran off to catch frogs or play some other boy game down by the brook.

Mama wouldn't be home until suppertime. The big old Plymouth would swing into the yard, and she'd reach across the front seat for her pocketbook, then head for the house, slamming the car door behind her. She'd be in the kitchen in an instant, tying her apron strings behind her as she crossed to the stove, banged open the cupboard doors.

It was hot. The air was thick, like warm gravy. Margie felt her chest heave, trying to drag in another breath. Her eyes slid shut, dark on dark.

She dreamed a little. She felt the water in the brook curling against her ankles. She heard the deep belch of cows chewing the cud. The sturdy thud of Daddy's footsteps in the tall grass—

"Daddy!" she wailed. "Daddydaddydaddy!" She kicked at the metal sides of the icebox, clawed at the panel on the door.

Sudden blinding light. "What the hell—" Strong arms lifted her out of the icebox and held her close, the good smells of sweat and pipe tobacco and Bag Balm.

□ □ □

Neither of them told. It was Daddy's unspoken request, and her unspoken promise.

She sat at the kitchen table, carefully eating every single one of her string beans. Mac lay on the floor under her feet, his long black tail thumping softly, making sad eyes up at her. Across the table, her two brothers discussed around great mouthfuls of mashed potato how if you clothes-pinned playing cards to the spokes of your bicycle wheels it would sound like a motorcycle.

"You're awfully quiet."

Margie glanced up. Mama was looking at her with those

calm blue eyes. Those eyes that saw everything.

"Are you feeling all right?"

"If she's quiet, she must be sick!" Under the table, Ted's foot connected with Margie's shin.

"Sick in the head, you mean!" Billy crowed.

"Hush, boys." Mama continued to look at Margie.

Margie tried. She tried so hard. But the hot tears began to slide down her cheeks. And almost against her will she looked to the head of the table, at Daddy.

"Walter?" Mama turned those calm blue eyes on him. She usually called him Honey. She never called him Walter unless something was wrong. "Walter, do you know what ails this child?"

The chair legs crunched against the floorboards as Daddy pushed away from the table. He sat staring at the floor, hands dangling between his knees, head sagging on his thin neck. "They were playing hide-and-seek," he said, "and she got herself locked in the old icebox."

Ted whistled. Billy whistled too, his brother's echo.

"The icebox?" Mama's eyes turned back to Margie, and now her eyes were the hard blue of the summer sky when the farmers needed rain bad and weren't going to get any. "Sweetie, you were trapped in the icebox?"

Margie swallowed. "I know you said we should never play in it but I thought it would be such a good hiding place they'd never find me but when the door shut I couldn't open it again I tried but there wasn't any handle—"

"Walter. You promised you would take the door off the hinges. You promised."

"I know. I thought I had. Thank God I brought the cows in for milking by going around back of the barn, just for the shade. They were feeling the heat, poor old things, so—"

"Walter." The single word cut him off as if she'd closed a

door in his face. "Walter, the child could have died."

And she stood up then, and her footsteps clapped across the kitchen floor, and the screen door sproinged open and slapped shut. Then in the distance there was a dull thud, and another, and another, slow and rhythmic in the summer evening. It took Margie a long moment to realize that her mother was chopping at the icebox with her father's axe.

Margie woke screaming, thrust away the suffocating pillow, clawed at the sheets twisted around her. She recognized her bedroom—the dark shape of the bureau, the open window outlining the ribbon of moonlit road below—but the panic still clutched at her heart. She pattered across the floor and down the hallway, and threw herself into her mother's arms as Mama rose from her own bed.

"There, there." Her mother's voice in her ear was soft, so as not to wake Daddy.

"It was squashing me!"

"It was just a dream, sweetheart."

"But I couldn't get out—"

"You were dreaming about the icebox, weren't you? But that old icebox will never close anyone up again. It went to the dump in the back of Daddy's truck. Now, back to bed."

"Can't I sleep with you?"

"Don't be silly. You're a big girl now. Why, you're almost six years old! Come along, now, and I'll tuck you in."

And a few nights later, when thunder rumbled over the hills and a sudden rain splattered against the roof over her head, Margie heard the cows tramping by. The cows made so much noise with their big splayed hooves that Daddy couldn't hear her shouting, "Daddy! Daddy! Don't leave me!" Her mother found her huddled against the bedroom door, shaking with sobs.

And again the next night, just as the first light of dawn silhouetted the trees beyond the pasture, Margie stood at her mother's bedside, begging to slip in beside her so she could breathe.

"What are we going to do with you, child?" her mother asked. But she lifted the covers and let Margie climb in.

□ □ □

"Where are you going, Mama?" Margie dashed out of the house just as her mother reached the Plymouth parked in the shade of the big elm.

"I'm just going downstreet for a can of Crisco. You can stay here. Daddy's in the milking parlor."

But Margie didn't want to let her mother out of her sight. She scrambled into the car, scooted across the bench seat, and sat with her legs dangling down. Sighing, Mama climbed in behind the wheel, and Margie patted the crook of her elbow, feeling her mother's skin warm and smooth under her fingers. She felt so safe next to her mother, especially as they slowed to let a car go by before they got onto the main road, and Mama reached across her to prevent her from slipping off the seat.

Besides, Margie loved going into Nesbitt's Store. The plate glass window next to the door looked like a church window, she thought, with *Lipton's Tea* spelled out in an arc of fancy letters, and under that, in smaller letters, the mysterious words *R. Nesbitt, Prop.* Just inside the door a big metal cooler grumbled, guarding the big cardboard buckets of ice cream. A scoop sat in a cup of water on the top, and above it the yellow cones poked out of a long, narrow box.

Sometimes Mama gave her a nickel, and then old Mr. Nesbitt would shuffle out from behind the counter in bedroom slippers all mashed down at the heels, his huge stomach curving his suspenders outwards, and open the cooler and lean way, way down to dig out a great dollop of ice cream and push it into the cone, giving an extra pat with the back of the scoop just for insurance. She always had strawberry.

No ice cream today. She'd been lucky to be allowed to come along. So while Mama asked Mr. Nesbitt to put the Crisco on their slip, Margie watched old Mr. Nesbitt's grandson lining up cans of Campbell's soup on the shelf.

The bell above the door tinkled, and Miss Willoughby walked in. Or swept in, like a queen.

She lived up the road from Margie's family. They could see her house just out beyond the vegetable garden, but they seldom saw her except when they met her on the narrow dirt road in her big, shiny Chrysler. She never gave way, just waited for Daddy to squeeze the Plymouth by as best he could.

Luckily she wasn't there in the winter. She'd arrive in June, and there'd be a flurry of cleaning over there, windows being washed and rugs beat out on the clothesline. They could hear her shouting at Nellie Hitchens and whatever unfortunate boy Nellie had brought with her to help that summer. Then all would fall into silence again.

In the evenings, her lights blazed long after Margie's family had gone to bed. She was all alone over there. No one ever came to call.

Miss Willoughby wasn't neighborly, Mama said. She kept herself to herself. She'd been to college, and now she taught at a ladies' finishing school out of state. Made her too good for the rest of us, Mama said.

Margie had always wondered how you went about finishing ladies. Now she leaned for safety against Mama's leg, and stared.

Miss Willoughby was tall, taller than Mr. Nesbitt, and she held her head high, as if she wished to be taller still. She wore her graying hair piled smoothly on the top of her head, held with tortoise-shell combs, and her eyes were the same gray as her hair. Her skirts swished importantly as she brushed by Mama and stepped up to the counter.

"I'm here to pick up my telephone order," she announced, "since you have *no one* available to deliver it." With this she eyed Mr. Nesbitt's grandson, who promptly edged down the shelf until he was out of sight among the cereal cartons.

Mr. Nesbitt lifted a cardboard box from behind the counter and set it in front of her. "Your order is ready," he said calmly. "And Erlon here isn't old enough for a driver's license."

"Well, I tell you, I'm frightened to leave my house," Miss Willoughby declared, "what with that man running around loose!"

Margie grabbed a double handful of her mother's skirt. Even old Mr. Nesbitt gritted his teeth as he asked, "Which man would that be, Miss Willoughby?"

"You know perfectly well whom I mean. That Winfield Pike person. When he first returned I understand he hired Nellie Hitchens to 'do' for him two days a week, but now she's living at his place as his common-law wife!"

Margie felt her mother's hand skim the top of her head. Mr. Nesbitt cleared his throat. "Children present, you know."

Miss Willoughby glanced at Mama, and then down at Margie, sniffed once, and turned her attention back to Mr. Nesbitt. "Well? Don't you think it's a disgrace? That man belongs in a hospital, not living among decent folks. In his condition, he could be dangerous!"

"Winfield Pike gave his all for his country in Korea, Miss Willoughby." Mr. Nesbitt shifted his suspenders into a more comfortable arc. "And I know it must have been a botheration for you, losing Nellie's services so sudden. But Nellie Hitchens is no spring chicken. Maybe she thought this was her last chance—" Suddenly his cheeks flamed. "I mean—"

"But that's exactly the point. This fellow Pike hardly counts as a man! Not a whole man, at any rate!"

Mama grabbed Margie by the hand and stalked out of the store, leaving the Crisco on the counter. "We don't need pies *that* badly," she muttered as she yanked open the door of the Plymouth.

Margie gasped. No pies?

□ □ □

Margie was forced to go to her brothers for information. At the lofty ages of eleven and nine, they knew everything.

"Who is the man who lives with Nellie Hitchens?"

Ted slapped shut the new Sears Roebuck catalog and kicked it to the edge of the living room rug, under the dust ruffle of Daddy's big chair. Margie knew he'd been looking at the ladies' underwear. But she also knew that if she told, Ted would put something slimy in her bed, or dump her teddy bear in the brook.

"You mean Winfield Pike?" Ted asked. He smirked at Billy, who was stretched out on his stomach reading a *Superman* comic book. "Why do you want to know about *him*?"

"Miss Willoughby said he wasn't a whole man. How can someone be part of a man? Was he supposed to go to finishing school?"

"No, silly, it's because he hasn't got a face!" Ted leaned toward Margie, his eyes gleaming. "His plane got shot down in Korea. He couldn't get out, and most of his face was burned right off. Ricky Bartlett saw him last month, going by in his truck. He's got eyes, but no eyebrows or anything. And where his nose and mouth ought to be"—Ted cupped his hands below his eyes in demonstration—"there's just a big, ugly, black *hole*!"

Margie backed away, horrified. "How—how can he eat?"

"I guess he just mushes up his food and drops it down the hole. I heard he was in New York City for years and years. He had lots of operations to try to get a face again, but the doctors couldn't help him much. So he came back here to his parents' old place up on Back Pond so's he could hide out."

"But Nellie Hitchens—"

"Yeah. I wonder how she kisses him." Ted made a great slobbery smacking sound and grabbed for Margie. Billy hooted with laughter as she dodged away.

"What are you boys going on about in here?" Mama stood in the doorway, hands on hips.

Margie ran to her and hid under her apron. "They said Winfield Pike has a big hole for a face," she wailed. "They said he has to mush up his food, and Nellie Hitchens has to kiss him!"

"Tsk! Theodore Parker, you're old enough to know better!"

"Mama, he was looking at the ladies in their underpants!" Margie cried, and dashed upstairs to hide her teddy bear.

□ □ □

"You'd better weigh it," Daddy said to the postmaster. "I don't know what the wife finds to tell her sister, but there's sure plenty of it."

Margie had come with Daddy to pick up some chicken grain at Nesbitt's and mail Mama's letter to Aunt Ellie out in Michigan. Mac waited in the Plymouth, black head out the open window, pink tongue lolling.

"Are these all the FBI notices you have?" asked a sharp voice. Margie whirled around to see Miss Willoughby surveying the Wanted posters tacked up on the end wall. "You haven't set any aside?"

Safe on his side of the grille, the postmaster glared at her. "I assure you that I post every notice that the United States Government sees fit to send to this office."

"Mm," Miss Willoughby said. "So you haven't seen any listing for—one of our newer residents?"

"No, ma'am. Nothing beyond what is right there."

"Ah." Miss Willoughby nodded her head knowingly. She strode over to the glass-fronted boxes, twisted the knob of her combination lock with long, efficient fingers, withdrew two letters from the box, slapped the door shut, and swept out of the post office.

The postmaster puffed out his cheeks beneath his half-glasses. "I hear she's after poor Winfield Pike. Thinks he ought to be locked up. After what he's been through!"

"Uh, Irving—" Daddy jerked his head at Margie.

But the postmaster didn't seem to hear him. "It's odd. They're saying Miss Willoughby was sweet on Winfield back along. Remember, he was a good-looking guy before he got burned and all. Well, she'd come visit her grandparents every summer when she was a teenager, and what I hear, one summer they were a pretty hot couple. They'd go to the dances at the fairgrounds, and then they'd go off in his jalopy until all hours. But she went off to college and he—"

Daddy cleared his throat. "Irving—"

"Oh, sorry, Walt." The postmaster looked down at Margie over the tops of his glasses. "Anyway, she's quite a piece of work. Did you hear that she suggested we all ought to go to church over to Whitneyville? We'd save a heap of money on the minister, she figured, and then we could turn our church here into a community center for the kids. She thought the sanctuary'd make a good basketball court."

Daddy grinned. "The church might get more use, at that."

The postmaster shook his head. "Your letter is overweight," he said gruffly. "That'll be twelve cents."

□ □ □

She was falling. Everything around her was falling, falling. But the sides were so tight around her, and she couldn't get out. "Daddy!" she screamed. "Daddydaddydaddy!" But when his strong arms reached for her, where his face should be there was only darkness, a great hole.

And now she dashed, shrieking, for her mother.

"Oh, lord," Mama said, sitting up in bed. She rubbed her hands across her face. "Walter, I do believe this child is marked for life."

Daddy grunted and turned his back to his womenfolk. "Get her settled down, will you? Morning comes early around here."

Margie threw herself into her mother's arms. "It fell! It fell out of the sky, and I was in it! I couldn't get out! And Daddy came, but he had no face!"

"My God, this dream is expanding!" Mama said. She thumped Daddy with the heel of her hand. "Have those boys been plaguing her about that poor Mr. Pike again?"

"Oh, that," Daddy murmured drowsily. "In the post office yesterday morning. Miss Willoughby was checking out the FBI's Most Wanted."

"That woman is a menace! Margie's never going to—"

"C'mon!" Daddy said, and pulled the pillow over his head.

Mama herded Margie back into her bedroom and tucked her in. But when her mother turned to go, Margie grasped at her nightgown. "Don't leave me!"

Her mother paused, a dim shape in the moonlight. "This is getting ridiculous, young lady." She stalked across the room and snapped on the lamp that sat on the bureau. "There. Now go to sleep. I don't want to hear another peep out of you."

Margie gazed at the lamp, at the reassuring glow cast by its frilly pink shade. The shade was decorated with a drawing of Little Miss Muffet with her bowl of curds and whey. Margie wasn't sure what Miss Muffet was eating, but it sounded disgusting.

She sat up in bed and looked out the window. The road was silvery in the moonlight, and so were the tall weeds at the edge of the pasture fence, and the fence itself.

When she leaned forward, she could see Miss Willoughby's house. As always, the downstairs windows blazed yellow. Of course, Miss Willoughby didn't have to get up early in the morning and milk the cows.

Margie wondered what Miss Willoughby did in the evening

all by herself over there. She couldn't have a television set, because there was no aerial on the roof. Did she listen to her favorite radio shows? Probably she read lots of fat, boring books.

Margie lay down again and went back to thinking about Miss Muffet's dinner, until the lampshade began to swim before her eyes, and her eyelids slid shut.

□ □ □

Friday was the end of the weeklong Vacation Bible School at church. All the children had Bible verses to recite for the evening program.

That morning, before she went to work, Mama set Margie's hair with crisscrossed bobby pins. Her scalp a mass of prickles, Margie practiced all day, reciting her verse—*ForGodsolovedthe-worldhegavehisonlybegottensonsowhoeverbelievethinhimshould-notperishbuthaveeverlastinglife*—for Daddy in the milking parlor, and even for her favorite cows.

The evening was magical. Margie's hair bounced in curls around her face, and she wore her best dress, the blue one with the big sash that tied in back. Even Daddy had come to church to hear her recite, fine in dark trousers with a crease down the legs, and a snowy white shirt and—a necktie.

Afterwards they all trooped into Nesbitt's, which had stayed open late for the occasion. The store was bursting with parents and children, stiff in their best clothes. Margie stood close to Daddy, who was talking to Mr. Wentworth, gesturing over Margie's head. She was afraid to grasp Daddy's dress-up trousers for fear of spoiling the crease, so she clenched her hands together in front of her blue dress and thought about strawberry ice cream.

More people pressed into the small space in front of the counter, and Daddy shifted backward, against the cooler. Margie couldn't see Mama anymore—she must have gone to fetch some margerine, because she always told Daddy she couldn't make butter after being on her feet working all day to help support the farm. Ted and Billy were busy shoving each other over by the wire rack of hunting magazines.

Suddenly a new figure appeared in the doorway. The door was propped open to let in the summer evening, so she was not heralded by the tinkle of the bell. She just appeared. And suddenly there was room for her. A space opened all the way from the ice cream cooler to the counter, like in the shootout in *High Noon.* Tall and proud as the marshall, Miss Willoughby strode in.

Her silk stockings whispered as she stalked to the counter to face Mr. Nesbitt, her narrow shoulders rigid, her elbows tucked in hard at her sides, her big black pocketbook swinging with each step. "That *monster* telephoned my house this evening!" Her voice rang out as if she were accusing old Mr. Nesbitt of doing the dialing himself. "Oh, it was Nellie Hitchens who began the call, whining some tommyrot about my leaving them in peace. As if *I've* done anything to disturb them! And then she put *him* on. I could hear him breathing! Well, I telephoned the sheriff's office immediately, and they said they'd get back to me. Get *back* to me! Has it come to this? A decent, upright woman, living alone, and the sheriff refuses to protect her!"

She stopped. There was a silence, a communal silence more profound than the shuffling, breathing quiet of the silent prayer in church.

"Well—" said old Mr. Nesbitt at last.

Miss Willoughby swung around to face the people grouped behind her. She addressed the adults only; the children below her eye level might as well have been so many mossy stumps. "I've been telling you for weeks, that man should be in a psychiatric hospital, not running about loose! Who knows what he'll do next?"

"Well, now—"

"Seems to me, Miss Willoughby—"

"Oh, my—"

A few people murmured scraps of answers. Looking up at them, Margie realized that even in their Sunday best they looked dowdy beside Miss Willougby in her elegant gray suit. Most everyone else just stood silent, waiting for the next scene in the drama.

That man, Mr. Pike. He'd been trapped, too. Shut up in the airplane, falling, falling out of the sky.

What were *his* dreams like?

Would Miss Willoughby make him be locked up? Then he'd be all alone, Margie thought, without even Nellie Hitchens.

And now Mr. Nesbitt came out from behind the counter, shuffled right past Miss Willoughby, and stopped in front of her. "What'll it be, young lady?"

Margie stood up straight in her blue dress with the sash, and her pretty curls. "Strawberry," she squeaked.

□ □ □

She sat between Mama and Daddy in the car, struggling to keep up with the ice cream melting stickily over her fingers.

"What *is* that woman's problem?" Daddy asked. "Nellie Hitchens isn't the only housekeeper in the state."

"What do you think, Dad?" Ted leaned forward in the back seat, his bow tie hanging crooked under his chin. "Is Miss Willoughby right about Winfield Pike being dangerous? I'll bet he got plenty of experience with guns and stuff in Korea."

"Shush, now, Ted. You'll frighten your sister."

"Yeah, but Miss Willoughby sounded real scared."

"Oh, I don't know," Mama said. "I think she just can't accept the idea that a man in Mr. Pike's condition would pass her by for the likes of Nellie Hitchens."

"Celeste!" Dad's voice sounded shocked, but Margie could hear the chuckle trying to rumble up from his throat.

Mama turned to glare at the boys in the back seat. "You didn't hear that," she said.

Ted's eyes widened in total innocence. "Hear what?"

Just at that moment the bottom of his cone soaked through, and a great glob of chocolate ice cream dropped onto his Sunday chinos.

□ □ □

It was hot, so hot. The air was too thick to breathe. The walls of her bedroom were clamping together, the slanting ceiling with its familiar patterns of cracks in the thin plaster was coming down, down toward her bed—she could not move—she could not scream, no sound would come out, she could not breathe.

She sat up, heart hammering in her chest. "Mama!"

She heard her mother's footsteps coming, the familiar creak of the loose floorboard halfway down the hall. She looked around her. In the moonlight, she could see the ceiling had raised itself back where it belonged, and the curtains hung limply on either side of the open window. Her nightgown was rucked up above the elastic of her underpants, twisted tight under her arms. She yanked it down.

She wished she hadn't cried out.

Her mother's voice came from the doorway, husky with fatigue. "Sweetie, this has to stop. You're almost six years old. How can Daddy and I believe that you're old enough for a bicycle when you can't even sleep in your own bed? Maybe we should think about getting you something else for your birthday."

Margie sniffled. This was a dilemma. Did Mama mean it? She wished she could see her mother's face.

"When you wake up, just tell yourself it's only a dream. *Please*, sweetie?"

Margie rubbed a knuckle hard under her nose. "Okay," she said with a gulp.

"That's my big girl. Good night, now."

Her mother's footsteps whispered away down the hall. Margie lay back down in her bed and pulled the covers up under her chin. The only sound now was the slow, familiar rise and fall of her father's snoring. A soft breeze from the window drifted soothingly like a cool hand across her hot face. She closed her eyes, and let the summer night wash against her skin.

□ □ □

Somewhere downstairs, Mac started to bark, a few sharp yaps followed by a low growl. Margie sat up, staring into the dark, frightened even to breathe.

She looked out the window. A figure was passing by on the road, dark in the silvery moonlight. The figure paused and turned toward the house, lifted his face.

Half a face.

Pricked out in the moonlight, eyes glowed under a strange shine of forehead. Below that, nothing. Nothing but a great, dark hole.

Margie's mouth leapt open, her chest heaved, ready to scream.

She grabbed the edge of her sheet and pushed it into her mouth. She would not scream. She would not, would not scream.

She was a big girl. A big six-year-old girl who was going to have a bicycle.

The figure passed by, walking on up the road in the moonlight. Downstairs, Mac left off growling.

Near the ceiling, one mosquito whined.

Margie leaned forward. She could see the windows of Miss Willoughby's house, brightly lit as usual. Now the figure stood on Miss Willoughby's doorstep. He knocked on the door, and the door opened. Margie could see just the hem of Miss Willoughby's skirt, swishing importantly. The light from inside shone out onto the man. The man with half a face.

Margie looked out her window at the distant figure. Her eyes were heavy. Her body wavered as she sat up in bed, like grass when the wind blows through it.

It was just a dream. Mama had said. It was just a dream.

She would not cry out. She would not call for her mother. She was a big girl.

She watched dreamily as the man stumbled backward, hands raised in front of him. The man had dreams of his own, she knew.

Just as Margie's eyes were slipping shut, Miss Willoughby stepped out into the pool of light from the open door, a long, straight, black line lifted to her shoulder.

The blast echoed in Margie's sleep as Miss Willoughby shut the door, and her doorstep went dark.

No Flowers for Stacey

Ruth M. McCarty

Reginald Stearns tucked himself in the shadows of the dumpster behind the Diamond Heights Mall and waited for the last store to close. He craved the nicotine rush a cigarette would bring, but couldn't afford to have anyone look in his direction. He'd staked out the employee parking lot for the past two nights, noting the patterns and habits of the "associates" as they made their way to their cars.

The parking lot edged the crummy side of the building. Potholes and poor lighting plagued it, and he'd helped it along by breaking two more of the overheard lights. A steady stream of shoppers had left at nine and as each store locked up for the night, Stearns had watched the employees head for their cars. The women, keys in hand, walked in pairs or groups. The men, cell phones to their ears, pressed the remote to their cars and drove off long before the engines were warm.

Just when Stearns thought Stacey wasn't coming out, he spotted her. He watched as the tall redhead with her flicked her lighter, and touched it to the cigarette already hanging from her lips. He knew she'd puff away as she walked toward her car. Stacey walked beside her, like the previous two nights. Her wavy blonde hair hung loose over her leather jacket. Stearns hadn't touched her hair in such a long time. He closed his eyes, took a deep breath and thought about her sweet smell.

She had on faded jeans and a black leather jacket, and the spike heels on her boots made her look taller than he'd remembered. Tall and thin and sexy.

They'd reached the redhead's car and Stacey had stopped to talk with her. Stearns couldn't make out what they were saying, but he heard them laugh. After a few minutes, Stacey adjusted her pocketbook on her shoulder and started for her car. The other woman watched Stacey, and so did Stearns.

Stacey turned and said, "I'll meet you there."

Stearns put his fingers to his temples. They were going to a bar! It had to be a bar. That's why Stacey had changed into her sexy clothes. Anger pounded through him. He'd followed the restraining order after getting out of prison. Read every paragraph with his parole officer. Every time they met they'd go over it again. He hadn't tried to call her. Not at her apartment or her mother's. Only at her new job. Only once! He bit on his knuckle to keep from punching the dumpster. He'd stayed away from her. He hadn't even sent her the roses he always sent after a fight. No flowers for Stacey they'd said!

Stacey got into her car, locked her doors, and started the engine. He saw her turn, give a thumbs-up to the redhead. Only then did the other woman drive away.

Stacey had parked her car in the same spot as the previous two nights—the nose of the car against the building, sheltered from the biting wind, perfect for his plan.

Stearns watched as the back-up lights came on when Stacey put the car in reverse and then watched them go out when she put the car back in park. He smiled at the perfection of his plan. He'd taped a promotional flyer to the rear window of her Chevy so when she looked in her mirror she couldn't see to back up. He knew she'd get out and remove it.

He started toward the car.

Stacey opened the car door and got out.

He wanted her to see him now, but she focused on getting the paper off her window and didn't look in his direction.

He stood behind her as she reached for the flyer. He grabbed for her hair and whispered in her ear, "Stacey."

An elbow jabbed him in the gut as a hand wrapped around his neck and flipped him over, flat on the ground. Stearns groaned as he looked at the object in his hand. Stacey's wavy blond hair.

A car screeched to a stop inches from his face; the redhead jumped out, gun pointed at Stearns, and shouted in a male voice, "Don't even move a finger. We got you this time, you bastard."

The woman dressed in Stacey's clothes smiled and said, "You have the right to remain silent . . ."

Tail

Stephen D. Rogers

And damned if somebody didn't grab my left breast. When witnesses lied, bureaucrats stonewalled, and law enforcement sneered, a PI had to keep from taking it personally. The job—the client—was all that mattered.

But one of the three men standing next me in this subway car had copped a feel, and maybe the other two noticed and maybe they didn't, but I wasn't going to let the crime pass unchallenged.

Except we were slowing as we approached the station and the subject of my surveillance was rising to her feet.

I followed Susan Bouchard up and out of Park Station, down Winter, and then dropped back as she turned right onto Chauncy.

Bouchard lowered her shoulders before entering the family planning clinic. I window-shopped, not the most successful of dodges, but my options were limited if I didn't want to lose her.

The name Chauncy made me think of a proper Bostonian, a staid and stern master of the house who, on one hand, denounced the evils of moral turpitude while groping the upstairs maid with the other.

Bitter about my experience on the subway? Who, me?

Why had Bouchard taken the T here when there were certainly clinics closer to where she worked? Unless she was afraid of being recognized. Or she'd come here to meet the person her husband feared.

My client couldn't stomach the idea of shadowing his wife himself but didn't mind hiring a professional. If he thought there was something wrong physically, he'd rush her to the hospital, wouldn't he? This was the same thing. Almost.

Twenty minutes after Bouchard went in, I stepped in front of her as she came out. "Susan? It's me, Dana, from Standish High. How long has it been? No, don't answer that."

"Dana." Her eyes were wide, uncertain, shiny with recent tears. They didn't go well with the severe suit, or the job in an English department.

"Are you still on the Cape?"

"No, we moved over the bridge after I had my daughter."

"Congratulations on that." I glanced at my watch. "Say, let me buy you a coffee." We'd passed a place on our way from the train station and I figured she might open up once she settled in somewhere.

Bouchard hesitated before accepting the offer. "I don't need to be back for a while yet."

And so we ordered coffees (deciding on size and blend and extras and lids) and split a blueberry muffin. Hunted for napkins. Picked a table that just happened to be the most private in the place.

I opened the conversation as I pried the lid off my cup. "Someone felt me up on the subway."

"How awful."

"Yes." After a quick swallow, I continued. "What could he have gotten out of it? Power, I suppose. Maybe the cheap thrill of an illicit act."

I paused, waiting to see if Bouchard would confess an affair, but she didn't.

Instead, she sat back and crossed her arms. "I know you didn't go to school with me."

"Then why are we sharing a muffin?"

"You're here because of your husband. You think I'm sleeping with him."

Interesting. Apparently I'd married since I left the house this morning. "Are you?"

"I have no intention of answering that."

I nodded as if I accepted Bouchard's answer as final. "How do you like working in academia?"

"Is that a threat?"

I shook my head. "I was just changing the subject."

"Some change." Law enforcement didn't have a monopoly on sneers.

"Your new house then. Or your daughter. How old is she?"

"Leave my daughter out of this."

So much for children as a bonding experience. I wet my finger to lift a crumb of muffin. Followed that with a sip of coffee. Smiled.

Bouchard filled the silence. "I want you to understand that I respect the work your husband does. I would do nothing to harm his reputation. His parsing of Old English is revolutionary."

Academics. "But."

Bouchard leaned forward. "The professor needs to stop with the under-grads. They can't stop him. Administration won't."

"The clinic . . ."

"Rosalie." Bouchard saddened. "So many of your husband's conquests ask me to be there when they abort. I can't do it anymore. Rosalie is probably still in there. From now on, I'm sending them to you."

"How did you get involved in the first place?"

Bouchard sniffed. "I'm the only female department member who isn't old enough to be their grandmothers. They think I'll understand, that I can somehow influence the professor."

"Do you suggest they come forward?"

"Your husband is a valued member of the college community, a source of endowments. We may live in enlightened times, but the ivory tower is still lit by torches."

"Torches can be very useful when driving away a monster."

When Bouchard merely blinked, I continued. "If the professor is—as you say—abusing his position, something should be done."

"Are you volunteering to head the committee?"

I thought for a moment before responding. "I think I am." Even if I couldn't protect anyone from whoever assaulted me on the subway, I could protect the professor's future students.

My client was concerned his wife was having an affair. Instead, she was patrolling the high moral ground, trying to do the right thing.

Bouchard continued. "He can't know I helped you."

"Afraid you'll lose your job?"

"No, I'm afraid your husband will get back at me by telling Jack about my lover."

Thursday night, while Professor Hilbert supposedly worked on his latest book with the help of Bouchard and a TA, I followed him to an apartment building where he honked the horn twice.

As an investigator, I appreciated people who kept to a strict schedule. Made the job easier. A young woman flounced from the doorway to the professor's car. Before I could even raise my camera, she was inside, and Professor was pulling away from the curb.

Well, after all, it had been a week.

They drove straight to what I assumed was the nearest motel where Hilbert disappeared into the office. He emerged a minute later and waved her toward a bank of rooms.

I snapped a string of pictures showing them coming together outside the door of room 112. Entering. Based on their agitated state, I doubted they'd bothered to lock the door behind them.

Now what? Without a client, I had no clear second act. Did I show the pictures to the professor? A school administrator whose response might be limited to a thin-lipped smile? A wife who may very well have been ignoring the situation for years?

How about the girl's parents? Could they cause enough of a stink to ensure the professor repented? Would they? Heck, the girl was probably boosting her grade-point average.

So where did that leave me?

Sitting alone outside a motel.

Needing to pee.

□ □ □

One week later, I followed Susan as she left the Middleboro train station, turned right up 105, and then turned right and then left into McDonald's.

The professor was still teaching, and may even now be driving to that apartment building to pick up his young charge. He'd been unimpressed by my photography. As had the college. As had his wife.

Bouchard wasn't going to run with it. She was too afraid of being exposed.

I decided to cut my losses and concentrate on paying jobs, sending prints to both the student and local paper. Let them compete for the scoop.

Bouchard parked, but didn't go inside the restaurant. Instead she walked past me and across the street. Reaching the tractor-trailer lot, she stopped and turned, her eyes pointing at 105.

I could understand Bouchard getting off the train and stopping at McDonald's to use the bathroom before meeting her lover. But if Bouchard was waiting for him to pick her up, why not have him do that at the train station?

Was he unwilling to drive the extra half mile?

Did she not want him to know she traveled on public transportation?

I snapped some photographs. At least the date/time stamps would prove to my client that his wife was not at work helping the professor with his book. I could even show him evidence of how Hilbert really spent his Thursday evenings.

A new white Toyota four-door sedan pulled to a stop in front of Bouchard.

My first photograph captured the driver's profile, the second the back of his head.

Bouchard stepped toward the car, leaned into the passenger window as it went down.

Full zoom allowed me to see her undoing her top two buttons.

The driver reached out and slipped something into her exposed bra. Black. Perhaps trimmed with lace. Tough to tell at this distance, in that light.

Bouchard withdrew from the window and then opened the door.

Kissed him before settling into the passenger seat.

The man I assumed to be her lover glanced over his shoulder to check for oncoming traffic.

The kiss had been both tender and hungry. Despite the pickup I'd just witnessed, no way were Bouchard and the handsome younger man strangers.

I captured him frontal and three-quarters before he accelerated. But would he continue down East Clark or turn around?

Stopping at the edge of the McDonald's parking lot, I glanced left just in time to see the Toyota pull into the hotel next door.

Why didn't Bouchard just meet him there?

Of course then they couldn't play their game.

Even illicit sex could stand a little additional spice.

I followed them into the lot and parked where I could both easily watch the empty Toyota and as many windows as possible. I'd already missed capturing a shot of them entering together.

Maybe they'd be given a room on this side of the building. Maybe they'd decide to slide back the curtains and grapple in front of the window. Maybe they'd stop right in front of me on their way back to the Toyota, turn slowly so that there would be no mistaking their identification.

What I needed was a clincher.

Jack suspected Bouchard was cheating on him but didn't want to believe. If I couldn't produce concrete proof of the infidelity, I knew my client would let his wife wiggle off the hook. He wanted to think his fears ungrounded.

She'd claim the professor had canceled their work this week, the Toyota had stopped to ask for directions, and the woman pictured inside the car was someone else. She'd been lying to my client for some time now.

He'd convince himself his gut feeling had been wrong.

I owed it to him to gather incontestable proof. Otherwise, I might as well just write him a report saying that everything was just fine.

For the next hour, I kept my eyes in sweep mode. Third floor, left to right. Second floor, right to left. First floor, left to right. Entrance. Toyota.

I was panning the second floor when Bouchard came out of the entrance. Zoom for the face. Wide for the setting.

The lover didn't follow her out the door.

Bouchard walked past the Toyota, through some low hedges, and on toward McDonald's.

From there I imagined she'd head home, arriving around the time my client said she returned home on Thursdays.

I still wanted a picture of the lover leaving the hotel, leaving Bouchard that much less wiggle room.

Third floor, left to right. Second floor, right to— There. He threw back the curtains and scratched his bare chest. Lowered his hand to scratch again.

Wide. Medium zoom. Zoom.

He was quite the hunk.

Not as young as the professor's missy, but not older by much. I could see what Bouchard saw in him.

She'd have a hard time explaining away the story these pictures told.

Just as I'd have a hard time explaining to myself the ones I didn't show my client.

Illicit. The word rolled off the tongue.

I snapped away.

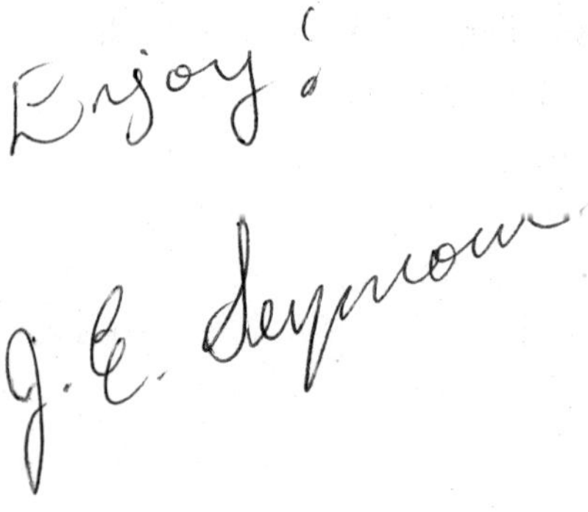

The Big Bash

J. E. Seymour

"This is embarrassing," Sally Barnard said to her boss.

"You know you're perfect for this. You're the smallest person in the office. Besides, the suit brings out the green in your eyes." He grinned at her.

She rolled those green eyes at him. "I'd better get extra pay."

"If this works, Sally, I'll make sure it goes in your file. You're really being a good sport."

"Right."

"Now you know what you're doing, correct?"

"Yes sir."

"Let's roll then."

Sally followed him out of his office and through the open expanse of desks, feeling her face get hot as the whistles and catcalls started. She'd spent six years here, struggling to get past the comments from her male co-workers, trying to get them to take her seriously despite her size and her sex, and this was going to ruin everything. She was sure her face was as red as her hair at this point.

"Hey, Sally, where's your Lucky Charms?"

She eyed Harry Austin with what she hoped passed for a death glare. "Shut up."

"Oooh, I'm so scared of the little leprechaun. You got your piece on under that suit, Sally?"

She did. Her Glock nine-millimeter semiautomatic was tucked nicely into the waistband of her green tights at the small of her back, well hidden under the top half of the suit. She didn't bother to mention that she was also wearing her vest, because that was a given on this kind of job. She offered Harry her middle finger.

Harry guffawed.

"You make a cute elf, Sally."

She focused her death glare in the direction of that comment, which came from Mark, the youngest member of the team.

"She's not an elf, you idiot, she's a leprechaun. You know, for St. Patrick's Day."

"Oh. Oh yeah. That's pretty good."

"But the accent's all wrong. Leprechauns come from Ireland, Sally, not Georgia."

She returned her gaze to the back of her boss's head as she followed him out the door. "Remind me again why I'm doing this, Dan."

"Fifty-two outstanding warrants, Sally. Ranging from bail skips to parole violations. Every one of them coming in for a big St. Patrick's Day bash, complete with green beer and great door prizes."

"Oh I get it, Sally's a door prize, right?"

Sally glared again. "Henry, if you don't shut up, I swear I'll take you apart."

Henry, at six feet and 210 pounds, laughed at the thought of Sally, who stood about five foot five and weighed probably 120 pounds soaking wet, taking him apart.

"Let's get this show on the road, folks." Dan Lancombe led his team of Deputy United States Marshals toward the event of the day. Invitations had been mailed out the month before to fifty-two select fugitives, none of them considered violent, all of them with outstanding warrants.

"Your name has been selected for our special St. Patrick's Day party, featuring an all-you-can-eat Irish buffet, green beer, and door prizes for all attending. Some of the great prizes include Big Screen TVs, VCRs, kitchen appliances and much, much more!"

Sally had her doubts about this sting, because this sort of thing was starting to get old. It'd been done to death by now. The original US Marshals' sting had been for Superbowl tickets. She wasn't sure kitchen appliances were going to be enough to entice the skips they were looking for to come out of hiding.

She was to situate herself at the door, greet the felons as they came in, give out green balloons to keep their hands busy, pat them down if she could. From there, the honored guests would be funneled to the ballroom, seated at tables, complete with pitchers of green-colored nonalcoholic beer. Once they were all seated, it would be up to Dan to make the announcement that they were all under arrest, and the big guys would come through the doors with their shotguns and submachine guns and it would be all over. Piece of cake.

They'd rented a restaurant, a big old place up in White Plains with a ballroom and plenty of parking. Sally wasn't looking forward to the evening's festivities. Being pawed over by felons was not her idea of fun.

It took several hours to get set up. Dan had come up with lots of creative ideas, including cleaning people with shotguns in their carts, waiters with submachine guns under their coats, greeters in tuxedos with handguns tucked in their fancy pants, and Sally, the little leprechaun, with her handgun, of course.

She was surprised at how many people actually showed up. They had only planned on the fifty-two, and there weren't that many, but it was a pretty good turnout just the same.

It was just after they had herded the whole bunch into the ballroom, just after the Special Ops guys had burst in there to start taking them down, that all hell broke loose at the entrance to the restaurant.

Three guys in black suits and ski masks came in through the front door with submachine guns in high ready. It rocked her back for a second, because first of all, the SOG guys weren't in their black suits tonight, and second of all, they were in the ballroom taking down the skips.

"Okay, little miss elf. Get your fucking hands in the air and you won't get hurt."

I'm not an elf, she started to say, then thought better of it. She raised her hands, slowly, staring at the guys, trying to memorize the visible features.

"What do you want?" It was the only logical thing she could think of to say.

The ninja at the front, the big one, who seemed to be the leader, answered her. "We want the big screen TVs, the VCRs and the kitchen appliances. Plus any spare cash you might happen to have lying around."

"You're kidding, right?" She could see the confusion in his eyes. Maybe he wasn't used to little ladies in leprechaun suits talking back.

"No, I'm not fucking kidding."

She wanted to ask him if he kissed his mother with that mouth, but she thought that perhaps discretion might be the better part of valor at this point, and she kept her mouth shut. She did turn her head, just to see if anybody else, the cleaning guys maybe, could see what was going on here. As luck would have it, they were all in the ballroom too, watching the fun. She was alone in this. Well, as alone as she could be with the three big guys in ninja suits. And their SMGs.

"Let's go, lady. You're going to show us where the stuff is."

Big guy again. Maybe the others were mutes. Maybe the three of them were sharing a brain and it was Big Guy's turn to use it.

"Well, uh . . ." She thought about what she was going to say. No loot, boys, just twenty Deputy United States Marshals in there with about thirty-five wanted felons.

Big Guy seemed to realize there was a problem. "Where is everybody?"

"They must be in the ballroom," said a smaller ninja with a squeaky voice.

Big Guy narrowed his eyes. She thought they might be brown. The skin around the eyes was white. She couldn't see any hair.

"Come on, elf lady. Where is everybody?"

"They're in the ballroom."

"So where's the loot?"

Where would the loot be? There was a bus in the parking lot, a big green bus with federal plates and mesh over the windows. Would the loot be there? Would they believe her if she said it was? If she could convince them to get into the bus, could she lock them in there? She wasn't sure there was any way to get out of this by herself. Any minute now, her buddies in the ballroom would be escorting the felons out in handcuffs and loading them into the bus. But they wouldn't be coming this way. They'd parked the bus by the back door for accessibility and to hide it from the arriving guests. Nobody would even notice she was missing.

Her arms were getting tired. She lowered them slightly, still keeping them away from her green lycra-clad body. "You know, uh, what should I call you, Mr., um?"

"Smith," growled the big guy.

"Let me guess, he's Mr. Jones?" She pointed at the smaller guy, who she thought might be black. "Anyway, Mr. Uh, Smith, see, I wasn't involved with the stuff. I can't carry any of that. We have, uh, you know, workers, laborers, for that sort of thing."

"Yeah, but you must know where it is." His voice was taking on a bit of an edge now.

The last thing she needed was for these idiots to get mad at her. If she led them into the ballroom, there'd be bloodshed, and it wouldn't be just from these guys. She had friends in there, and she wasn't going to spring this gang on them.

"The kitchen."

"The kitchen?" Mr. Smith sounded skeptical.

"Well, we have to go through the kitchen, to get out back, out to the truck."

"Oh, that sounds perfect, we won't even need to use our truck." This came from the third ninja, who was somewhere in the middle of the pack, slightly shorter than Mr. Smith, slightly taller than Mr. Jones. His voice was muffled, because for some reason, he had chosen a ski mask that covered his entire face except for two small slits for his eyes. He seemed to be wearing glasses under his mask. This had to be the biggest gang of idiots she had ever seen.

"Uh, right," she said. "I can get you the keys."

"Good." Mr. Smith lowered his weapon slightly and aimed it right at her chest. "You go first."

When she pushed open the door to the kitchen, she realized that she wasn't the only one not in the ballroom. Mark, dressed as a busboy, was actually washing dishes, or at least he had his hands in the sink.

"Mark? Are you insane?"

He turned to look at her. He must have seen Mr. Smith behind her, because he turned completely white. Mark O'Brien was a pale guy to start with, but every bit of color he had drained right out of his face. He licked his lips.

"What the hell is this?" asked Mr. Smith, forcing his way into the narrow aisle of the kitchen and stopping dead.

Sally turned on him and tripped him, bringing her foot into his ankles and her hands on the back of his neck at the same time. His submachine gun went skittering across the floor. Mr. Jones, distracted by Mark, fell over Mr. Smith, leaving the guy in the glasses to lower his weapon and pull the trigger. Fortunately, it appeared that the guy in the glasses had forgotten to take the safety off his weapon.

"US Marshals, get your hands up." That was what Mark was yelling, and he didn't actually have soapsuds on his hands. What he had was his weapon, hidden out of sight until he saw a chance to use it.

The guy with the glasses dropped his weapon on Mr. Jones, who was just trying to get up when the gun hit him on the head.

Sally had her weapon out now, but it looked like she wasn't even going to need it. She looked over at Mark, who was actually shaking. Then she kicked the guns away from the three guys.

"Y'all got cuffs on you, Mark?"

"Uh, yeah, I got one set."

"Hand 'em over. You have a radio?"

He nodded.

"Call some backup on in here, would you?" She leaned over toward Mr. Smith, her green-slippered foot planted on the back of his neck. "By the way, asshole, I'm not an elf. I'm a fucking leprechaun."

By the time they sorted it all out, it was after midnight. Sally was sitting in Dan's office, finally wearing a pair of jeans instead of green tights.

"I tell you, Sally, that was nice work you did."

"It wasn't just me, Dan. Mark spotted them and hid in the kitchen."

"How'd you like to move up in the world?"

"To what?"

"I'm looking for someone to work fugitives full time. You

want it?"

She didn't have to answer him. Her grin told him how she felt about his offer. She got to her feet and shook his hand. "Thank you, sir."

"You're very welcome, Deputy Barnard."

Courtesy Call

John Urban

Sergeant Jim Hannafin liked working the department's three-to-eleven shift, especially in mid-August, when a good portion of the town's residents fled Western Mass. for the Cape or Connecticut shore.

Hannafin was covering the front desk when he heard a truck outside down-shift. He spun his chair around toward the closed circuit monitor and watched a big Ford flatbed pull up in front. The deep blue cab was unmarked, but Hannafin knew the type. He was the one who instituted the town's "repo sign-in policy" three years prior. Turn off someone's electricity and they get mad. Cut off cable TV and they get really mad. Reclaim a car and you risk entering the realm of guns, knives, and baseball bats, even in suburbia.

Hannafin swung back around toward the front door and watched the driver walk in, clipboard in hand. He looked young and on the clean-cut side. "I've got a repossession. Figured I'd give you folks a courtesy call."

Hannafin nodded as he stood. It took all of his six-foot, four-inch height to reach the entry book they kept on the top shelf. "What's the address?"

"251 Birch Bend Lane. Guy named Chris Noble. Know him?"

"It's not a him; it's a her."

The driver looked at his paperwork. "Right. Should have figured. A baby-blue Mustang ragtop. Definite chick car. She got a rap sheet?"

Hannafin sat back in his chair and used his elbow to push down on the butt of his handgun so it wouldn't jab him in the side, but he said nothing.

"A husband or boyfriend that'll try to stop me?"

"No," Hannafin said. "How far behind is she?"

The driver flipped through the legal-size sheets attached to his clipboard. "Too far. Doesn't even give me the number of months. Paperwork says I'm supposed to get the car no matter what, not even cash accepted. They only do that after you've bounced a whole book of checks. I'm not going to have any trouble with her, am I?"

"No. Don't think so. Might not even be home."

"All the better. Just as long as the Mustang is there." The driver slid Hannafin a business card under the thick glass partition. "You guys ever need some help with towing impounded cars, give me a call."

Hannafin looked at the card—company logo, address, telephone number. "You new to the job?"

"A year next week."

"We met before?"

The young repo man's hand brushed across his mouth. "No."

Hannafin looked beyond him and out at the truck. "What's your name?"

"Rob."

Hannafin's eyes turned to the driver. "Last name?"

"Labonte."

Hannafin slid the book under the separating glass and said, "Okay, Rob. Sign here."

The driver said, "Mostly I haul cars around Hartford. Won't be at this much longer, either. Going back to school. Get a degree."

Hannafin took the book. "Good luck with that. You know how to get to Birch Bend?"

"All set," the driver said and he headed for the door.

□ □ □

Jim Hannafin walked to the back of the station where two young patrolmen were in the break room jawing about changes needed in the Red Sox bullpen. He shook his head. Twenty-somethings two years out of the Academy with PhDs in the science of baseball. Hannafin tossed a photocopied menu on the table. They were halfway though the shift and even though he had seniority he said he'd pick up dinner. When Hannafin was a patrol officer he would have had the smarts to drive the sergeant, or at least offer, but not these two.

While one of the men eyed the menu the other one said, "I was watching the camera and saw that young repo guy pull in. Who's he putting the grab on?"

"Christine Noble."

Both patrolmen laughed and one of them said, "Sweet-talking Chrissie?"

"She's a good kid."

"Anything you say, Sarge."

"Just got messed up along the way. When you two dopes are older you might have a better sense of how that can happen."

The first patrolman passed the menu to the other. "Oh, she's a good kid. No question about that. Word is she's a lot more than good. Generous, too, you know."

"Can it," Hannafin said.

"Doesn't really qualify as being a kid in my book," the

other patrolman said.

Hannafin set his shoulders back. "I told you two to can it. Now what do you want for dinner?"

"Okay, but one question, Sarge."

"Enough already."

"Come on, Sarge, how come a hard-ass like you is so soft on her? The two of you go out when you were in high school? The jock and the town hottie?"

"Do you know what you want for dinner?"

"Okay, Sarge. One question, though: were drugs and stripping what people expected of her back then?"

The question seemed to hang in the air a moment before Hannafin said, "No." There was another silent moment before the sergeant added, "And what you two may not know is that she's trying to clean herself up."

"Not so sure, Sarge. I pulled her over not that long ago and she seemed screwed up to me."

Hannafin nodded. He had seen enough to know that when you put years of shit in your body it messes up the way your brain is wired, even when you're clean. He picked up the deli menu and said, "Enough about Christine Noble. Now what do you two clowns want for dinner?"

□ □ □

Jim Hannafin took their orders and called it in. Fifteen minutes later he searched among the keys on the board and grabbed a set for one of the unmarked Crown Vics.

Ten minutes later, he pulled up in front of the Center Deli and walked in. Sal Gereke was with a young kid who was working the phone. Sal gave Hannafin a wave and went back to work sliding pizzas in and out a double-stacked oven. He used a long wooden paddle to place one of the pies on the counter and he looked at an order sheet. "A salad? Jimmy, don't tell me you're on some lettuce-eating diet."

"I've got a salad and two meatball grinders."

"I know your order. I'm thinking the salad is you. Rabbits eat salad, Jimmy. The town's finest should be eating meat."

"Sal, why'd you wait twenty years to give me grief?"

"Grief? I'm looking out for you. I got you covered, bud." It was Sal's way of referring to his days of playing offensive tackle Hannafin's senior year. They went to the states and a good part of their success was Sal blocking for Hannafin.

"Sal, you ever see Chrissie Noble in here?"

"What, that salad's for her? I'll feel better if that's what you're telling me."

"No, Sal. I'm just asking."

Sal was back sliding pies in and out of the oven. "Chrissie? Sure. Not so often. Every once in a while."

"How's she doing?"

Sal shut the oven door and turned toward Hannafin. He wiped his big hands on a towel tied to his chef's smock. "Jimmy, I've got to figure you're more in the know about those things than me."

"Yeah, I guess," Hannafin said.

"Why you asking? She all right?"

"Forget I mentioned it."

"Prettiest girl in the school, wasn't she. Hell, prettiest girl I'd ever seen. You date her back then?"

"No," Hannafin said. He didn't mention the day in elementary school when he walked her home and she kissed him when they were among the trees. Hell, he never told anyone. Never needed to, because that's all that ever happened.

Sal placed a large white paper bag on the counter and poked at the register with an oversized finger. "I put an extra grinder in there in case one of you salad lovers needs to fill up. I know you always want to pay, Jimmy, and that's okay but this time the grinder's on me."

"I'm not going to eat it," Hannafin said. "Ten more pounds gets me back to 205."

Sal put Hannafin's cash in the register drawer and counted out his change. "So if you don't eat it we're even."

Hannafin smiled and reached around the back of his sidearm and slid the change into his pant's pocket.

"You see Chrissie, say hello for me, Jimmy."

"Okay, Sal."

Hannafin was almost to the door when Sal Gereke said, "It's tough being a cop in your home town, isn't it, Jimmy."

Hannafin turned. He thought to say something like, why do you say that, but he didn't.

"You've got to be the law but part of you wants to make it right for the people you grew up with, or at least look after them."

Hannafin said nothing.

"I'm just saying, that's all. Gotta be tough, especially for a stand-up guy like you. You're a good cop for this town, Jimmy."

"From your lips to the Town Council's ears, Sal. See you later."

□ □ □

Hannafin set the deli bag on the passenger seat and walked around to the other side of the car. Once he was in, he lowered the driver's side window and rested his left arm on the door. For a moment it felt like stepping back in time and for some reason he thought back to when Sal's father ran the deli. All their friends from high school would meet up there in their parents' cars on a Friday night. He could almost smell the Bacardi and cola. If he turned on a classic hits station the memory would be complete. He turned on his police radio instead. "Supervisor Two, returning to station."

Hannafin lowered the transmission shift and headed out of

the parking lot, but he steered left, rather than right. He decided to take the back way.

When he passed the road leading to Birch Bend Lane he laughed to himself thinking about Chrissie and his high-school days. Like every guy friend he had, he'd say "If I knew then what I know now."

At the next intersection he caught the tail end of a yellow light and he stopped. His mind went back to a night three years earlier when he responded to a call at the Noble house. She was slumped against the bathroom wall, halfway gone from an overdose. After a shift like that, Hannafin usually went home and watched TV with a six pack of talls by his side. Not that night, though. He went upstairs and woke his wife and two daughters, just long enough so he could hear their responses when he said he loved them.

He paused when the light changed. He figured he had a few extra minutes so he made a U-turn, backtracked, turned right onto North Main, and took a left onto Birch Bend. Just to make sure everything was okay, he told himself.

It was just past dusk and the sun's afterglow was fading against the deep-blue sky. When he was a block from the Noble house he turned off his headlights and slowed. Rob Labonte's truck was parked at the foot of the driveway, backed in. Two large lamps mounted to the back of the truck shone on the blue Mustang convertible already on the flatbed.

Hannafin squinted to get a better look. When Chrissie Noble emerged from behind the truck he felt a sense of sadness come over him, but it was replaced by confusion. Chrissie was smiling and joking. Then the front of the flatbed rose and slid back. The driver was taking the car off the truck.

Jesus, Hannafin said to himself as he started the unmarked cruiser and backed out, the lights still off. He turned the Crown Vic around and shook his head while he watched in the rear-view mirror.

Chrissie was walking Rob Labonte toward her side door.

When Hannafin reached the end of the street he turned on the driving lights, took a right onto North Main, and headed to the station. Hannafin thought, Sal was right, being a cop in your own home town can draw you in too far.

His window was still down and he was almost to the station when for the first time he heard the cicadas. The sound reminded him of when he was young. It was the same background noise, what must have been hundreds, maybe thousands, of cicadas filling the night. That memory stayed with him until it was ripped away by the dispatcher's voice. "Supervisor Two, shots fired at 251 Birch Bend."

What happened next became a blur, a flash of time. Hannafin spun the Crown Vic's steering wheel and the car fishtailed across the double yellow line. The paper bag of food flew across the seat, then back again and onto the floor. "Shit," he said. He didn't bother looking; he knew there would be a mess. He worked the wheel, straightened out, and gunned the accelerator. With his right hand he flipped on the lights and siren and reached for the radio mic.

"Two is on, can you repeat that?"

"A neighbor called in. Three, maybe four, shots believed to have been fired from within 251 Birch Bend."

"Dispatch, did the neighbor say anything about a flatbed truck?"

"Negative."

"Can you ask?"

"Two, again?"

Hannafin's foot was hard on the floor and the Crown Vic was doing almost eighty in a forty-mile-per-hour zone. "Dispatch, ask the neighbor if there's a blue flatbed truck in the driveway at 251."

Hannafin slammed on the brakes and his unmarked car slid sideways as he turned onto a side street that gave him a shortcut to

Birch Bend. Again, his accelerator foot hit the floor.

"Affirmative, Two. The truck is there. The neighbor reports a Caucasian female, mid to late thirties, in front of the house. She may have been shot. We have an ambulance responding."

"Anyone else, dispatch?"

"Negative. Already asked. Just the female."

Chrissie, he thought. No question about that. Then it came to him. The recollection that had slipped him earlier. Rob Labonte. He hadn't met him before, but he'd seen his picture, probably something from a neighboring jurisdiction that passed in front of him one day while he was working the desk. A dropped assault charge. Hannafin gassed the car even more.

"Supervisor Two, what's your ETA?"

"I'm turning onto Birch Bend. Tell the neighbor to stay in his house."

"Roger that. You have two backups leaving the station now, Two."

Backups, Hannafin thought. Those two should have left immediately.

He was almost a block away from the house when he saw her. She was leaning up against the far side of the flatbed. The cab lights were still on, lighting up the driveway. His view of Chrissie was partially blocked by the cab, so he couldn't tell if she'd been shot and he couldn't see Labonte.

He flipped the siren switch off, but he could still hear wailing in the distance. The other two cars were coming from across town.

Hannafin spun the wheel over and jammed the brakes, swerving the Crown Vic to a stop in the middle of the street. He opened the driver's door and crouched behind it, his gun out, his forearm on the door to level his aim.

He yelled, "Chrissie, are you okay?"

Her words were unintelligible.

He could hear his blood pumping. Pounding really, adrenalin. He was trained to slow things down at these moments. He tried. He assessed the area. The side door to her house was open. A light on inside. Everything still. The driver's side door of the truck was open, too, but he couldn't see Labonte anywhere. Hannafin got low to get an angle under the truck. Labonte wasn't there, either. He yelled, "Chrissie, where's the truck driver?"

She was crying uncontrollably. It was a horrible sound, more like a hurt animal than a human cry.

Where the fuck are you, he said to himself. The house backed up to woods. Hell, he could already be on the run. Yeah, or he could be right there, waiting.

Hannafin shouted again, "Labonte, come out with your hands up!"

Chrissie's freakish cries continued.

Hannafin knew the neighbor was probably watching from a window, maybe someone who could see Labonte, but Hannafin didn't want to draw anyone else into the scene. Again, he yelled, "Where is he, Chrissie?"

She screamed, but made no sense.

"Where?" he yelled.

This time he understood her words. She cried out, "He's dead!" And she came around the side of the truck, a pistol, pointed down, held with both hands.

Jesus, Hannafin said to himself. He stood partially, but stayed behind the door. "Drop the gun, Chrissie."

She didn't. If anything, her grip seemed to tighten. "The fucker hit me," she said.

"Chrissie, put down the gun. It's me. Jim Hannafin. Everything is going to be okay, but you have to put down the gun."

"Okay?" she said. "Okay? I killed him!"

"Where is he, Chrissie?"

"He's on the kitchen floor, dead! The fucker hit me—he came at me with a gun!"

She stepped alongside the truck and as she did, she shifted the pistol in her hand. The flatbed was tilted down, but straps still held the car. She was trying to release them with her left hand.

"Chrissie, everything is going to be okay," Hannafin said. He watched her closely. At first he assumed she was high, but now he realized that her physical movement seemed normal.

She still hadn't answered him. It was as if she couldn't hear him. Then she put the gun on the car carrier, placing it behind the Mustang's tires so it wouldn't slip off the angled platform. She was using both hands to work at the holding straps.

Hannafin stood and slowly walked toward her. He could hear the sirens getting closer. "I'll help you with that, Chrissie. Let me give you a hand."

The sirens were just down the street. She looked at him long enough for him to be certain she wasn't high. Messed up, but not high. He saw, too, that her blouse was torn. He lowered his gun, but kept it ready. Just calm her down and get the weapon, he told himself. "Let me help you, Chrissie."

She looked up at him. "Jimmy, is that you? Jimmy Hannafin?"

"Yes, it's me" were his words, but before they were spoken a voice behind him called out. "Gun!" It was one of the patrolmen. The other men had just arrived. Hannafin knew Chrissie had a gun, but they were seeing it for the first time. At almost the same moment the second patrolman yelled, "Sarge, down!"

Hannafin was close to her and it was his voice that now let out a wailing sound. "NO!" It was as if all three screams—*Gun, Sarge Down, No*—were said in the quick cadence of a second, no more.

Chrissie's eyes widened and she reached across the flatbed

and began to sweep the barrel toward the other two men in what may have been the work of a messed-up mind or a misplaced sense of self-defense. Whatever it was, it triggered events that could no more be undone than the earlier assault on her, or every other mishap and mistake that shaped her adult life. Her gun never fired, but the threatening move was enough. The patrolmen did what they were trained to do. Hannafin, who had dropped to the ground as he raised his weapon, did, as well.

Quickly, one of the patrolmen came to Hannafin's side. "Sarge, you okay? She was going to shoot." The other ran to Christine Noble's body.

Neighbors came running out of their houses. Hannafin looked away from the men and away from Chrissie. He closed his eyes. In the numbness he heard the cicadas for what was the briefest moment before the air was filled with the siren of an unneeded ambulance.

Bob and Lynne,
Thank you for your support
I hope you enjoy the story.
Vaughn

Bagging the Trophy

Vaughn C. Hardacker

At a young age, I learned that there are times when patience is more than a virtue—it is a necessity. Every living thing needs time to grow and mature. A good trap is no different.

When I was ten, my uncle Cy spotted a trophy buck in his pasture. Every morning he got up before the sun and watched that deer through his kitchen window while he drank his first coffee of the day. He knew the buck was wily; a wild animal does not grow to be that magnificent if it's stupid. Cy knew if he was to have any chance at it he would need to get close enough for a sure shot.

He put his plan into action that spring. Every couple of weeks he placed a single bale of hay in the pasture, allowing the whitetail time to adjust to the growing shooting blind. By mid-October, Cy had built a small fort from which he could bag his trophy. On opening day, Cy got up, drank his coffee and waited for sunrise—when he could legally hunt. As he stepped out of his house, he heard a shot. He raced to the blind and found his neighbor standing over the buck with a proud grin on his face.

□ □ □

I had not a clue why Assistant State Attorney General Harry Coyle called me to his office. One thing was certain though, if the boss called me, he had something on his mind. I walked in and took a chair across from his desk. "Counselor."

"Gordon." He closed the file he was reading and sat back. "I'd offer you some coffee, but I know you don't drink the stuff. You still on the health kick?"

"You know me; I like to stay in shape."

Harry is addicted to Dunkin' Donuts. If he had his way, the chain would be designated the official restaurant of the state of Maine. He considers doughnuts to be one of the basic food groups. When he dies, he wants his remains entombed in a DD restaurant.

On the other hand, I try to spend at least an hour in the health club three times a week. Now that I'm getting on in years it doesn't take much for my midsection to look like a globe.

Harry pushed the file aside and sat back in his chair. Harry's office was as cluttered and unhealthy as his diet. Somewhere beneath his girth and piles of files lay a leather chair with mahogany arms that was rumored to match his desk—even the framed degrees on his wall were canted and uneven. I would have used a dab of putty to hold the corners in place. When Harry steepled his fingers in front of his face, I knew he was ready to get to the point.

"What have you got on that shooting in Ludlow the other night?"

"Not much right now."

"Was it an accident?"

"That's highly unlikely."

"If it wasn't an accident, that means it must be a homicide. You have any suspects?"

"I got one strong possibility. He's a local bag of pus I've been trying to nail for a couple of years now."

The door behind me opened and Shirley, Harry's secretary, poked her head in. Harry motioned her to enter. She quietly handed me a glass of grapefruit juice and then departed as silently as she'd arrived.

"Okay, let's get back to business. Who's this suspect?"

"Romaine Daigneault."

"Romaine? Sounds like a vegetable."

"Lettuce."

"Let us what?"

"Romaine, it's a type of lettuce."

"People actually name their kids after stuff like that?"

"At least this guy's folks did."

Harry slurped his coffee. "You going to tell me what's happening or am I going to have to pull everything out with a pair of pliers?"

"Okay. Here's the story. The vic, a kid from Chicago named Giordano, was in a fancy rehab; he was a coke and meth addict. Either he decided he was cured, or simply had it with therapy; he walked out and never went back. Somewhere along the line, he met up with Romaine and his current live-with, Louise Michaud."

"She a local?"

I nodded and placed the glass of juice on the only open corner of Harry's desk. "Louise lives in a run-down house on Saco Road, although calling that place a house is a stretch. It appears this Giordano kid got an eye-full of Louise's sixteen-year-old daughter, Pat. He obviously liked what he saw and moved in with Romaine and Louise and from what I can learn, set up housekeeping with the daughter."

"Wait a minute, are you saying?"

"Yup, full connubial rights—right down to sharing the same bed."

"These people make rednecks sound like high society."

"The only thing keeping them from being trailer park trash is there's no trailer. There's nothing they won't do for an easy buck.

Romaine isn't the smartest person you'll ever meet, but he's crafty, like a fox. In an earlier era he'd have been a good chicken thief. I know he sells drugs, among other things."

"Such as?"

"He's not above anything—B and E, fencing stolen goods, anything that doesn't involve holding down a real job is okay with Romaine."

"What about the girlfriend and her daughter?"

"I don't think Louise is anything but a moll. At best, she's intellectually challenged. However, I think Pat's been doing some business."

"Selling drugs?"

"Her body."

"You got to be kidding me. Are these people for real?" Harry bit into a donut and absently wiped at the strawberry jelly that dribbled onto his chin.

"I'm afraid so. The only way you'd meet them at the country club is if they were cutting the fairway grass.

"Somehow or another, Giordano lived with them for three days, then, and this is conjecture on my part, his money either ran out or Romaine ripped him off. Two days ago I got a call about an accidental death—Giordano's. By the time I got there and questioned the suspects, they had already concocted their story. They say Romaine was cleaning his handgun."

"Handgun? Did he get it legal?"

"Yes, the gun is legal, although with Romaine's history, I don't know how he got it.

"Romaine said he was cleaning the gun and Giordano wanted to see it. When Giordano grabbed the pistol, it went off—twice. He was hit in the chest, DOA when the paramedics arrived."

Harry glanced at his notes. "So, the girlfriend, Louise, and her daughter, Patricia, verify his story."

"Patience."

Harry raised his eyebrows and rolled his eyes. "I'm trying, but sometimes talking to you tests it."

"No, *the daughter*; her name is Patience."

Harry gave me a hard look. I saw his skepticism. "Hey," I said, "I didn't name the kid. If you met Louise, you'd see that making sure her socks match is all she can handle most days."

Harry shook his head.

"Whatever happened to good *American* names like Diane or Amy?"

"Beats me. Based on some of the names I come across these days, Patience isn't so bad."

"You think it was an accident?"

"No, I think Louise meant to name her that."

"The shooting; do you think it was intentional? Damn, Gordon, I think sometimes you intentionally play mind games with me."

"Well, I don't have that many friends to play with—I was an only child."

Harry rolled his eyes again.

"Yes," I said, "I think it was intentional; it's difficult to clean a loaded automatic."

Harry finished his coffee and reached below his desk. He placed a huge take-out container of coffee, I think they call it a Box of Joe, on his desk and refilled his mug, splattering the contents of his open file with coffee drops. "Okay, Gordon, do what you can. But don't spend a lot of time on this; we've got a ton of cases backed up. This sounds like one sociopath offing another."

"Okay, boss, I'll do my best to wrap it up quick."

As I walked out of Harry's office, I thought about Uncle Cy's deer blind. That trophy buck might have gotten away from him, but I was not about to let Romaine get away. All I had to do was figure out a way to construct my hay fort.

□ □ □

They all stuck to their story. If I was going to get Romaine for Danny Giordano's killing, I needed a confession. The obvious problem was how to get it. Romaine was never going to be a contestant on *Jeopardy*, but he wasn't dumb enough to confess to murder.

I was sitting at home wondering how I could get him to spill his guts. Stymied, I snapped on the television and found myself watching a rerun of the *Untouchables*. When the idea came to me, I thought it was beautiful.

It was time to start placing my hay—one bale at a time.

The next night I dropped by Romaine's favorite haunt, a local dive called the Log Cabin. I ordered a club soda with a twist and watched the Celtics murder the Philadelphia 76ers. It wasn't long before some of Romaine's entourage of bottom-feeders showed up. Romaine's best friend, Charlie Duffy, walked to the bar and stood next to me waiting for the bartender to pour him a beer and a shot.

Duffy isn't a bad guy for a scumbag. He lives in a rusted-out doublewide on a dirt road so remote the state doesn't even plow it in the winter. In summer, he drives a rusted-out Chevy four-by-four and, when the snow gets too deep for the truck, an old Ski-Doo snowmobile. If he spent as much money on family and home as he did on tattoos, body piercing, booze, cigarettes, dope, and keeping his worn-out truck and sled running, he'd have the biggest and nicest home in the county. Duffy, however, has a different set of priorities from the rest of the world. His kids are at risk of becoming feral, their diet consisting almost exclusively of venison and wild fish. Duffy is also reputed to be the most proficient poacher in the area.

Duffy stared at my drink and snorted with contempt. "Hittin' the sauce pretty hard there, Officer Burgess."

"Hey, Duffy, what's up?"

The bartender placed a mug of beer and a shot in front of Duffy, then deftly scooped his ten-spot off the bar. Duffy belted down the shot and motioned for another. "Never thought I'd see you in here."

"I'm looking for Romaine. You know where I can find him?"

"Ain't seen him all day."

"Too bad, I really need to talk with him."

"I'm gonna meet him later. You want I should tell him you're lookin' for him?"

"Either that or I can give you the message and go home to my wife and kids."

Duffy picked up his beer chaser and chuckled into the mug—he was obviously amused by anybody who would want to spend time with his family. He only went home when he was broke or too drunk to go anywhere else. "What you want me to tell him?"

"You know the kid who was killed at Louise's place?"

"What about him?"

"It seems his old man is some kind of bigwig in the Chicago mob. You know, connected to some serious bad boys." The truth of the matter is Giordano's father was wealthy, but he had nothing to do with organized crime; he owned several up-scale restaurants. However, I knew Duffy wouldn't see past the Italian name and Chicago before he started imagining *Godfather* movies.

Duffy downed his second shot and chased it with a big swallow of beer. "So?"

"They aren't buying that it was an accident. If they don't get some kind of proof, other than the word of Romaine's friends, they'll be sending their own people out here to look into the situation. I imagine they'll be looking to even the score."

Duffy motioned for a third round and leaned closer to me. I tried to maintain eye contact; it wasn't easy. When Duffy spoke black gaps where teeth used to be and the musky aroma of whiskey kept distracting me. "What you saying?" he asked.

"I think you know."

"Hell, man, you're the cops; give them what they want."

Having placed the bale of hay in my fort, I stood up and tossed a five on the bar. "All I got is the word of Louise and Pat. If you see Romaine, tell him those Chicago people know he's lying and Louise and Pat are swearing to it. Might not be a bad idea for him to start watching his back." I started for the door. When I reached it, I waved goodbye. "See you around, Duffy."

□ □ □

For the next two weeks, I neither saw nor talked to Romaine. I stayed busy working a couple of other cases. Harry called me a couple of times, asking if I had anything more on Giordano's shooting. I told him, "No, I'm still looking into it."

"Well," he said, "don't spend forever on this. If you don't have anything new, drop it. We're too busy to spend a lot of time on a case we may never crack."

"Sure."

I continued working. Another week went by. Finally, I got a call from Romaine.

"What's up?" he asked.

"The sun, the moon. What do you mean, what's up?"

"Don't screw with me, Burgess. You know. The Chicago mob—they still think I done it?"

"I guess so." Another bale added. "Your problem is that all I have is statements from Louise and Pat. Those boys in Chicago figure they'd do or say anything to protect you. Besides, the women have an interest in this too. No doubt they've seen enough TV to know they could be considered accomplices."

I could almost hear him sweating through the phone. I leaned back in my chair, glad he couldn't see the big grin on my face. As I said, I always knew that when it came to thinking, Romaine had a hard time keeping up with the human race, but now I believed he was still standing at the starting blocks. It was hard for me to keep from laughing.

"Ain't there anything we can do?" The pitch of Romaine's voice increased. He sounded as if he was being squeezed in a vice.

"Well, the way I see it there's only one thing you can do."

For a few seconds, all I heard was the hiss of the phone line. I thought of Uncle Cy. Whenever I told him I was thinking he would say, "Thought so; I could smell wood burning." The air around Romaine must have smelt like a forest fire.

"You name it, man. I got to get them guys off my back!" His voice boomed.

I visualized perspiration pouring from his greasy face as he shouted into the phone. As calmly as possible, I answered, "Take a polygraph test."

I imagined that I heard crackling sounds on the phone and smelt the smoke. He doesn't know what a polygraph is, I thought. So I told him. "It's a Lie Detector test, Romaine."

"I know that. You think I'm some kind of moron? I saw them used in a television show once. They ain't allowed in court, right?"

I didn't want to scare him off, so I told him the truth. "Usually that's the case. But look at it this way, if it went down as you say, this will prove it. It'll give me something for Don Giordano."

When I said "Don," Romaine inhaled sharply. After a few seconds he said, "When can I do it?"

"We can do it as soon as you get your lawyer."

"I ain't got a lawyer."

I carefully added another bale to the blind; neither Harry nor I would be happy if this got messed up. "We'd better stop talking right now, Romaine."

"Why?"

"Without a lawyer present, it isn't smart for us to be communicating, let alone discussing your situation."

"Why for I need a lawyer? I ain't done nothing. It was a friggin' accident."

I knew I had him; the final bale was in place.

"Are you willing to sign a waiver?"

"A what?"

"A letter saying you don't want a lawyer and are taking the test without being under duress."

"Burgess, stop using words I don't know—what in hell you mean, 'under dress'? I ain't no fag that goes around wearing no women's clothes."

"I said, 'under duress.' It means you aren't being forced to take the test."

"That's a bunch of crap, man, I'm asking you, ain't I?"

"Okay. If you'll sign, we'll do it."

"I said I'll sign. You think I'd put you on about this?" Romaine was shouting, letting me know I was getting under his skin.

"Where are you?" I asked.

"Louise's place."

I referred to my notes, read the phone number to him to make sure I had it right. "I'll call you right back. It'll probably be best if we do this quick. Are you available tonight?"

He hesitated for a second. "Sure."

"Be right back at you." I hung up and called Harry on his cell phone.

"I got Romaine Daigneault prepped to take a poly."

"I don't believe it. Does this idiot have an attorney?"

"No, he thinks if he gets a lawyer everyone will think he's guilty. He swears he did nothing wrong so he doesn't need one."

"Gordon, make sure the idiot signs a waiver before you do anything."

"Already asked him about that. He'll do it."

"Just in case, I'd better be there."

I called Romaine and told him I would be over to get him in twenty minutes.

□ □ □

Harry was waiting when Romaine and I arrived. I took Romaine into the testing room and then joined Harry in the small room behind the two-way mirror.

"How'd you get him in here to do a polygraph?" Harry asked.

I told Harry about my little scam.

"He actually fell for that?"

"Yeah."

"If his defense attorney is worth anything, he'll try to get him off on mental incompetence."

"You think it would fly?"

"Probably not, but if I had a client this stupid, I'd try."

Harry settled down in front of the video monitor and placed his Box of Joe on the floor. "You know, there are times when watching an interrogation is better than reality television."

I left for the interrogation room. As I walked, I reviewed the protocol for administering a polygraph test. If the exam is to have any validity, you cannot deviate from it. I've been certified to administer the tests for ten years, but still take great care when doing one.

Before picking Romaine up I had made sure the video camera was set up—we always tape all polygraph tests. Down the road, we might have to prove we haven't violated the suspect's rights during the testing process. Today, though, I had an agenda—and appeasing the court system wasn't it.

The testing room was set up and the camera positioned so the polygraph was not visible on the tape. If the video got into court, even a glimpse of the machine will make the tape inadmissible. Should a juror see it, he or she may become biased. Since there are very few instances where polygraph test results are admissible in court, we do not want to lose the video should something important come from it.

I sat with my back to the camera and started the pretest interview. "Okay, Romaine, let's get this show on the road."

"Yeah, you know I'm an important guy; I ain't got all night." He reached into his shirt pocket and pulled out a pack of cigarettes.

"I'm sorry, Romaine, there's no smoking allowed in the building."

Romaine muttered something I couldn't hear. I let it ride; I didn't want to risk making him angrier than he already was.

"All right," I said, "before we start I need to know some things about you."

"What kind of things?" Romaine shot me a suspicious look. I knew I had to tread lightly or my prize buck might spook.

"The sort of things that will interfere with the test's validity."

"What are you talking about, man?"

I was in no mood to educate Romaine on the concepts of testing reliability and validity—I doubt he would have understood anyway. I minimized the concept. "We want you to feel safe and keep everything above board."

Romaine's doubts ratcheted up a few notches; he became antagonistic. "What for? You told me these tests ain't allowed in court."

"In most cases, that's true. Still, we have to make sure no one violates your civil rights; the test will be videotaped."

Romaine looked around, trying to locate the camera. "Do

you wish to continue?"

"Yeah, what the hell."

I began to read him his Miranda rights, but he cut me off.

"I know all that stuff; I seen it on TV, in the same show where I saw the lie detector. I know you guys can use anything I say and about having the right to a lawyer. But I ain't done nothing, so let's get on with it."

I ignored his impatience and finished reading him his rights. "You understand what I just read, Romaine?"

"I said so, didn't I?" He began to squirm in his chair. "Can we get this over with?" He folded his arms across his chest and rolled his head backward. "I'd kill for a cigarette."

"Relax, Romaine. I don't want to overlook anything here." I was not about to lose Romaine like Uncle Cy had lost his trophy buck.

We talked for the better part of an hour. I asked questions about his childhood, life experiences, run-ins he'd had with authorities—anything that could lead to misinterpretation of the collected data. I also explained how we would conduct the test.

"Are you ever going to hook me up to that machine?" he groaned.

"One last piece of business and we'll be ready to go, Romaine."

I slid a typed letter in front of him. "This is a statement stating you are here voluntarily and are a willing participant in this process. It also states that I have informed you of your right to have counsel present. I can read it to you if you'd like."

"I ain't stupid. I can read."

"Fine, take your time and read it carefully. If you agree with it, please sign and date it at the bottom."

Romaine spent an excruciating five minutes reading the form. While he struggled, I began to get nervous; sweat beaded my forehead and tickled as it rolled down my face. Afraid he'd notice, I got up and walked behind him before yanking a handkerchief out of my rear pocket and wiping my brow.

Everything was on the line. If he decided he did not want to proceed, he could walk and would be within his rights. There was no way we could hold him because he was here of his own accord.

Romaine suddenly turned and stared at me. More sweat poured out of my body, soaking my shirt. I wiped my forehead again. "Hot in here."

Romaine looked at me as if I was crazy.

I muttered, "I must be coming down with something."

"Hell, don't get me sick, man." He pointed at the form and asked, "What do they mean by that?"

I told myself to remain calm; I had him in my sights. I leaned over to see what he was talking about and he shifted aside.

"You sure you ain't catching?"

"I'll be fine." I reassured him. "They are just saying that you're here voluntarily."

"Why don't they just say that?"

"You know how lawyers are, always using big words."

"Ain't that the truth?" He bent over the form and signed.

I relaxed. The fort was complete.

I returned to my chair and spent another twenty minutes interviewing Romaine, giving him opportunity to divulge anything that could screw up the interpretation of the charts. At the end of the interview, I reviewed the questions I would be asking.

"I didn't expect to be here all night. I want a smoke."

"The worst is behind us, Romaine. The test only takes a few minutes."

All the pretest requirements out of the way, I rolled the machine over and hooked Romaine to it. Police departments with more money than ours use computers, but Maine is not a rich state;

we still used the old type, with pens and graph paper.

When I had the sensors attached, the machine would measure body functions such as heart and respiratory rate and sweat gland activity, to record reactions to nine questions

The questions fall into three categories: generic questions, which we call symptomatic questions, designed to see how he responds to generally nonthreatening questions. These questions give the operator a feel for how the subject's body will react when not pressured.

The second category is control questions, which set the subject up for the third category, relevancy questions, which get right to the matter: did the subject do the crime.

Usually questions one through three are symptomatic; four, eight, and six are control and five, seven, and nine are relevancy—they would tell me whether or not Romaine had murdered Giordano.

I took a breath. I had to fire my questions fast and furious at Romaine—completing the test in about two minutes. A good liar, and Romaine was an accomplished one, could sometimes fool the machine. I wasn't about to let that happen. I wasn't going to give him time to think about the question and adjust.

We started the test.

"Is your name Romaine Daigneault?"

"You know me, man."

"Answer yes or no, please."

"Yeah."

"Yes or no, please."

"Yes."

I fired the questions at him as fast as possible. "Do you think I'll ask you a question that you and I did not review?"

"No."

"Are you going to answer each question in this test truthfully?"

"Yes."

The pens jumped.

"During the first twenty-five years of your life, besides what you've told me, do you recall ever having lied to anyone in authority to stay out of trouble?"

"Y—No."

"Did you shoot Danny Giordano?"

"No."

Another jump.

"During the first twenty-five years of your life, besides the childhood fights you described to me earlier, do you remember ever having intentionally hurt someone?"

"No."

"Were you the one who shot Danny Giordano?"

"No."

Yet another spike.

"During the first twenty-five years of your life have you ever committed a crime and not been caught?"

"No."

The graph spiked again.

"Did you shoot Danny Giordano with a nine-millimeter pistol?"

"No."

The largest spike of all this time.

"Okay, Romaine, that's all." I turned off the machine, unhooked him, and removed the chart paper. "Just relax for a few minutes. I'll analyze this and then we'll discuss the results."

I walked out of the room, leaving Romaine alone. When I entered the viewing room, Harry was still watching the monitor, his ever-present Dunkin' Donuts container beside him. "He's like a caged cat," Harry said.

I glanced at the monitor; Romaine was sullen, fidgeting in

the chair. After a few seconds, he got up and began to pace back and forth.

I said, "I'll grab a drink."

Harry refilled his coffee cup. "You want some Dunkin' coffee?"

"No, thanks, Harry. That stuff is as lethal as drinking battery acid."

"Good though."

"I'll be right back."

I got a bottle of water from the vending machine and returned to the viewing room. I spread the chart paper across the table.

"Well?" Harry asked.

"He lied like a rug. He killed that kid as sure as you and I are standing here," I said. "Look at this." I bent over the print-out and circled the spikes on the key responses. "He lied on every question where I asked if he'd killed the kid: 5, 7, and 9, where the rubber meets the road, really hang the son of a gun. I thought the pen was going to break off the machine."

Harry shook his head. "Don't get too excited, Gordon. I'll never get this into court. We need more."

We heard Romaine talking, and looked at the monitor. He was on his cell phone. We stood before the monitor and I turned the volume up.

". . . frigging test was a joke. They got nothing."

He listened for a few seconds.

"Cool it, babe. They'll never pin anything on me. Besides the jerk needed killing; for three days all he done was use my dope and roll around in bed with Pat."

Another pause.

"Look, once I get out of here, we'll take the money and split."

Romaine listened again.

"No, they can't trace the money, but we need to get out of state in case the mob comes after me."

Romaine kicked the chair and his voice became louder. "Damn it, Louise, I told you, they'll never prove I done it. B'sides, even if I flunked the test, it ain't no good in court."

He became quiet, then even on the video monitor we could see his face turn red and the veins in his neck become pronounced.

"For Chrissake, Louise, there ain't no way to study for a lie detector test. What kind of stupit question is that? Don't be igorant; you know I hate igorants!"

Louise must have groveled, because Romaine settled down.

"I only did this to get the mob off our backs . . . listen, I ain't had a smoke since they brought me in here. I got to go."

I heard Harry inhale sharply. "Damn, Gordon, we just got a confession."

"Sure sounded like it to me."

"Is the camera still recording?"

"It's good for several hours yet. I put a fresh tape in when we started."

"Take him outside and let him have his smoke."

"And?"

"Once he gets his nicotine fix, bust his ass." He pointed at the video monitor. "You bagged him."

Wherever Uncle Cy is, I know he smiled.

Rat

Woody Hanstein

Charlie French tossed Kelvin Parker's criminal record down on the dented metal table that separated the two of them in the tiny visiting room of the Jefferson County jail. The room smelled of disinfectant, and the turquoise paint on the cinder block walls was peeling in pieces the size of postage stamps. French's back was bothering him again, and he had trouble getting comfortable in the cheap plastic visiting room chair.

He took another long look at Parker and shook his head, dismayed that suddenly his hope of convicting the murderer of a lovely nineteen-year-old college girl now rested almost entirely on a scumbag who answered to the name of "Shaky." Just two weeks ago, French had a solid case that was going to send Jerry Bell off to prison for twenty-five-years-to-life, and at the same time put an end to French's short losing streak that had his boss in the homicide division saying once again that at French's age he should move on to something less stressful, like prosecuting welfare fraud or maybe health code violations.

French still had witnesses who knew that Bell had been dating Erin Waters since the fall semester and some who heard the pair arguing loudly earlier on the evening she died. He still had Bell's fingerprints all over the dead girl's dorm room and the $1,000 in Bell's wallet that even he had admitted came from the $5,400 student loan check the girl had cashed that morning at the college credit union. What he didn't have was his eyewitness. He didn't have Kyle Thomas, a local kid and former student at the college who, at the time of Erin Waters's death, was taking a break from classes and delivering pizzas to pay the bills. Thomas had delivered a couple of pies down the hall and stopped in to say hello to Erin, but instead found Bell standing over the poor girl's body, his hand in her purse. He testified well at Grand Jury, explaining how Bell knocked him down and sprinted off down the stairway and how he had recognized him from the semester before when they took the same English class.

But two weeks ago, Thomas died in a crash out on Route 6, and that left Charlie French with just some circumstantial evidence that by itself Judge Quinn probably wouldn't even let go to a jury. That's where Parker came in. French knew from the man's SBI printout that he was only thirty-three, but those years looked like they had been hard ones. Parker's sallow skin looked translucent in the bright overhead lighting, and his dark hair was already starting to turn grey. He was short with a rugged build and a faint scar on his forehead that ran all the way up into his scalp from the center of his left eyebrow. A dozen small, badly drawn jailhouse tattoos covered his arms and sides of his neck, and on his left forearm was a bigger, professionally done one of a dagger dripping drops of red blood and below it, in blue ink, the words *NOBODY WINS*.

"So, tell me. Why does everybody call you Shaky?" Charlie French asked.

Parker shook his head. "Never knew exactly. One of my mom's boyfriends started it and it just stuck."

"Doesn't sound real complimentary."

"Don't think it was meant to be."

The lawyer tapped Parker's criminal record with two fingers. "Tell me why I should even consider believing a weasel like you?" he asked.

"Hey, I resemble that remark," Parker said and then he laughed. His teeth were brown and a couple lower ones were missing.

"Answer the question."

"From what I've been reading in the paper, it seems like you really don't have much choice," he said.

"You a big newspaper reader?" French asked.

"I read it when the guards get done. That's not a crime yet, is it?"

"No, reading the paper's still fine. But studying up on a case to learn enough details to fake a cellmate's confession . . . now that's something the law continues to frown upon."

Parker shrugged. "Do you want to talk to me or not? You can start your trial next week without me, for all I care."

"From your lawyer's call this morning I got the impression you cared quite a bit."

Parker shrugged, but he didn't speak.

"How much time did you get the first time they caught you selling Oxy to minors?"

Parker scratched his chin. "Four years, but that was near a school. And I had Judge Kutcher. They don't call him The Butcher for nothing."

"So what will they start calling Judge Quinn after she tees you up next month? And this time did I read it right that you were on probation when this drug stuff went down?"

"Just for an assault."

"Just an assault? You broke a nurse's jaw over in the ER. You think Judge Quinn is going to think that was just an assault?

Hell, you'll get five years on the PV alone." French shook his head. "I think you've got bigger problems than I do, my friend."

Shaky Parker straightened in his chair and the smile left his face. "Look, I know I'm a rat," he said. "And I know my record sucks. But that don't mean I'm not telling the truth. We both know we need each other. Your trial starts Monday and the guy who saw Jerry Bell running out of that girl's room is dead. My problem is I got guys waiting down at Warren that think I ratted them out on a thing a couple of years back. So we can try to make this work or we can call it a day."

"Keep going," French said.

Parker held up one finger like he was scolding a young child. "First thing is, I'm not testifying without a time-served deal. In writing from the AG herself. I'll plead to everything they got on me, but it's gotta be time served. With no probation."

French shook his head. "How's that going to look to Bell's jurors?" he asked. "When they see your record and then learn you're just getting time-served?"

"It's going to look fishy as hell, of course. Which is why we both know I'm not getting anything unless I'm telling the truth. Unless I know things that only Bell could know. If I give you stuff that had to come from Bell, those jurors will know I'm telling it straight."

Charlie French set a legal pad down on top of Parker's criminal record and took a cheap ballpoint out of his shirt pocket. "So convince me," he said. "Convince me that Jerry Bell told you he killed Erin Waters. Especially after he's denied it to everybody else for the past year."

Parker's eyes narrowed. "Who was he going to tell? That campus cop who arrested him two hours later with a thousand bucks of the dead girl's money in his pocket? You see him just turning that money over to Deputy Donut and saying *Hey, I just strangled my girlfriend and stole this*?"

French wrote one word down on the yellow pad and underlined it twice. "So why would Bell choose *you*?" he asked.

"We were high, for one thing."

French looked around the dingy, cinder-blocked little room. "On what?"

"Marijuana."

French didn't say anything but there was a question in the hard way he set his mouth.

"There's a guy on A-block goes out every day on work release," Parker said.

"What's his name?"

Parker shook his head. "You don't need to know. We're talking about Jerry Bell."

"So I should just trust you?"

"Piss-test me if you want. I been in here more than three months, so I should piss clean if I'm lying. And piss-test Bell while you're at it. If we don't both piss hot, you can forget the whole thing."

"So you and Bell are smoking pot, and what? He just has to get it off his chest how he killed Erin Waters?"

"It wasn't that easy, believe me. He didn't want to talk about it at all, so we started talking about my case. He was saying how it was too bad I didn't have a better lawyer, like the one his folks hired for him. He's got Julie Kramer from down in Augusta, the one with the nice legs."

French looked down at his watch and took a deep breath. "Keep going," he said.

"Understand now, Jerry's getting pretty high on account of I don't think he's smoked a blunt for a while. So I told him about a guy I knew who had Kramer on an armed robbery charge. I told him how she screwed the guy's trial up so bad that after his jury found him guilty the Feds came after him for the firearm he used and he ended up with an extra two years down in Danbury on top of his state sentence."

"That sounds like total bullshit," French said.

Parker shook his head and laughed. "Of course it is. But what does Bell know? He got upset enough that after a while he wanted a second opinion about his case. Before long he's telling me the whole story."

"Which is?"

"Which is how he met this girl on the field hockey team last fall and how they started dating. I got lots of juicy details on how good the sex was, if you care about that. Bell told me about visiting her folks over Christmas break and helping her dad fiberglass an old canoe and even how he buried the family dog so none of them would have to. He made it sound like him and the girl were happy as pigs in shit right up until the end."

French stopped taking notes and looked across the table at Parker. "What happened at the end?" he asked.

"The chick got pregnant."

French set his pen down on the yellow pad. "How far along was she?" he asked.

"She couldn't have been too far, because she just found out that day—the day Bell killed her. He said she bought one of those test kits at the drugstore and had learned the results right before he'd come to her dorm to have supper."

"And he told you all this?"

"How else would I know it? Or know that she had cashed her entire student loan check that morning to look for a car, and that Bell had taken the money after he killed her."

French stared hard at Parker, but he didn't say anything.

"I guess none of that was in the newspaper," Parker said.

"Don't worry about the newspaper. Did Bell say why he

didn't have the whole $5,400 on him when he got caught? He told the police the $1,000 he had was a loan from Erin so he could pay his tuition in the morning. He said she still had the rest of the money to pay for a car she was picking up the next day."

"Bell told me he hid the rest of the money. He said he kept the grand on him in case he needed to take off quick."

"What else did he say?"

"He said he just lost it. He wanted the girl to get the problem fixed and even said he'd pay for the doctor. I guess she wasn't too keen on that idea. The two of them got yelling so loud he said people from down the hall came in to calm things down. So he split and went for a long walk. He said he went back a couple of hours later to try to talk to her but that only got her even uglier. He said she had been drinking and was pretty drunk."

"She just finds out she's pregnant and she starts drinking?" French asked.

Parker shrugged. "That's what he told me. Should be easy to check—don't they look into that when they do the autopsy?"

French didn't answer and tried to look bored. The medical examiner's report listed Erin Waters's BAC level at .13% at the time of her death, but none of that information had ever been made public. Neither had anything about the pregnancy. "So Bell goes back and the girl is drunk," French finally said. "What happened next?"

"Bell says the girl turned on him big-time. She started saying how she'll have the baby alone because he'd be a shitty dad anyway and how he's wasting his time in college because they both know he'll end up working in his dad's body shop and then she starts ragging him how he's no good in bed." Parker shook his head. "No man wants to hear that."

"So then what?"

"He says he got mad. He just wanted her to shut up but she wouldn't, so he covered her mouth and she started struggling and when he finally got her quiet he could see she wasn't breathing. After he knew she was dead he was getting the rest of her money when that pizza guy came in."

"Did he say why nobody in the whole dorm heard any of this?"

"He said there was music blaring from the room next door. Jimi Hendrix he said."

"So he just grabbed the rest of her money and took off?" French asked.

"That's what he said. He told me he didn't mean to kill her and said he still didn't understand how the charge could be murder when it was just an accident."

"What else did he say?"

"The rest was mostly just personal stuff after that. How the case was affecting his family and things like that."

"Things like what?" French said. He picked up his pen and got ready to write. "Tell me in detail all the personal stuff. Tell me every bit of it."

Parker rubbed a hand across his face. "I'll try but I wasn't really keeping track of this part of the conversation. . . . He said he felt bad his dad had to put up the deed to his body shop to get the $75,000 loan for his lawyer's retainer. And that his mom has been so depressed since he got arrested that they started her on happy pills—I think he said Zoloft but don't hold me to that. He feels pretty responsible for all of it."

French looked up from his notes. "Anything else?"

"His sister. I guess she lives out west somewhere. I think he said Portland . . . or maybe Seattle. A couple of months ago she wrote him that she and her husband were expecting their first baby and that got him pretty upset about where things with his girl would have been if he hadn't been so freaked out about her having a bun in the oven."

"Anything else?" French asked.

Shaky Parker exhaled slowly and shook his head. "That's all I can remember."

French looked down at his notes and then put his ballpoint back in his shirt pocket.

"So, do we have a deal?" Parker asked.

French stood up slowly and felt the pain in his lower back clamp his hips like a girdle. "I'll get back to your lawyer by tomorrow," he said, and he headed for the door.

"But tomorrow's Friday," Parker said.

French turned back to face him. "Don't push it," he said. Then he walked over to the intercom on the wall and pushed the red button. "Get me the fuck out of here," he said into the speaker. A few seconds later the lock on the steel door that led to the waiting room buzzed and Charlie French pulled it open and walked through it.

When French got outside in the fresh spring air he stood for a long time by his open car door with his arms on the roof rack and his back arched against the pain. He knew what he needed to do next. He knew he needed to get a warrant to make Parker and Bell both provide urine samples, which he had no doubt would test positive. Then he had to drive back to his office across from the capitol building and fax Julie Kramer a letter containing all of the admissions Jerry Bell had made to Kelvin Parker. He would include Parker's full criminal record and the plea bargain he'd be getting, and then French would wait by the phone for the volcanic eruption of a call he'd get from Kramer as soon she had learned that just four days before a murder trial that her client's full confession had suddenly appeared.

French knew that after Kramer got nowhere with him that she'd file a motion *in limine* asking Judge Quinn to keep the statements out, but that eventually Bell's confession would come in and that the case would go forward. At trial, Kramer would certainly have plenty to work with against Parker, but in the end the intimate things Bell had told him and those positive urine tests were likely to overcome even the great distaste all twelve jurors would surely feel toward a jailhouse rat like Shaky Parker.

□ □ □

A couple of minutes after Charlie French had escaped the little visiting room, a guard came and took Parker back to his cell. Jerry Bell was sitting on his bunk reading a letter. Their third cellmate was still down at Riverview undergoing another psychological evaluation, so he and Bell had the block to themselves. In a little while, lunch got served and the two of them ate without talking. At two o'clock a guard came by to say it was time for outdoor rec and that it was so nice they wouldn't need jackets. The sun was shining and the warm, fresh air would have felt good, but Parker told the guard he was having another migraine so he'd probably just lie down and miss rec once again.

Jerry Bell left the cell to join the other prisoners in the hallway. Parker could hear one of them bouncing a ball and then the sounds of the whole group heading out to the fenced-in basketball court butted up to the side of the old brick jail. Parker climbed onto the upper bunk by the window, and he could see nearly a dozen prisoners and one guard out in the sunshine. Three or four of them were shooting baskets and one was jumping rope and the rest just stood talking in groups of two or three.

Parker slid off the bunk and listened for a minute for sounds in the hallway. Hearing nothing, he went over to the shelf by Bell's bunk and extracted the medical examiner's report from the discovery file Bell kept neatly stacked in chronological order. Parker also grabbed the letter from home that Bell had been reading that morning. In the medical report he double-checked the dead girl's BAC level to make sure he hadn't laid things on too thick with French and also verified that her pregnancy had only just begun. Then he carefully put the ME's report back exactly where he'd found it. He lay down on his bunk and slowly read the note Bell's mom had written earlier that week to her only son on thick, off-white stationary with her initials *WKB* embossed at the top of every page.

The letter was mostly boring news from home, but at the end there was one part that Parker could maybe use. Bell's father had been having prostate problems for a while and his latest PSA test had come back and everyone was relieved because it was low and the doctor said things were looking good. Parker finished the letter and put it away exactly as he'd found it. He made a mental note to tell French about Bell's dad's PSA result when they met to prepare for trial. Then he lifted up the far end of his bunk and checked to make sure he still had weed left in a sandwich bag stuffed inside the bed frame's hollow leg.

If nobody from the state police came up to piss-test the two of them today, he decided he'd smoke one more time tonight with Bell, but that would be it. Last night, once Bell got stoned, all he could talk about was how after Kyle Thomas's death he'd never have the chance to prove that Thomas was the one who killed Erin and stole the rest of her money. Shaky Parker had actually seen a little of Kyle Thomas a couple summers back when Parker was seeing a girl who managed the campground at Miller's Beach where Thomas did odd jobs. The kid certainly had a temper back then and also a strong taste for PCP, so maybe Bell's theory was even right.

Parker picked up the old *National Geographic* that he'd gotten out of the jail library earlier that morning. He didn't read the articles, but he did enjoy the photographs of faraway places he'd never been. There was a piece in the magazine about Galveston, Texas, and the pictures made the place seem nice. Parker thought after he got done testifying next week and his case pled out that maybe he'd try things out down there. Maybe try Texas and see what that was like.

Double Dare

Mo Walsh

"Paula, I need more Pot o' Golds." I smiled shyly at the bookkeeper for St. Dismas's weekly bingo and handed her the cash from the instant game tickets I'd just sold.

"Sure, Mindy. Just a sec." Paula banded another fifty-dollar packet of ones and tossed it into an open trunk already half-filled with money. She made a note of the serial numbers on a new pack of instant game tickets and passed them to me.

"Feeling lucky, Sarge?" I turned to the police officer sprawled in the folding chair between Paula's desk and the doorway to the tiny office.

"Nah."

The weekly bingo night was easy private duty, a plum for the cops with seniority. Dillon figured we'd need a bazooka to get the attention of Sergeant Snooze. Tonight the Red Sox were playing Game of the Week, and all his attention was fixed on the old black and white TV on top of a battered file cabinet.

I fanned the packet of tickets practically under the cop's nose. "Come on, Sarge. Pick any one you want. Only a dollar."

"Nah." The baseball game went to commercial and the cop

smirked at me. "Go rob some more old ladies."

"You want a drink?" I crossed to the refrigerator behind him.

"Nah. Thanks." His attention was fixed on the TV again.

I grabbed the first can I touched—diet lemon-lime, and me with no bourbon. I leaned back against the fridge, pretending to watch the video of the hottest hitter in the Sox line-up.

I studied the gun holstered three feet in front of me.

How much time would I need to close that distance, pop the snaps and get my finger on the trigger before Sergeant Snooze clicked to what was going on? Dillon insisted I couldn't do it, even after weeks of practice on the three holsters we bought off the Internet.

"Too many variations," he'd said, trapping my wrist and wrestling me onto his lap. "You're hitting the thumb breaks, but too slow on the safety snaps. Take him down first. One smack, side of the head."

I felt in my apron pocket for the homemade sap, a pound of lead shot stitched into a toy caterpillar. I'd liberated the bug from a beanbag zoo that wasn't bringing any noticeable luck to one of my instant-game addicts.

I checked the TV. The Red Sox had two men on base and a 2-2 count on the batter.

I dropped the soda can into the recycling bin. Sergeant Snooze didn't budge.

The count was 3-2, and the batter grounded another foul down the third base line. I inched forward.

"Paula!" The sound exploded through the office doorway. A split second later, Richie Doolin, all five-foot-three and 250 pounds of him, barreled in with two other workers I called the bingo twins trotting at his heels. "We got twelve winners on that four corners game at nine bucks apiece. We need ones." He winked at me. "We'll get 'em right back on the Pot o' Golds, won't we, Min?"

"You know it." I smiled. The payout tonight was a hundred bucks a game split among the winners. The players didn't consider the one-dollar bills real money. "I better get back out there."

I slipped down the hall and through the double doors into the old cafeteria. The church school had closed ten years ago, but St. Dismas still pulled in a big crowd for bingo. The challenge was finding enough volunteer workers. Enter "Mindy," the shy little secretary Dillon and I had invented.

□ □ □

"You're new to town and anxious to fit in." Dillon drilled me on my character. "Your granny loved bingo, played every week at the VFW on the Cape, took you along from the time you were five."

Actually it was Great-Aunt Louisa and a well-heeled church in Chestnut Hill. I'd been grounded for the summer after the junior prom and sentenced to chauffeur the Wheeze.

I sighed and batted my eyelashes. "Granny called me her little good-luck charm."

Dillon kissed me, and there was laughter in his voice as he nuzzled my ear. "Bingo was the first word you could read or spell. At six, you could count to seventy-five by fifteens."

"I hung up my bingo dauber when Granny died," I improvised. "I couldn't bear the memories."

"For awhile. Now you just remember how happy she was playing bingo. And being such a sweet person yourself . . ." Dillon licked the corner of my mouth. ". . . you want to help spread the joy of gambling to other greedy old grannies."

So for six weeks "Mindy" hawked tickets, sold rubber pizza and ran prize money between the cashier and the winners. Our payday was going to be the annual SuperBingo with the prize stakes doubled, two Big Money cover-alls, a fifty-fifty drawing, and a weekend casino package to raffle. The cash-on-hand would be at least ten thousand.

"It's still not much of a pot for the risk," I'd told Dillon, when we first planned the big-gun gamble.

"Nope." He grinned. For Dillon, as for me, it was never just about the money. He'd boosted his first car at twelve and parked it in front of the Quincy police station. Three years later, he stole a patrol car from in front of the Quincy station and parked it in the spot reserved for the police chief—in Milton, the next town over. Dillon's dad was a cop in New Hampshire. They didn't get along.

□ □ □

I worked my way down the center tables, selling instant-game tickets. These didn't even need to be scratched. There was a paper strip to rip off to uncover each row. Match three symbols and win, just like the slots.

"I'll take five," called a brown gnome with purple lipstick and a bad black-dye job. She shoved a five-dollar bill at me and continued marking the free spaces on a new sheet of bingo games for the next set. "Wait!" She rearranged her lucky assortment of saint statues, kitschy figurines, and cologne bottles. "All right. Got the tickets?"

Rip, rip, rip. Instant-game strips fluttered to the floor around her chair. "Nothing. Give me five more." Rip, rip, rip. "Two dollars and one dollar." She handed me the winning tickets and some crumpled bills. "Ten more."

I moved down the tables, a lily-shaped cologne bottle now tucked into my apron pocket. I'd itched for it for weeks, but Dillon had warned me, "You don't lift nothing, Bev, not one kewpie doll or silver-plated horseshoe. Wait for payday."

I reached the last table, where an old geezer daubed listlessly at a single three-game strip. A young man about my own age sat next to him, playing his own three-strip and pointing out the numbers the old guy forgot to mark. His long-sleeve oxford shirt was buttoned at the cuffs, and I could see the outline of the T-shirt he wore underneath. His hair was cut just a little too short, his glasses were tinted a little too pink, and he sat just a little too straight. Young studs don't play bingo.

"Five, please." Our fingers brushed as Dillon passed me a bill for the tickets. He'd found the geezer in a local roach motel and was paying him fifty bucks to play Grandpa tonight. "How's it going?"

"Going good. Any luck tonight?" We kept our voices casual.

"Not yet, but I feel it coming." He tossed the tickets to the geezer. "Good luck, pal."

☐ ☐ ☐

We'd met eight years ago in juvenile court: same prosecutor, same parole officer, same mandatory group counseling sessions. I was Macy's Enemy Number One, and Dillon had gotten caught at last, snatching the tips jar off the counter at Starbuck's at the peak of the latte-fix hour. The additional possession charge was a frame, he insisted, laughing. He'd left *his* stash in his other pants.

My folks packed me off to a college with a tolerant admissions policy in the Berkshires, where I failed to earn a degree in five years, but landed a ninety-day stretch in the house of correction for larceny. My parents didn't show up on my release date, maybe because I didn't tell them when it was. I had a ride with an old friend, a graduate of the Dedham HOC school of technology. Dillon picked me up in a Hummer.

"It's not stolen, Bev. It's rented," he said. Of course, the credit card number on the contract was stolen, and the driver's license was forged. One week later, at 3:00 A.M., we abandoned the Hummer in the middle of the old Prison Point Bridge.

In the two years I'd teamed with Dillon, we'd worked the T, the airport, and the courthouse, lifting credit cards, cell phones, and laptops. We'd gone from shoplifting to smash-and-grabs to breaking-and-entering. We'd lived for weeks in vacation homes while their owners were away. We'd stolen a limousine, a trolley, and a boat we didn't even know how to run. We'd become bored.

"Too much like taking candy from a baby," said Dillon, when we set the "Shark Byte" adrift less than a mile from her berth on the Fore River. "We've got to shoot for something tougher."

"Or something that shoots back," I teased.

That was the start of the big-gun gamble, and since I thought it up, I got to go first.

□ □ □

"Good luck, pal" was our signal to go. The mental rehearsal upstairs had gone well until Richie Doolin's interruption. I'd make my move for real in just a few minutes, when the caller and Richie and the bingo twins were tied up paying out door prizes. At this time of night, Paula was setting aside the Big Money prizes to give Richie after the drawings. Then she'd leave with Sergeant Snooze to deposit the rest.

"Bingo!" A hand shot up, and Richie headed for the far corner to verify the winning numbers. The twins were getting ready to draw the ten tickets for the cash door prizes. I strolled down the other side of the center tables. In two seconds, I'd be through the doors to the hallway and the office.

"I've got bingo, too!" An ancient walrus of a man grabbed my apron. If I had to call back the guy's numbers and cut across to Richie for the payout, I'd miss my shot.

At the other end of the room, Dillon pushed back his chair, stood up and stretched. He joined the pack of smokers heading for an outside door. He had four minutes to boost a car. I had six minutes to meet him on the corner with the cash.

I waved over one of the bingo twins. "Can you help this gentleman, please?" I leaned closer and whispered, "I really need the bathroom."

I was through the doors before she finished saying, "Sure."

Every nerve in my body was firing and twitching, but I forced myself to walk slowly and keep my breathing under control. My fingers trembled with anticipation as they passed over the cologne bottle in my pocket and closed around the sap.

In the dim hallway, I counted every floor tile between me and the office. I expected any second to see the cop escorting the cash out the door, but when I peeped into the office, Paula was just locking up the night deposit bag. I had four minutes.

Sergeant Snooze stood with his back to me, arms crossed, eyes still glued to the baseball game on the TV above the filing cabinet. The score was 7 to 5 in the eighth inning. I didn't know who was winning. I didn't care.

"Do you need something, Mindy? I'm just locking up." Paula's smile faltered as I swung the sap at the cop's head with my left hand and went for his gun with my right.

The cop was going down, but I hadn't hit him yet. My right hand closed over air where the holster should have been. I staggered forward, carried by the momentum of the swinging sap.

The cop ducked under my arm and caught my right wrist in a crushing grip. He twisted my arm up and back till I thought he'd rip it off at the shoulder. I choked as his other arm slammed into my upper back and he pulled my collar tight across my throat. He kicked my feet out from under me. Sergeant Snooze was awake.

"Eat floor, bitch!" the cop screamed, and I was down, chewing grimy carpet as he cuffed my arms behind me. He was sucking in air, and the hand splayed between my shoulder blades was shaking. We both knew I'd almost had him.

"Almost" doesn't count in the games Dillon and I play, and I didn't much care how this one went wrong. My six minutes were up, and Dillon wouldn't hang around. That was our deal. There was no reason the cops should be looking for him, and they wouldn't get anything from me.

As the not-so-snoozy sergeant hauled me to my feet, I saw two more cops coming through the office door. I saw them as Sergeant Sonofagun must have seen me, clearly reflected in the screen of the old TV. I hoped the Sox lost the game

"Your ride to the station is here, Miiindy." The sergeant pushed me a little harder than necessary toward the door. "Hope you like our jail."

They had my prints in the system, so what the hell. I smiled at him. "You can call me Bev."

The three cops hustled me down the hall and out the rear door to the parking lot. We paraded past the St. Dismas regulars, past Paula and Richie and the bingo twins, past the brown gnome and the walrus and the old geezer.

I didn't dare look for Dillon. I didn't need to. The patrol car was gone.

To Lynne + Bob
Enjoy my creepy side.
Libby Mussman

The Name Game

Libby Mussman

Dreams float through her mind as she sinks deeper into her bed of browned pine needles. She gazes up tall, spiny trunks to the bushy green branches that huddle high above her. A slow dusk darkens the branches, mutes the light, or perhaps it is the dreamy state she's drifted into that blurs her focus and imitates twilight. At any rate, she feels safe here in the forest of her childhood. Not "safe" exactly, but at peace.

As a child she skipped along the springy trails. Seldom was she still. But even then she would sometimes seek solitude in the deepest places known to her, nestling into the needles as she is now, concocting fantasies of her future life. *And how are those dreams turning out?* She chuckles softly to herself, although there is no one else to hear. *No prince gallops in to sweep me off my feet. No royal wedding dazzles readers at the newsstand.* In fact, normality dulls her life: high school, college, elementary teaching. The most fairy-tale aspect emerges in her hobby, creating life-like, fanciful dolls.

Pine smell fills her nose, her mouth, her head. She feels swaddled, satiated by the plush padding, and turns her thoughts to the fine points of basic comfort. Beneath her, she feels a thick, damp substance gathering in a puddle around her head and shoulders. *Is it pine sap?* She slips deeper into the sleepy fog. Wonderful peace.

A sudden tremor jostles her thoughts. She remembers him. She remembers hollering her last silent words to him as he drove away, *You can do anything to me, anything, but please, oh please don't leave me in 'dis here briar patch!* A faint smile curls her lips, her inward giggle bubbles through and stirs the pine needles.

The headlines of the future, I can hear the newsroom banter now. 'Debbie Dearborn . . .' She clenches the muscles at the back of her throat, but manages only a gurgle. *'Debbie Dearborn, Doll Designer . . .' 'Debbie Dearborn, Distinguished . . .'* That's better. *'. . . Designer of Dolls . . .'* Her mind pauses, then jerks forward, *'. . . from Dracut . . . '* Slowly her fingertips touch her throat and dab at the ring of congealed sap. *'. . . Discovered Dead.'* Her mouth twitches at the corners, gapes, then tightens in a flat line. Her eyelids roll wide open, to stare, unseeing, at the sky of needles above her.

□ □ □

"Dear Mother," Ed wrote, "It's time for me to be moving on again. My landlady has been very kind. I'll miss this apartment, but I do get restless, you know. Construction crews are cropping up everywhere. I'm heading to New Jersey. Maybe Elizabeth. It's near the coast, and my atlas shows it on Newark Bay. It's an old port city. I'll follow the Hudson River along the New Jersey side. I've seen the New York side plenty in my trucking days."

He nodded his head in short, quick bobs. "Mother will be pleased that I'm using the Atlas she gave me." He lifted his gaze to his bookcase. It was the only other piece of furniture in his efficiency apartment besides the creaky brown recliner, where he sat to write. Here he also slept, coaxing the Naugahide to retain the mold of his body. He rose and stood beside the bookcase, his eyes gleaming with enjoyment, chin firm with pride. Running a finger lightly across the smooth surface of the uppermost edge, a thrill surged through his arm, tingling it with goose bumps, and causing a sudden shudder throughout his body. "So smooth," he thought. "Smoother than kid leather. Smoother than skin. Not a blemish. Not a scratch."

He stood tall with pride and admiration, his chest lifted, spine straightened, and shoulders thrust back. He patted the top shelf as if he were patting the head of a beloved child. "One of a kind, and it's mine." A satisfied smile crept across his face, dimpling one cheek. His whole body swelled with importance. Even in private, he was embarrassed to snap at his fly to reduce the swelling.

Classic lines and fine oak construction held his invaluable collection of phonebooks of each town and city in these United States. A collection that took him years as a truck driver to complete and keep updated, until that day the Powers That Be called him in to talk. "There are rumors," they had told him, "coincidences." They were "sure he wasn't involved, but there is the company's reputation to consider." Hah. He had his collection filled by then. He'd find another job. Construction work was always available somewhere. Moving the bookcase and its contents would be a chore, but one must pay his dues to maintain the most valuable source of connection a man can have. He'd move on and show them he wouldn't be prohibited from the joys of life . . . and death.

And he had shown them, thanks to his own diligence, and thanks to Mother's constant support. She had even provided some phone books for him from towns near her. He hadn't ripped any pages out of the books she had given him. He was sorry to keep any secrets from her, but she wouldn't like to know that he had torn one page each out of the Ohio, New York, New Hampshire, and Massachusetts phone books. "Oh yes, and one page out of the Elizabeth, New Jersey, phone book. Emily Erickson, a soft first name and a strong last name." The veins at his temples began to throb. "Better not think of that now. Don't want any headaches.

Must finish my letter to Mother."

"Page two," he continued.

I added a new name to our name game list:

Alice Abbey, Akron
Barbara Brooks, Buffalo
Carolyn Croft, Concord
And
Debbie Dearborn, Dracut

I'll write again soon.

Your Loving Son,

Eddie

Vacationland

Mike Wiecek

One of Paul Carrington's biggest surprises, when he moved to Carlyle-by-the-Sea, was how much big-city life followed him. Not that he was expecting Norman Rockwell's hometown, of course. But after running a supermarket in Bridgeport, where typical customer complaints involved homeless addicts shooting up in the restroom or gunfire in the parking lot, Paul had hoped that an organic food co-op in a wealthy artists' colony might be a little more relaxed.

True, he no longer had to deal with bullet holes in the walls, or armed robbers stealing crates of steak from the loading dock. But shoplifting was an even bigger problem than in Bridgeport. The co-op's board of directors refused to consider hiring a uniformed guard, naturally—symbol of hierarchical oppression, and all that. So Paul wandered the floor whenever he could, warning off the light-fingered grannies and teenagers weak on the basics of capitalist economics.

"Seitan is next to soy milk, in the cooler," he told a customer, one bright sunny morning. "Veggie burgers are in the freezer."

The front doors jangled, and a man walked in, briefly obscured by the sun's glare. He paused by the community bulletin board. Paul glanced at him once, then looked back sharply.

"Excuse me." He left the customer

The newcomer was average height but wide and slabsided, with a face that had run into too many cinderblock walls. He wore a dusty, light gray suit, the narrow tie loose at what must have been a twenty-one-inch collar.

"Good morning," said Paul. From hard-won habit, he kept his eyes on the man's shoes and hands—which were all rough and scarred.

"I was wondering." The man had a low, raspy voice. "Aromatherapy. Think it'd do me any good?"

"Pardon?"

"I get tired of the same stink all the time. You know—cordite, sweat, blood, that kinda thing."

Paul considered. The young cashier nearby watched open-mouthed, her tongue piercings all visible.

"Well," Paul said carefully, "you might try the florist next door. An armful of lilies, say, could refresh your kitchen nicely."

The man laughed, a sort of growling cough, and put out his hand. "I'm Gresko. Annie's cousin. You know, the black sheep?"

"Ah." Annie was Paul's sister-in-law, and Gresko's name often came up, in a furtive sort of way, at Thanksgivings and Christmases. "I thought Annie said you lived in Newark."

"Up on vacation. Needed a little time away." He winked. "You know."

Paul sighed, wondering if he'd ever be free of Bridgeport. "Come on upstairs," he said. "We can talk in my office."

"Okay." Gresko looked at his watch, which was big and metal on a wide leather band. "But you might want to check the alley out back first."

"Oh?"

"Some guy's lying under the dock," Gresko said. "He looked pretty dead."

□ □ □

Fifteen minutes later three patrolmen, one detective, and the chief himself were on the scene: Carlyle-by-the-Sea's entire police force. Paul was quiet, still stunned—for all the violence he'd had to deal with, it usually involved strangers. Harold Hopper, who had a lifetime of opinions, no sense of humor, and far too much free time, was hardly a friend. But he was a fixture at the co-op, and Paul knew him well.

"Think he'll live?" Chief Vandell asked one of the paramedics, who was helping shift the unconscious man onto the ambulance gurney.

"Hard to say. Not waking up yet, that's not good—subdural hemorrhage would be my guess." The medic pulled a pair of straps around and gently belted the victim's legs and torso. "The doctors can tell you more."

"You taking him to County General?"

"St. Mary's. They got a better trauma unit."

As the ambulance departed in code two, lights and siren, Vandell sighed and turned to Paul.

"So long as he lives, he's our case," he said. "But if he dies, the state police'll take over."

"Harold's as hard-headed as they come," said Paul. "If his performance at our board meetings is any indication, I wouldn't count on handing off the investigation."

"You weren't pals, eh?"

"I didn't say that." Paul liked the chief; they'd gone shore-fishing once, had breakfast now and then at the diner. But he'd only moved to Carlyle-by-the-Sea a year ago, not nearly long enough to become a real part of the community. "You knew Harold, surely."

"Oh, yes, indeed. I don't think he's missed a council meeting in twenty years. Always has a resolution of some sort, and lots to say. He was on about the dolphins, lately. Wanted the school to stop serving tuna melt on Fridays."

"I guess it's a good thing we don't sell fish."

"And the casino—which isn't even ours. The Malinakit have federal recognition, so they can do whatever they want no matter how many letters Harold writes."

"Harold likes an uphill struggle." Paul watched the crowd of bystanders slowly diminish, now that the show had lost its leading man. "He thought the co-op wasn't democratic enough—which as far as I could tell meant that someone other than him was making decisions."

Vandell smiled briefly. "Tell me about your relative, Mr. Gresko." The change in topic was swift.

"I never met him before." Gresko was sitting in one of the patrol cars, not handcuffed but not really free to leave, either. Through the window Paul could see him sitting folded into the narrow seat, head tipped back and eyes closed. "He said he was here on vacation."

"Just coincidence, him showing up ten minutes after our first attempted murder in two years, eh?"

Paul shrugged. "He's my cousin-in-law, but he's your suspect."

"One of them," said Vandell. "Just one of our suspects."

□ □ □

Paul worked the remainder of the day worried about Harold, distracted by unwanted attention from gossipy shoppers, and more than a little irritated by the whole thing. The board had been leery enough of his urban, big-grocery background; having relatives like Gresko pop up wasn't going to help. It was too much to hope that Vandell would simply clear him and send him back to Newark.

Sure enough, in late afternoon, just when the busy hour started, Gresko reappeared. He waited politely by the customer service desk, no more out of place than, say, a howitzer. A small girl wandered over from the checkout and stared at him.

As Paul approached he watched the child's mother whisk her away, glancing suspiciously back over her shoulder.

"They let you out?" he said.

"Nothing to charge." Gresko leaned against the desk. "Your chief needed some time to get comfortable with that."

"Hmm." Paul noticed other customers trying not to eavesdrop too openly. "Look, don't take this the wrong way, but let's go for a walk."

Outside cars backed up the street, waiting for the light. An onshore breeze cooled the air. Paul led them to a bench on the town common.

"You're still a suspect," he said.

"Yup."

"Which means you're staying here for awhile."

"The chief happened to mention he'd appreciate it if I did." Gresko's growly voice sounded amused.

"Wonderful." A pause. "We need to clear you, don't we? Prove you're innocent."

"We?"

"Otherwise you'll be around all summer."

"Well, I *am* on vacation."

"Oh, right, I forgot." Paul sighed. "No doubt you'll be shopping at the co-op every day, buying your wheatgrass smoothies and so forth."

"Annie did say I should eat better, last time I saw her."

"I bet." Paul grimaced. "She'll never forgive me if you get sent up to Warren for a few years."

Before he could reply a man in workboots and faded jeans

interrupted them, walking up from behind the Great War monument. For an instant Paul saw Gresko go tense with surprise, but he immediately brought himself under control.

"Eh, Paul." The man was in his early thirties, his T-shirt dusty with plaster.

"You're early, Matt. Board meeting doesn't start for another thirty minutes."

"Ayuh. On time for once, then." He looked warily at Gresko. "You're from away?"

"New Jersey." Paul introduced them.

"On vacation?"

Gresko made a guttural sound that could have been a chuckle. "Everyone's been very friendly." When they shook hands, both men held on a little too long, examining each other.

"Matt's got a masonry business," said Paul. "He volunteered some work when we expanded the cafe, in fact."

Matt finally let go. "I was up at the Malinakit tribal hall. They're looking for bids on the new casino."

"Don't lowball," Paul said. "They've got more money than God now." Gresko chuckled again.

Late afternoon sunshine slanted through the trees, golden on the lawn. Children's shouts drifted from the playground on the other side of the common.

"I wanted to tell you, I think we got a spy," said Matt.

"What?" Gresko perked up.

"I know," said Paul. "I've noticed him too. Dark hair, really long sideburns, usually carrying an iPod or a cellphone or something?"

"A gawmy one, he is." Matt nodded. "I seen him last week, then again Sunday, walking around the co-op for an hour both times."

"Always muttering into his phone." Paul noticed Gresko's

curious stare. "Probably from the Whole Foods in Ogunquit," he said. "They can't stand the idea we're still in business. They have to know what our prices are, to undercut us properly, so this guy walks through reading the shelf tags into his recorder."

"I confronted the numb bastard," said Matt. "No, no, nothing like that—just a little talk, told him he could join up and we'd send him a flyer every week so he could do his comparison shopping at home."

"And?" Paul frowned.

"A jerk, he was. Raised his voice, poked me in the chest, then stomped out of the store without buying a picked thing."

"Probably lots of customers around, watching all that?"

"Well." Matt hesitated. "Some."

Paul shook his head. "You know what I'm going to say, right?"

"I know, I'm sorry. I just don't think we need to let people like that into the co-op at all. Like Harold—you had him on a blacklist for a while, eh? After he harangued that poor old lady about organic-versus-local for twenty minutes?"

"It didn't work." Paul eyed Matt for a moment. "You haven't heard?"

"I was with the Malinakit all afternoon. Heard what?"

"About Harold . . ."

Matt raised his eyebrows, and Paul explained.

"I gotta admit, I'm feeling mixed emotions here," Matt said. "I've had to listen to that meatball lunatic's ranting a few too many times—he thinks he can call up board members any time he wants, yell at us for an hour."

"Yes—"

"Maybe the old coot just finally ticked off the wrong guy."

Paul looked at him. "If that reporter for the *Advertiser* finds you, don't give an interview, okay?"

Gresko cleared his throat, a kind of deep, attention-catching rumble. "You have a board meeting tonight?"

"Yes." Paul looked at his watch. "Matt, maybe you can head on over, tell the others I'll be there soon."

"Sure." Matt nodded goodbye, his gaze lingering on Gresko a moment, then walked off. Crossing the street he waved at a driver, called a greeting to someone else, and disappeared around the corner.

"It's a small town," said Paul. He'd have to talk to Matt privately, maybe before the meeting, and explain what Gresko was doing here.

If he could figure it out himself, that is.

Gresko said, "He's done some boxing, that guy."

"What?"

"You can tell. Someone's been in the fights, they move . . . different." He caught Paul's skeptical glance. "Hard to explain."

"I guess."

Gresko stood up. "I was hoping you might be going to the Planning Council meeting later on."

Paul had started to rise, but he stopped and squinted up at Gresko from the bench. There was a long pause. "About the LNG terminal?" he said.

"That's what's on the agenda."

"I was thinking of attending, yes, after our board meeting." Paul finally stood, slowly. "It won't be the same without Harold, though. He always livened up the public comments."

"I can see why you all would be opposed." Gresko made a small gesture that nonetheless took in the common, the town hall, the commercial square—everything around them. "You got a real nice town here. Unloading liquid natural gas two miles up the coast, well, that's not a neighbor I'd want either."

"Do you . . . does this have anything to do with why you're

in town?"

"Of course not." Gresko smiled, and Paul almost took a step back. "But I never been much of one for TV, or an early bedtime. I thought I might take in the show."

A church bell rang five o'clock from across the common, and they listened to the carillon for a minute.

"Would you like to tell me what you're really doing up here?" Paul asked. "Besides wrack and ruin all around, that is?"

Gresko laughed out loud. "Vacation," he said. "Why doesn't anyone believe me?"

□ □ □

The committee room at Town Hall was far too small for the overflow crowds that had been showing up ever since plans for the terminal had been announced, six months earlier. The project's architects—Greensward Energy LLC—had reams of optimistic impact studies, beautiful four-color posterboards of the pipeline, and, most importantly, the whole-hearted backing of the state government. Gadflies like Harold Hopper might suggest tangled financial connections tantamount to bribery, but others were far more interested in the promised six hundred jobs. Audiences at the Planning Council meetings had grown testy and argumentative.

Paul arrived a few minutes before eight, Gresko ambling along beside him. A fading sunset still glowed orange against the purple sky, though the high school parking lot lay in deep shadow from surrounding conifers. Cars filled the lot, and a pair of police cruisers were backed in on either side of the school auditorium's entrance.

Vandell leaned against a pillar, relaxed, watching the crowd. When he saw Paul he held up a hand in greeting, then pointed to the side.

"Mr. Gresko," he said.

"Hiya, Chief."

"You seem to have a wide interest in local issues."

"Just looking for something to do." Gresko stood relaxed.

"Paul?"

"He said he'd be bored sitting in a bar."

Vandell jerked his head at the door. "All right. Don't cause any trouble."

Inside, the bleachers were folded up against the walls, leaving room for rows of chairs arranged on the wooden floor. Under the basketball hoop at one end, a low dais held a folding table with five chairs and microphones waiting. Chatter and laughter echoed noisily off the painted cinderblock walls. Most of the seats were taken.

As Paul scanned the crowd, two men stepped in front of them.

"Gresko," said the first. He was even broader and blockier and more scarred, if that was possible, and his voice was soft. "I didn't believe it, did I, Tommy?" He nodded to his rangy, jittery companion. "I said, that couldn't be Gresko, because everyone knows he hasn't been out of the Ironbound in fifteen years. What could possibly have brought him up here?"

Paul was three feet away before he even realized the other man had moved. Gresko had slipped one foot backward, evenly balanced, his hands loose and open. The tension between the three men was an almost visible force.

"Like it says on the license plate," said Gresko. "Vacationland."

Tommy, who had the gaunt face and empty eyes of a habitual meth user, grunted a sort of laugh. "Us too," he said.

"Interested in the gas terminal?"

"Funny coincidence, that." The first man glanced at the dais, where a woman in a severe black outfit was taking her seat. "We have a little seaside cottage, lobster traps on the wall, quaint as all hell, Tommy's in heaven of course, and we discover—what do you know!—an operation in which our organization has a small business stake is the subject of public interest. A meeting. We decided to come see, sort of keep an eye on our investment." His voice suddenly turned hard, though it was no louder. "To see that no one has any ideas of interfering. That there is no opposition."

"Ah." Gresko nodded slightly. "Who is it again—Greenland? Greenway? Whatever, it appears they have a silent partner."

"I like to think of ourselves as, how would you say . . . *expediters*." The man smiled, without humor. "I heard that word on TV. Good, huh?"

"So you, ah, expedite the opposition away, so to speak."

"So to speak," the man said, "that's right."

Paul wondered what he should do—run for help? Pull the fire alarm? Suggest a time-out and a group hug? But he just stood there, frozen by the drama.

Feedback squealed through the auditorium as the woman up front tapped her microphone. Someone at the soundboard shouted "Sorry!" as the crowd winced. "Hello? Hello?" The woman started again, more cautiously.

The general chitchat died away. Gresko lowered his voice nearly to a whisper.

"I don't know where you're looking for . . . opposition," he said. "But I'm not it."

"Oh?"

"I'm completely uninterested in this terminal."

"So you read the calendar wrong." The man showed his teeth. "Bingo's tomorrow night."

Gresko, without moving, abruptly seemed to loom even larger. "If you don't believe me," he said, so quietly Paul could barely hear him, "then we should talk it over outside."

The only noise was the shuffling and coughing of the crowd.

"No," said the man. "I don't think so. Not now."

Another feedback screech, immediately suppressed. "Thank you all for coming," the woman's amplified voice boomed. "This is a special session of the Tri-County Area Planning Council . . ."

Suddenly, without Paul seeing how, Vandell and two uniformed officers materialized beside them, surrounding their little group.

"Gentlemen?" said Vandell, quietly.

"Excuse me," said Gresko. The speaker's voice droned on in the background. They were at the back of the auditorium, behind the audience, and no one had noticed their smaller drama. The other two just looked at the policemen, wary but neither surprised nor apparently concerned.

"It's a pleasant evening," said Vandell. "Let's keep it that way, shall we?"

"Sure," said Gresko. "I was just leaving."

"Already?"

"I made a mistake." He nodded at Tommy and the other man. "It's not bingo night after all, I've been told."

□ □ □

For two days Paul's life returned to its usual routine. Gresko found a room somewhere on Route 9, and only came by the co-op once, early in the morning, when few customers were around to be disconcerted by his presence. He chose some peanut butter and a baguette.

"Harold's still in a coma," Paul told him.

"I heard." Gresko added a pomegranate to his basket. "The chief makes sure I'm up to date. I think he's hoping I'll crack."

"Pomegranates are loaded with antioxidants," said Paul. "Good choice."

On the third day the weather turned gray, spitting rain, the smell of sea and salt heavy in the air. The lunch rush was slow, but the cafe sold twice as much go-cup coffee as usual.

Paul was helping stock the vegetables when Vandell walked in, his long slicker dripping rain, the reflective silver stripes bright under the fluorescents.

"We get to keep the case," he said to Paul after shaking water from his hat.

"Sorry?"

"The state police don't get it after all. Harold woke up."

"That's great." Paul hesitated. "For Harold, anyhow."

"He doesn't remember a thing. His last memory is getting on his bicycle, fifteen minutes before he came downtown. Traumatic amnesia—the doctors doubt he'll ever get it back."

"So that's a dead end."

"Maybe." Vandell placed his hat carefully back on his head and surveyed the store. The sole cashier was checking a regular, joking as she ran his items past the scanner. No one else was nearby.

"Your cousin's free to go," he said.

"Not *my* cousin," said Paul automatically. "Wait—he didn't do it?"

"Those two goombahs at the planning meeting. It seems they were here to convince people the LNG terminal would be just perfect in their backyard. We had a number of citizen complaints about their tactics."

"They tried to whack Harold because he spoke up at the meetings?" It was hardly a surprise, but Paul found it hard to believe.

"That's what we figure. Of course it didn't work out that way—Harold survived, and now he's a hero. You should see the fruit baskets piled up in his room."

"Oh my God." Paul rubbed his head. "He's going to be insufferable."

Vandell cracked a smile, but it faded quickly. "One of them disappeared after the meeting the other night. Right off the map. Tommy Shanks—the skinny one. His pal won't say a word."

Paul waited. Rain hammered the roof. Finally he said, "You think Gresko—"

Vandell shrugged. "I doubt we'll ever know."

"What are you doing about it?"

"Everything I can do, which is exactly nothing. I told Gresko he needs to go home. He's had his vacation, and I never want to see him again." He stared unblinking at Paul. "Ever."

"I'll mention that," said Paul. "At the next family reunion."

□ □ □

But Paul saw him once more. Not fifteen minutes after the chief left, off to mediate another confrontation between the Malinakit's casino developers and their opponents, Gresko walked in. He was carrying an enormous umbrella with blue and white panels and the Merrill Lynch bull printed on it.

"It's like Noah's ark out there," he said, stamping his feet to shake water from his pants.

"Just a summer shower." Paul finished straightening the kale and collards and brushed his hands on his apron. "Come on, we can sit in my office."

When the door closed, Gresko stood carefully in the small space before Paul's desk, keeping the steady drips away from the files and boxes of paper.

"I'm leaving," he said.

"Business done?"

"I told you—this was my vacation. Annie was right, it's nice up here. I mean, except for the rain."

Paul looked at him. "The police think you had something to do with Tommy Shanks' disappearance."

Gresko nodded. "Of course I did."

"Huh?" Paul stared. "You're admitting it?"

"To you? Sure. You saw him. He was a cranked-up weasel. Not the kind of trash you need up here in God's own little acre."

"But . . ." Paul, for once, was at a loss for words.

"I found him later that night." Gresko spoke quietly, to keep his voice inside the office. "They really *did* have lobster pots on their wall . . . gave him a good talking to and sent him on his way."

Paul frowned. "Sent him where?"

"Back to the Ironbound. Told him to leave immediately. See, his pal was smart enough to finish up in a quiet way, but Tommy was a loose cannon—he might actually have hurt someone. You all don't need that."

"So you didn't . . . he's not actually . . ."

"Dead?" Gresko laughed, a kind of scary raspy noise. "Nah. No need."

Rain fell even harder. The phone rang, was picked up elsewhere.

"Come on," said Paul. "I'll buy you a coffee in the cafe. You'll need a clear head while you're driving in this."

□ □ □

As Gresko prepared to open his monster umbrella and depart into the lashing torrent, Paul detained him for a moment.

"I wasn't sure if I was going to ask," he said. "But I think Annie would want me to."

Gresko looked around. They were at the far entrance to the cafe, music on the stereo, the tables empty and no one close enough to overhear. "Yeah?" he said.

"Did you mean to hit Harold so hard?"

A long pause. Paul found, to his surprise, that he wasn't particularly scared. Gresko studied his face.

"Why would you think I did?" he asked softly.

"I'm guessing it's the casino." Paul sighed. "Greensward

already has one set of, um, private investors. I don't think your lot would be involved too. So it couldn't be the LNG terminal. The casino's the only other deal going up here—and it's just the kind of thing that might attract . . . Newark-based liquidity, let's say. Harold was even more hot about the gambling than he was about the gas, when I think back on it."

Gresko's face had no expression. "Tommy Shanks?"

"I believe you. No other reason to go to that meeting, so you must have expected him—or someone, I guess—and it was a nice, neat way of getting the chief off your back."

A woman ran up to the door from the parking lot, soaking wet, and pushed through with an apology. They watched her move through the cafe into the store proper.

"People have harder heads back home," Gresko said. "I might of forgot that."

"Maybe so." Paul nodded. "Thank you."

"Of course, it could just be the people I happen to run into. Maybe I need to get away more." Gresko smiled. "How about I come visit again next summer?"

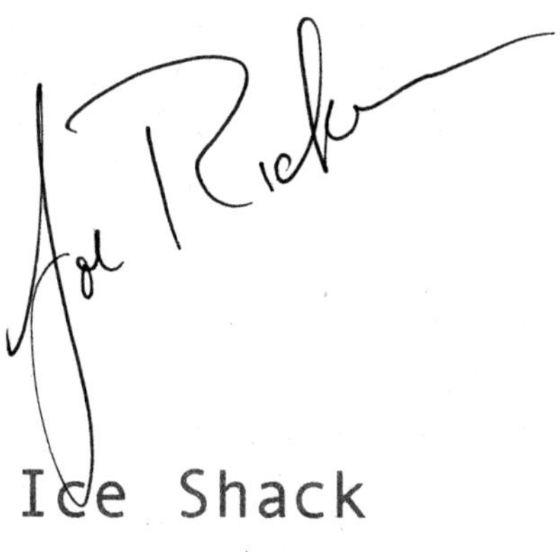

Ice Shack

Joe Ricker

If you go through the ice, water soaks through the layers of clothes and pulls you down. It forces the air out of your lungs and you drown by the time you hit the bottom and you're gone until they find your body in the spring—*if* they find your body.

There's no one but us walking on the lake. Falling snow makes it difficult to see the ice shack, four hundred yards out. That's where Louie is waiting for us. That's where the Boss told Louie and me to bring Jimmy because I vouched for Jimmy. And Jimmy owes too much money.

When we were kids, Jimmy fell through the ice, in the middle of Square Pond where the water was thirty feet deep. The cold water and the sudden pull downward came and his face went to the color of the chunks of ice he'd broken through. I lunged and caught his hand. His fingernails dug into my palms. He begged me, and God, at the same time, to save him as his head dipped under and he choked on mouthfuls of water. I could feel the toes of my rubber boots sliding over the ice as the weight of him and his drenched layers pulled me toward the hole. My fingers clawed at the ice until Jimmy, somehow, shucked off his boots and bottom layers and kicked and I pulled until we were lying on the ice panting and scared.

This lake is deeper. Jimmy walks a few feet in front of me pulling the toboggan loaded with ice traps, the auger, bait, beer, and food. My top thermal has shifted up on the small of my back and I feel the icy metal against my flesh—pale with the indentation of the safety on the forty-five.

Jimmy puts a cigarette to his lips and checks his pockets. "You got a light?" he asks looking back at me. I can't look Jimmy in the eyes. I light his smoke. He turns and I adjust the gun.

Three days ago I slept with Jimmy's wife. She pulled me into her softness with her legs, thighs squeezing against my ribs—used her heels to push into the small of my back. Her red hair was tangled in my fingers as I pulled it—hair I smelled while biting the side of her chin. The same hair that sometimes left a hint of its fragrance on Jimmy that I can smell the wind blowing off his shoulders—sweat, and white wine. I've been sleeping with Jimmy's wife for a while—collapsing on top of her on starched hotel sheets with love and guilt swirling in my stomach like the baby she's carrying—my baby.

"We're almost there," I tell Jimmy.

He pushes on. The sliding toboggan whispers against the snow behind him.

The ice shack is fifty yards away. Louie has his snowmobile parked beside it. Behind the ice shack is the hole. It's the hole exposing water—dark, cold, black—like shadows inside the barrel of a gun. It's the hole we're supposed to dump Jimmy's body in after I kill him.

The snow collects against the seams of my boots and the straps at the cuffs of my jacket. Cold creeps over my nose across my cheekbones, down the sides of my neck, inside my jacket—curls into a ball against my chest, then rolls down my ribs and the insides of my arms—around my wrists where it spins into my palms, between my fingers and over my knuckles like something curious and colorful.

We step up to the door of the ice shack and Louie comes out.

"Hey, Jimmy," he says. He hands Jimmy a small pouch with some tools in it. "Take a look at the sled, will ya, Jimmy? It's been stalling out."

Jimmy drops the rope from the toboggan. He looks me in the eyes as he takes the tools. He turns and squats near the engine of the sled. I slip the forty-five from my pants, click the safety off and hold the muzzle against the back of my leg. Louie takes a step back and moves behind me. I hear his jacket rustling like he's reaching for something. He taps my left shoulder and points at the back of Jimmy's head. Jimmy's breath rolls over his shoulder and I can see the side of his face, the windburn on his cheeks, and the snow falling against his neck. I look at Louie and bring the gun up.

I slide the gun across my chest, put the barrel against Louie's jaw, and pull the trigger.

The shot blows the hearing out of my left ear. Louie spins and I step away from him. He falls to the snow on his hands and knees, blood spattering from the bottom of his jawless face. Jimmy is crouched on the ice covering his ears. I turn toward Louie and his babbling howl enters my right ear. Snow is clinging to my eyelashes, making my eyelids quiver to shake them off. I push the barrel against the back of Louie's head.

I pull the trigger again and watch a scarlet burst spray onto his outstretched fingers and the snow. His body collapses. The echo of the gunshot rumbles to the edges of the lake.

Jimmy grabs Louie's feet and I take an arm. We drag him around the ice shack to the hole. When we roll Louie in, water spills out over the ice making slush out of the snow. Air bubbles inside his jacket, then the faceless body sinks out of sight.

I pull the set of keys from my pocket. There's a red camp on the other side of the lake—a pick-up in the driveway. Jimmy takes the keys. He puts them in his pocket.

"You can never come back, Jimmy," I say.

"I know," he says.

Circulation

Pat Remick

It was the kind of heat that could turn deadly. Edward Philbrick traced watery trails through the condensation clouding his beer mug and wondered how long it would be before the blistering temperatures took their toll.

His looked up as his uninvited supper companion plopped down on the red plastic stool beside him and said, "Hot enuff fer ya?"

"What the hell do you think?" Edward grumbled. He turned his attention back to his steaming plate of "Tonight's Special" at the Pines Café: overcooked pot roast, yellow mashed potatoes covered with lumpy brown gravy, and washed-out green beans bathed in far too much butter.

Even the coldest beer wouldn't counteract the heat rising from his plate. But the $5.99 "Special" was affordable, an important consideration given two ex-wives and five children scattered across the country. They despised him, but not the money he sent faithfully each month. Edward understood obligation all too well.

Tonight he had little appetite for his supper or another conversation about a sweltering New England summer day. Edward had heard "Hot enuff fer ya?" too many times already.

He realized Cocheco Mills was no different from small towns everywhere with their citizenry connected by endless discussion about the weather because they often had little in common beyond their shared geography. But what did these New Englanders expect? It was August, for chrissakes. They were just too cheap to embrace air conditioning in their belief that scorching heat was as rare as a blizzard in May.

They seemed to forget that every summer brought a few days when their homes became stifling boxes filled with the sound of whirring fans that barely circulated the heavy air. Heat shimmered off the blacktop and threatened to ignite the dry brown needles alongside the roadways, creating a pungent combination of pine and tar. Limp clothing clung to sweaty bodies. It resulted in a common irritability aggravated by constant complaining about the oppressive heat. Even the churches prayed for an end to the searing temperatures.

"A real scorcher, ain't it? Get this hot in Texas, Eddie?"

Edward hated to be called Eddie by anyone and especially by Bill Wykoff. It implied a familiarity that did not exist. Sharing space at the café's worn Formica counter didn't make them friends. If it had, the friendship would have been one-sided, since the retired postal carrier generally talked nonstop, primarily about himself. Most nights, Edward found it easier to daydream than try and fight his way into Bill's monologue. But tonight he was too irritated to keep quiet.

"Are you kidding? Back in Texas, it was hotter than this in the middle of winter, for chrissakes. That's why there were so many murders—too frigging hot."

"Well, I reckon we'd rather have heat and mosquitoes than murdahs," Bill said, his New Hampshire accent destroying the "r's" on some words and adding them to others.

He waved over the new part-time waitress, a perky high school student named Brittany, and asked for a lemonade refill. "Of course, some would say the mosquitoes are murdah enough, right, Brittany?" he chortled.

The teenager politely smiled. Edward was too hot to be amused. "Hey, Missy, any chance you can find another fan to get some air circulating? It's too damn hot in here to eat." Brittany's smile vanished as she scurried off.

"Give her a break, Eddie. The heat's not her fault," Bill said.

"If you call me Eddie one more time, I just might murder you. Maybe that way you'd get the point."

Come to think of it, a murder would definitely be more exciting than what qualified as news in this former factory town. Edward was weary of running stories about the never-ending squabbles of the volunteer selectmen, the recurring—and thus far unfounded—panic that a big-box store would move in to drive out local businesses, and the infinite number of local sports that changed only with the players' names.

Neither Bill nor the general population of Cocheco Mills realized it, but the byline of Edward T. Philbrick II once stood tall atop scores of major news stories. In his day, Edward had toppled the arrogant, humbled the elected, and exposed the entrusted.

Cocheco Mills saw only a pot-bellied, middle-aged newspaper editor who ate supper every evening at the town's sole year-round restaurant because there was no one at home to cook for him. In three short years, Edward had become part of the town's daily rhythm, someone who showed up at Rotary meetings and other local events, and made sure their lives were chronicled.

He hated this town.

Edward's misery was interrupted by the sound of angry voices coming from the small office off the café's dining room. He could see its "manager," a tall, skinny twenty-year-old named Jimmy Jones, arguing with his pregnant wife who had arrived minutes earlier. From the few words Edward could make out above the clatter, Tiffany was resisting Jimmy's demands that she go home to clean in preparation for entertaining his parents the following evening.

"What are you lookin' at?" Bill asked.

Edward pointed toward the office. "Looks like the new Mrs. Jones may be thinking better of her decision to marry our esteemed manager. Wanna bet how long this marriage lasts?"

"Until he's a big basketball star. Everyone's says he's goin' to make it to the big time," Bill said.

"Yeah, right."

Edward didn't like Jimmy. There were rumors the cocky young man had a history of bullying and brushes with the law that his parents used their financial influence to conceal. Edward knew people resented Jimmy getting away with so much over the years. But not even his family could save him from the rule that two failing grades made him ineligible to play basketball his senior year, so Jimmy dropped out of Cochecho Mills High.

After hearing so much praise over the years, Jimmy considered it only a minor setback on the road to a professional basketball career. He played in all the regional leagues and supported himself with "temporary" employment at the Pines Café. In two years he had advanced from line cook to manager of the restaurant now decorated with his sports trophies. There were rumors cocaine made it easier for Jimmy to believe the pro scouts would come.

Brittany returned from the kitchen with another box fan and plugged it in near the end of the counter.

"About time," Edward said.

Brittany managed a weak smile. "Another beer, Mr. Philbrick?"

"Better make it a tall one. I need something to cool me down before I go back to the newsroom. It's like a sauna."

"More lemonade, Mr. Wykoff?" Brittany asked.

"Please make mine a tall one, too, my dear." Bill removed his faded U.S. Postal Service cap and used a paper napkin to wipe his bald head. Then he launched into a lengthy series of anecdotes about his hottest days as a mail carrier.

Edward tried to appear interested even though he had heard all the stories before. He preferred to drink his beer in peace rather than deal with the agitation that followed if Bill realized he wasn't listening.

He had just fifteen minutes of his supper break left, but Edward needed more liquid fortification to face another frustrating evening of dealing with rookie reporters who couldn't spell or find the lead of a news story unless it bit them in the butt. He was tired of training these ungrateful beginners only to watch them leave for higher-paying jobs and more glory than he had enjoyed in years.

He also dreaded tomorrow's meeting with the out-of-state publisher, who arrived like clockwork twice a year to "look at ourselves on paper" and gauge the newspaper's financial health. Edward avoided the advertising side of the business, but sensed things were not going well.

"What in tarnation is going on?" Bill asked, nodding toward the office.

The shouting was louder. Edward thought he saw Jimmy raise his hand to Tiffany before he slammed the door shut. Seconds later, a sobbing Tiffany ran out of the restaurant, hands covering her pretty face.

"Sure you don't want to place a bet on that marriage?" Edward asked.

Bill used his napkin to wipe his glasses and blot the moisture off his head again. "Every couple has squabbles, you know that.

Even me and my beautiful wife, Ann, God rest her soul, had some doozies over the years."

As Bill launched into a lengthy narrative about the many qualities of his late wife, Edward watched Brittany place her order pad on the counter, walk quickly to the office, slip inside and close the door. Less than ten minutes later, she and Jimmy emerged, faces flushed and clothing slightly askew. He thought Jimmy looked well comforted.

Edward sighed and put a ten-dollar bill and change on the counter. "Duty calls. See you tomorrow, Bill."

Bill nodded and, still talking about his beloved late wife, turned toward the truck driver eating silently beside him.

Jimmy leaned against the doorframe inside the entrance, a smirk on his face. Edward stopped and pointed at him. "Hey, Mr. Manager, think maybe you could check the thermometer—and the calendar—and find some specials that are slightly more appropriate for the weather?"

"Sure thing, Mr. Philbrick," Jimmy said, still grinning. "And when do you think you'll run a story on the summer league and all the points I'm scoring?"

"When it's news, Jimmy," Edward muttered as he walked outside. He felt the slightest hint of an evening breeze. Maybe things were about to change.

He glanced toward the river and noticed a shiny black sedan with tinted windows and Massachusetts plates approaching on Main Street. It slowed in front of the café and turned down the narrow driveway that led to the employees' parking lot. The vehicle resembled a limousine, but Edward doubted its mission was upscale.

The next day's meeting with the publisher went even more poorly than Edward could have imagined. Examining the *Daily News* "on paper" produced far more financial negatives than positives. The young publisher warned Edward he had three months to turn things around or the newspaper would become history—along with his job.

"Maybe I should just fire you now and put us both out of our misery," the publisher groaned. "But I've never forgotten how you treated me like a regular reporter instead of the publisher's son back in Texas all those years ago. You better pull this off, Edward. We can't keep bleeding cash."

Edward had weathered many ups and downs during his lengthy career. But he wasn't sure how much lower he could go. The *Daily News* was pretty much at the bottom of the other side of "over the hill." No decent large newspaper would ever hire him as an editor if he got fired from this job. And he was just too old, too broke and too jaded to start over as a reporter.

Maybe he should sell out for a public relations job. The price would be higher than any small-town newspaper could pay. But journalism was the only thing that ever excited Edward. His ten years of working as a reporter in Texas were the most thrilling of his life. The adventure ended prematurely when family obligations forced his return to New England. With his parents—and marriages—now dead, the *Daily News* was all he had left.

This weighed on his mind as he slid onto his regular stool at the café counter a few hours after the depressing meeting with the publisher. There was no reason to rush back from supper. The edition had been put to bed. Only a tragedy of major proportions could wake it up—like a couple of drunken teenagers wrapping their car around a telephone pole.

Jimmy and Brittany smiled at him. "Hey, Mr. Philbrick, we got some pretty 'cool' specials for you tonight." Jimmy winked as Brittany giggled and gave her boss an adoring look. "Maybe you'll be in a better mood to discuss me and the summer league now."

"We'll see." Edward grabbed the list of specials from Brittany. He was pleased to discover that someone had figured out that cold chicken salad and gazpacho were better summer fare than steaming pot roast. Maybe cocaine hadn't totally destroyed Jimmy's brain yet.

"I thought you might find these more to your liking, sir," Jimmy said with a small bow. "And as they say, the customer is always right."

"You come up with these yourself, Jimmy?"

"Of course I did." He grinned.

Edward saw a flicker of disappointment cross Brittany's face before she turned and walked away. Jimmy didn't seem to notice. Instead, he turned his attention to Bill Wykoff, who had just come through the front door.

"Hey, Mr. Mailman, what big fat lies are you delivering this evening?" Jimmy said loudly. "By the way, is it true you guys used to open all the packages and take out what you wanted before you delivered them?"

"You know damn well the Postal Service doesn't allow that."

Even from a distance, Edward knew Bill was seething. Everyone, including Jimmy, knew Bill's retirement had not lessened his allegiance to the United States Postal Service. From his first day of employment, Bill Wykoff had put the Postal Service on the same pedestal as God, country, and his sainted mother.

"Well, I do know that when my grandmother sent me cookies, one of them had a bite taken out of it and you delivered the box," Jimmy said.

"Are you accusing me of violating federal law by opening your mail? If so, you better have proof, buddy," Bill said, his voice rising.

"Chill, you old coot. I'm just yanking your chain. Don't go postal on me."

Bill glared at the young man. "It's not a joke to accuse someone of a federal crime. Say something like that again and I'll give you postal with my fist."

"Whatever you say, Mr. Mailman," Jimmy said. "But you better cool down before you give yourself a heart attack. Let me get you some lemonade." He turned away to get Bill's drink.

"He thinks I'm kidding," Bill said, taking the empty stool next to Edward. "I could knock the spit out of that kid in a minute. And I will, too, if he doesn't stop harassing me."

"What makes you think he's harassing you?" Edward said.

"He's been making cracks about the Postal Service all week. I oughta smack him around on general principles. Think that would knock some sense into him, Eddie?"

Edward grimaced and signaled Brittany to bring him a beer. "How many times do I have to tell you to call me Edward? How would you like it if I went around calling you Billy or Billy W?"

"Heat's making everyone cranky, ain't it? How about we head down to the tavern after supper and see if we can improve that nasty mood of yours, old man?"

Edward wasn't fond of the Corner Tavern, but it was one of the few places that might be tolerable tonight. No sunlight entered the bar and there were enough air-conditioning units to counteract the heat and heavy fog of cigarette smoke. Plus, the beer was cold and the music decent. He had nothing better to do—why not?

As they left, Edward noticed the same black sedan from the day before approach and turn into the driveway beside the café.

"Who's that?" Bill said. "Looks like out-of-state plates."

"Probably some friend of Jimmy's. I doubt he's here for the food."

It was still early for the regular tavern crowd. Edward and Bill took a booth in the back. The air conditioning was such a relief it was easy to ignore the darkness and the stale smell of alcohol and cigarettes.

"What'll it be, boys? And where you been?" asked Kathy, a rough-looking waitress who had been slinging beers as long as anyone could remember.

"Here and there and back again." Bill winked at Kathy, but she ignored him.

"If you've been reading the paper, you've got a pretty good idea what I've been doing—a big fat nothing," Edward said.

Two hours and three pitchers of beer later, Bill had pretty much run out of things to say about himself and his lovely (but deceased) wife. He also ranted about how Jimmy Jones insulted not only him but thousands of Postal Service employees. "Someone really needs to teach that jerk a lesson," Bill declared more than once. Edward nodded and continued drinking.

Having exhausted his usual topics and with no new potential listeners in sight, Bill asked Edward about his time in Texas.

"Did it all: Tornadoes, rodeos, oil, and cotton. Courts and crime. But the murders were the best," Edward said. He felt a slight beer buzz.

Bill drained his glass. "That's sick."

"It was great. When I was in West Texas, there was at least one murder a week. They were all different. One time a woman went to the bathroom at this cowboy bar and came out to find another gal in her seat. Pulled out a gun and blew the chair-stealer away. Got her seat back, though," Edward said.

"Are you serious?" Bill slurred. "Heat make 'em all crazy or just the wild, wild West?"

Edward laughed. "Probably both. Everyone has a gun in Texas. Back then, if a black man was murdered, there might be a couple paragraphs in the back of the newspaper. But if the victim was white, always front page. That's why I liked white murders the best—guaranteed byline on page one above the fold. A real rush."

Bill refilled their glasses while Edward continued reminiscing. "I'll never forget this new bride was shot to death outside her apartment building in 1979—wedding gown still on her bed inside. The managing editor vowed there would be a front-page story every day until her murder was solved. Circulation went through the roof."

Bill was surprised the beer had loosened more words from Edward than three years of eating supper together.

"I wrote so many stories about 'beautiful blushing bride Mary-Alice Oatman' that it got to the point that I cared more about finding a new angle for the next story than the fact that a twenty-two-year-old girl was brutally murdered," Edward said. "Sad to say, Mary-Alice Oatman made my career."

"Did they evah find out who did it?"

"Nope. Eventually the readers got tired of the front-page stories. So did the cops. I went to a bigger newspaper but there's an anniversary story every year. Some people think the husband did it, but no one could prove it."

"Why the husband?"

"Turned out he had a girlfriend on the side. Cops also wondered if maybe she did it. Couldn't prove that, either." Edward lifted his glass: "To beautiful blushing bride Mary-Alice Oatman. May she rest in peace."

"Were there murdahs in the other places you worked?" Bill asked.

"Oh, sure. Bar fights, domestics, drug deals gone bad. You name it. But they were never front-page stories like the unsolved cases, especially if the victim was young or attractive. Better if they were both."

Edward took another swig. "We had a preschool teacher fatally shot coming home from her bachelorette party. Even the wire services picked up that story. My byline was in newspapers all over the country. It was great."

Bill couldn't believe what he was hearing. "Great?"

"Not the murder, but the play," Edward said.

"The play?"

"Yeah, play. That's what you call it when a story gets into a lot of newspapers and on the TV and radio news. Murder always gets big play."

"Oh." Bill frowned, obviously trying his best to understand despite increasing inebriation.

"Anyway, another time this handsome all-American-type was shot when he went out to get ice cream for his new wife. Got interviewed on TV for that one."

"That's terrible. Did they find any of the killers?"

Edward stared into his glass. "A few years later, a whacko serial killer named Timothy Lee Zilker claimed he killed Mary-Alice and the other two, plus about twenty others across the country. They executed him, but the families never believed he was the one. Cops didn't either."

Bill was quiet for a moment and then raised his mug. "To all those poor young people." Then he passed out, spilling his beer on Edward.

It was time to go home.

□ □ □

At 3:00 A.M., the ringing interrupted Edward's drunken stare at the blank television screen. "What?" he grunted into the telephone, fighting to sound sober.

It was Police Chief Len Adkins. A patrolman had discovered the battered and bloodied body of Jimmy Jones outside the Pines Café just after midnight. He was shot twice in the back and a shattered basketball trophy was nearby. The state attorney general's office was sending someone down to help with the investigation. "I thought maybe you'd want to get down here before the big papers," Adkins said.

Edward changed into fresh clothes. The streets were clear of traffic and the crackling of emergency radios outside the restaurant interrupted the predawn silence. Edward would not be the only newsman here for long.

He joined Adkins and a group of policemen near Jimmy's bloody corpse. "Looks like Mrs. Jones was a tad unhappy with her basketball star hubby," Edward offered.

"What makes you think Tiffany did this? They're newly-weds, for God's sake," Adkins said.

Edward hesitated. "Doesn't mean she didn't do it. They were fighting a couple nights ago and things got pretty heated. He may have even hit her."

Adkins stared at Edward. "Did you see him hit her?"

"No, but I'm pretty sure he did. She ran out with her hands over her face."

"Why didn't you report it? Spousal abuse is a crime in this state."

"I wasn't sure."

"Then you can't be sure now, either, can you? Jimmy was an asshole sometimes, but murdered by his own wife? That's crazy."

"I think he was fooling around with that new waitress, Brittany. With a baby on the way, Tiffany might have been mad enough to kill him. Even if she didn't, there's always the cocaine angle. I can't be the only one who's seen those black sedans from Mass."

"Jaysus. Jimmy's body ain't even cold and you're making up crap," Adkins said. "We best just wait and see how this thing plays out."

They didn't have to wait long. All of Cocheco Mills soon knew that Jimmy was not only shot but also bludgeoned with one of his prized trophies. They read about it in a *Daily News* special edition beneath the byline of Edward T. Philbrick II.

Edward told his young reporters that covering Jimmy's killing required experience, preferably someone who had written about murders before. This kind of story was important to a newspaper.

In the days that followed, Edward churned out page one stories with new angles and not-so-vague references to unsavory activities involving Jimmy and those around him. Edward knew the authorities had no idea who killed Jimmy or why.

Daily News circulation soared. New subscriptions were at an all-time high. Newspaper vending boxes were emptied by eager readers. Advertising sales skyrocketed.

The heat spell had broken, but there was still plenty to talk about. Cocheco Mills couldn't get enough of the murder of Jimmy Jones and the search for his killer ("or killers" as Edward speculated).

Chief Adkins repeatedly tried to reassure the populace, saying it was unlikely Jimmy was the victim of random violence. (A theory unsupported by evidence, the *Daily News* noted.)

Edward used all his journalism skills to keep the saga twisting and turning. If there was nothing official to report, he posed leading questions to authorities. When they refused to answer, Edward used their nonresponses to raise suspicions.

He asked Chief Adkins if anyone ever investigated domestic abuse allegations against Jimmy. As expected, the chief declined comment. So Edward wrote "Chief Adkins refused to confirm or deny reports of domestic abuse, or to comment on reports Tiffany Jones spent the night at her parents' home following a newlywed spat hours before her husband's murder." It caused readers to wonder if Jimmy was killed for hitting his wife.

Another day, Edward reported authorities refused to confirm that Jimmy was having an affair with a co-worker who reportedly worked late the night he died. Edward quoted the co-worker's parents as saying she was home early to finish her homework, making her identity obvious to café regulars while giving readers another suspect and motive to consider.

When Edward learned police planned to question everyone in the café the night of Jimmy's death, he published his own account of Jimmy's final hours. He related in painstaking detail Jimmy's comments to Bill Wykoff but sanitized Bill's reaction, for which the retired postal carrier was grateful.

Another day, Edward quoted unnamed sources who shared stories about Jimmy's bullying past. He even contacted drug authorities so he could write they refused comment on a possible drug connection, providing the first public hint of Jimmy's substance abuse and sparking rumors he was the victim of a drug deal gone bad.

Edward also cited "reports that a black sedan with tinted windows and Massachusetts license plates was seen at the Café the day of the murder, as well as the day before." He found "an expert" who said Massachusetts was the source of most illegal drugs coming into New Hampshire. Chief Adkins demanded Edward provide additional details. Edward refused but used their conversation for a story the next day.

Salaciousness sold far more newspapers than sympathy ever could. Edward did everything possible to ensure the dirty linen of Jimmy Jones—and everyone around him—was on display each morning.

Although the café closed out of respect for Jimmy's funeral, it quickly reopened to serve the hungry mourners. By the next day, Jimmy and his trophies were replaced. Brittany was said to be too distraught to return. Other than the gossip about each morning's *Daily News* story, life seemed to return to normal.

□ □ □

But Bill Wykoff felt unsettled. There was a change in his supper routine. Most evenings, Edward was so involved in writing about

Jimmy's murder he didn't eat at the café. On the rare occasions when he did, Edward gave only a brief greeting to Bill and the rest of the regulars as he quickly walked to a rear booth. He ate alone, cell phone beside his plate, and left as soon as he was finished.

Chief Adkins was now Bill's more frequent companion at the counter, too busy investigating Jimmy's slaying (and dealing with the rumors sparked by Edward's stories) to drive home for supper with his family.

"Hey, Chief, this thing ever gonna be solved?" Bill asked one evening a few weeks later.

"Sure as hell hope so," Adkins said. "The police databases haven't turned up anything. I'm getting so desperate I even tried the Internet to see if I can locate similar cases."

"Find anything?"

"Not one case so far where a gun and a basketball trophy were used to kill someone. I don't have much time to search, though, being so busy responding to the *Daily News* stories. I'm getting pretty tired of seeing Edward T. Philbrick II's name, and mine, on page one every day."

"He really likes writin' about these kinds of murdahs. Told me that's how he made his name in Texas, said they were good for business."

The Chief put down his coffee cup. "What do you mean by 'these kinds of murders'?"

"You know, young people, just startin' out, like Jimmy and Tiffany."

The Chief was about to respond when he saw Edward enter the café behind a slickly dressed younger man whom Bill identified as the newspaper's out-of-state publisher. Edward looked away from the counter as the duo headed for a booth by the window. He seemed happy, something that never happened when the publisher was in town.

Bill felt the hairs stand up on the back of his neck. Now he knew why he felt so uneasy. The circumstances were too familiar. He leaned toward the Chief and whispered, "Have you tried searching the Web for 'newlywed murdahs'?"

□ □ □

Across the café, Edward put down his menu and looked up expectantly. The publisher smiled. "Edward, I met with the advertising side. There's been a phenomenal turnaround. As usual, murder has done wonders for circulation and our profit margin."

Edward was relieved. Maybe he wouldn't lose his job after all.

The publisher played with his fork. "I've been doing a lot of thinking. I'm keeping the *Daily News* open, but replacing you."

Edward felt like he had been sucker-punched. All the effort and long hours, and this was his reward? He had put the newspaper first, pushed things to the edge and beyond. Edward felt his face turning red. He didn't know if he could control his rage, even if he wanted to.

The publisher laughed. "I can see you're surprised. You shouldn't be. You done good, Edward. I need you in Montpelier. The *Beacon* needs a new managing editor."

Edward was stunned.

"And do you know why I want you there, Edward?" the amused publisher asked.

"Because I hate being here?"

"No, Edward. It's because you understand there are circumstances that can require an extraordinary commitment to boost circulation numbers."

Edward waited for his boss to continue.

"I was afraid you'd lost that commitment," the publisher said. "It took awhile, but you proved once again that you're not afraid to do what it takes for the good of the newspaper. That's the kind of managing editor I need in Montpelier. What do you say?"

Edward struggled to find the right words. Finally he said, "Have I ever let you down?"

Susie Cue

Steve Liskow

I'm sweeping out Rudy's Rack & Cue like I always do on Friday afternoon. Rudy lets me stay in his back room for free if I do good, like Vinnie lets me sweep out his bar most nights. Since Mama went away, I got nowhere else.

Then Susie Cue walks in, hair like a brand new red crayon and about as skinny except in girl places. She's wearing a red tank top and jeans that fit like a fresh Band-Aid. She's carrying a suitcase in one hand and a little leather case in the other, and her arms is white as spaghetti.

I wonder who drove her here 'cause the only way you can get to Zachariah Gap is by car. The railroad don't stop since the meat-packing plant moved to Medville, twenty miles north. The Greyhound don't neither unless they got a flat or something. Susie told me later she was hitching and made the guy drop her off here, some guy who tried to do bad things to her. She held him off with the swift army knife in her jeans.

She asks Jerry Kraft if he wants a game. Jerry's real good, and he tells her he only plays for money. She gives him a smile like fresh lemonade and tells him she's got something better than money.

All the guys laugh like they do when someone sends me to the store for a new buzz for the saw, and Rudy tells them to cool it with the kid around, which is me.

The next thing I know Jerry's racking up the balls, a hard round rainbow in the triangle. He puts a five-dollar bill on the side of the table and tells her to break. She opens up the little leather case and puts together her own three-piece pool cue. Then she bends over the table and every man in the place lets out a sigh like he's just got a taste of something sweet. I see her bottom, round like two cue balls under denim, a little bulge on one hip like she's got a wallet in there, but it don't got much in it, not like her jeans, and suddenly I understand what she's got.

Everyone crowds around to watch, and she clears the table before Jerry even gets to take a shot. Then they try double or nothing and most of his balls is still lying on the table when she finishes again. Some of the other guys step up, and she takes them, too. They offer to buy her a drink, but she just unscrews her cue and walks out.

Her wallet's fat in her pocket now.

At the bar that night, all the guys talk about how she leans over the table so you can see down her tank top and how she strokes that cue with her fingers, like something she loves.

Vinnie asks me what I seen, and I tell him about Susie's hair like a red jawbreaker and those jeans. I don't tell him about her smile, but he looks at me like he already knows about it anyway. When I curl up in the sleeping bag in his back room, her smile still watches me in the dark like I'm waiting for Santa Claus again.

Saturday, all the guys who work in the meat-packing plant come into Rudy's. There's nothing else to do, no movies or nothing, and they talk about baseball and the girl that cleaned everyone's clock yesterday. Then Susie walks through the door and the sudden quiet is like the way I used to feel in class when teacher asks me to do a problem but the numbers is too big.

She talks to a few of the guys, but just polite, not really looking at them close. She plays a few games with the ones she didn't beat yesterday and they want to buy her a beer, but she keeps saying no thank you.

Then she looks over at me and it feels like I'm in Mama's car and she just slammed on the brakes. I hold onto my broom real tight so I don't fall over.

"What's your name, Tiger?" Her voice is like my fuzzy blue blanket. I tell her my name's not Tiger, it's Johnny.

"I'm real glad to know you, Johnny. Mine's Susie. Would you be an angel and get me a Coke? Classic if they got it?"

All the men look at me like they're mad, but I didn't do nothing. She hands me a warm five-dollar bill, and I put down my broom next to the door and go over to the Mobil station across the street and get her a Coke. I get her a bag of chips, too, out of my own money. Then I look both ways even though the light's red and go back to Rudy's.

When I get back, Susie and Larry Heavenrich are laughing a little even though he's got four balls left and she's trying to get a shot at the eight ball to finish him off, too. Larry never calls me dummy or nothing. He's going away to college in the fall and told me he wants to be a vet. I thought that was a soldier, but he told me no, it was a doctor that takes care of horses and cows and puppies. Larry's nice, I can see him liking pets, but most people don't have pet cows. I bet they's really hard to housebreak.

Then Tom Vandy comes in, and I don't like him. Once, after Mama went away, he told me there was a way God would make me smart. He told me if I took off all my clothes and stood under the traffic light at midnight under the full moon and asked God to help me, He would. But when I did it, Tom Vandy was there and he had some other big men with him. They put me in a pick-up truck and took me a long ways out of town and made me drink out of their bottles until I couldn't stand up anymore. They kept calling me "retard" and laughing and making me drink until I fell asleep.

When I woke up the next morning, my head hurt real bad and I was lying in a puddle that smelled like going to the bathroom and I threw up until I thought I turned inside out. Rudy found me along the road and wrapped me in a blanket and gave me a ride back to Mama's house. But there was different people there because Mama went away and they looked real mad when I tried to go in. That was when Rudy said I could stay in his back room if I wanted. Vinnie told me the same thing a few days later. They're my friends.

So Tom Vandy comes in and says something about a pussy whipping everyone, but I don't see a cat anywhere. I'm trying to get out of there before he sees me, but he comes right over and clamps his big rough hand on the back of my neck like he always does, and it hurts.

"Hey, Dumbo," he says, and his voice sounds like a can opener. "How they hanging?"

I look around and the curtains are okay, but he starts shaking me till my teeth bump together.

"You getting any, Dumbo? A big stud like you?"

"That's enough, Vandy," Rudy tells him. His voice is like one of the teachers at school telling the boys in the back to stop fooling around.

"I'm just having a little fun, Rudy," he says. "No harm in that."

"Leave him alone."

Then Susie comes over. Today, she's wearing a yellow top, round white mounds peeking out under a blue work shirt, the prettiest lady I ever seen.

"Johnny, would you do something for me?"

"Sure," I say. Tom Vandy turns to her and his grip loosens on my neck.

"Hey, baby," he says. "We haven't been introduced, but I'm Tom, and this is your lucky day."

"Or not." She don't even look at him. She reaches into her jeans and hands me a ten-dollar bill. "Johnny, would you get me a cheeseburger and a Coke? And get whatever you want, too. Please?"

"Hey," Vandy says again.

"You're not saying anything important," Susie tells him. "Just apologize for being an asshole and get on with your life."

His hand slides off my neck. She don't weigh as much as one of his arms like fireplace logs, but she looks at him like she's swatted bigger flies.

"You probably came in here to play pool," she says. Larry Heavenrich has his cue turned around like a baseball bat, his hands gripping it tight. "You want to give me a shot?"

Tom Vandy says he came in to give her a shot, then I get out of there. I stay away until my neck don't hurt anymore and eat a cheeseburger and fries, then take another burger and a Coke back to Susie.

When I get back, she's bent over the corner of the table and Tom Vandy's biting his lip and watching her wallet dance. There's a soft click and a thunk when the eight ball drops into a pocket, then Susie picks a bill from the edge of the table. She has to wiggle her bottom to get the wallet back into her pocket now. Tom Vandy's face is red and pinched up like he's got a stomachache.

"I need to take a break now," Susie tells him. "I'll be back in a little while."

Then she takes me by the hand and leads me out the door. Tom Vandy's eyes drive nails into my back.

Susie walks me around the corner and down to Mrs. Terwilliger's Boarding House. She's got a room there now and she lets me in and shows me to a big soft chair and sits down on the bed across the room. There's red roses on the wallpaper, almost as red as her hair and even bigger than her head. A half-full bottle on the dresser's got a cork in it. She pulls that swift army knife out of her jeans and opens the bottle, but I say no thank you. She pours a little dark juice into a glass and opens her wallet. Then she pulls out a whole bunch of money and I look away when I see her tucking it in the drawer with her underpants.

That's when she tells me about the man in the car that wanted to do bad things to her. And I tell her about Mama and how I quit school when it got too hard. She asks me how old I am, but I don't remember for sure when my birthday is, it was a long time ago. She says hers, too. She says she's just staying here for a week or two until she figures out where she's going to go next. Then she asks me if I go to church and I tell her about God not listening to me under the full moon and her face gets real old.

"Would you show me where the church is tomorrow, Johnny?"

I know then I'd do anything for her, and I better hurry if she's only going to be here for a week or two.

But the next day she talks to Larry Heavenrich at church. Her eyes get all soft when she listens to him, and then they get into his car and drive off. I go over to Rudy's and sweep the whole place four times and don't listen to the ball game on the big TV. Then I go over to Vinnie's even though he's closed on Sunday and sweep there four times, too. I even clean the ashtrays on the bar. I don't listen to the ball game there, too.

After dark, Larry Heavenrich's car glides up in front of Mrs. Terwilliger's and he opens his door and walks around to the other side. He holds that door open for Susie and I can see her smile from across the street. They walk up the steps with his arm touching hers soft like she's a soap bubble, and at the door she turns back to him. He leans his head down and their faces touch for just a minute. Then Susie goes through the door and Larry walks back down the steps like he's listening to happy music. The light in Susie's room stays on a real long time and I don't go away until she turns it out.

That night, I dream of Susie and Larry and how happy they look.

The next three nights, Susie plays pool with everyone and takes their money, except for Larry. When they play, nobody puts money on the table. They play pool like they're dancing to that same happy music.

One night, someone puts money in the jukebox and when real loud music comes out, Susie nods her head. "Oh," she says. "Iron Made in Japan." Everybody laughs, I guess 'cause they's singing in English.

I watch Larry drive her home. Their faces touch longer every night.

The next night, Larry puts money in the jukebox, Cretins Clearwater Revival singing about Susie Cue and how he loves the way she walks and talks. She gives him that lemonade smile and clears the table, the balls clicking like teeth. At the next table, Tom Vandy's face is like a blizzard coming out of the west.

That night is Saturday, and Larry goes inside Susie's room with her. I go close to the window. The lights is off and I hear little sounds like a puppy crying. I worry until I remember Larry wants to be a vet and take care of puppies and kittens and stuff.

It's almost morning when he comes out and he looks like he's dancing to even more happy music than before. I knock on Susie's door real soft in case she's asleep, but her voice drifts through the wood like cotton candy. I tell her it's me and she tells me to come in. Her hair is all mussed up like a red ball of string, and there's a funny smell in the room like I remember a long time ago before my daddy went away on Mama. She looks soft as a kitten.

"I seen Larry bring you home," I tell her. "I just wanted to see you're all right."

"I am," she says. She's sitting on the bed wrapped in a sheet, but she looks like she's dancing, too. Her eyes look like she hears Larry's music.

"I had to be sure," I tell her. "I heard a puppy crying from outside your window, and I wanted to know it was okay, but Larry's gonna be a vet, so he musta made it all better."

Her face gets red, almost like her hair. "Yeah," she says. "He did. And I made his ol' puppy bark, too."

I wonder about that 'cause Mrs. Terwilliger don't allow pets.

Susie's looking out the window. "I'm gonna stay around here a lot longer than I thought, Johnny." I can feel the music coming off her. "I want to help Larry take care of his dogs."

She's really saying something else, but I know sort of what she means and I feel real happy, 'cause I like Larry, too. After a few minutes, I figure out she's waiting for me to leave so she can take off the bed sheet.

When I sweep out Vinnie's bar that afternoon, I tell him that Susie wants to take care of Larry Heavenrich's dogs, and he gives me a funny look and asks me where I was last night. I tell him and his forehead bunches up and he tells me I shouldn't spy on people. I go over to Rudy's and he asks me why I left so early last night and I say I been taking care of Susie but now Larry's taking care of her, too. Rudy's eyes flick like he's watching a fly behind me and I turn and see Tom Vandy looking at us. His eyes feel like barbed wire. Then he puts down the pool cue and walks out real loud. I try holding my broom like Susie holds her pool cue, flicking my wrist like she does.

When Susie and Larry come in that night, they stuff a whole bunch of quarters in the jukebox. Then they play a game and Susie wins. Then one of the other guys asks her for a game and puts a bill on the table. Larry moves over and plays with some other guys.

Susie wins her game and another guy steps up. Then another.

Susie sees me with my broom. "Johnny?"

I go over and she pulls a bill from her pocket. "Would you get me a cheeseburger and a Coke? And something you like for yourself?"

I go to the diner and eat french fries with lots of ketchup like Susie's red hair. Then I remember her food and start back.

Tom Vandy walks in ahead of me and takes the table next to Susie. I can smell liquor like he swimmed in it. She's playing with a man in a sweatshirt and a John Deere hat, and he's pretty good. They's only four balls left on the table.

"Gonna get yours tonight, baby," Tom Vandy says. His voice sounds like he wants to kick a puppy. Susie don't look at him, but she misses an easy shot and the guy beats her. She sees me with her food and comes over to me.

"Thanks, Johnny. Did you get anything for yourself?"

"I had french fries," I tell her. "A king size. With lotsa ketchup 'cause it makes me think of your hair."

She gives me a look like Mama used to till I quit school, then Larry comes over and says hi. He and Susie sit and talk for a long time and she keeps nodding. They go out the door like they's dancing again.

I see Tom Vandy isn't there anymore. I put down my broom and go out into the street. Larry's taillights are gone and suddenly I'm afraid. I walk down to the traffic light and turn toward the rooming house and then I'm running, past the laundromat and the post office and through the alley behind the Cash 'n Carry and the doctor's office, the wind in my ears and my heels banging the pavement. I see Mrs. Terwilliger's house up ahead and I run even faster, my side hurting and my breath cold in my throat. My heart beats like Iron Made in Japan.

Larry's car is parked in front, but nobody's in it. I go up to

Susie's window and the shade is down so the window's just a big yellow box. I hear a voice growling like a big dog. I go up the steps and through the door and down the hall to Susie's room. My hand turns the knob without my telling it and I step into the yellow light and trip over Larry.

Susie's crying against the dresser, trying to push herself upright, but her arms is like wet string. A line of blood drips from the corner of her mouth and her tank top is ripped so I see her white mounds like cupcakes. Her jeans are pushed down, and I see a little red patch between her legs before I look away, too.

Tom Vandy lies across her bed, and his pants is down. His man thing hangs loose and angry between his legs and I want to tell him not do bad things in front of a lady. He's gargling and his hands is waving like he's fighting off mosquitoes.

Then I stand up and see the stick in his mouth. He tries to pull it out, and I know it's part of Susie's pool cue. Then he stops gargling and his eyes look at me before they roll back in his head like big white cue balls. I pull the stick out and blood splashes all over my hands and face, on the rug, on my shirt, everywhere. Tom Vandy slides off the bed and his shoulder knocks me down.

When I put the stick down, Susie is over next to Larry and he's trying to get up. There's a big lump on his forehead and his eyes look funny, but he gets his hands flat on the floor and pushes himself to his knees. He turns his face to Susie and she puts her arms around him. She's still crying.

"Mrs. Terwilliger's gonna be real mad when she sees this mess," I say. "You go back to the pool hall and I'll clean it up."

"We can't go back there, Johnny," Susie says. "You should go away, too. You'll be in a lot of trouble because you came in here and touched things."

"I always clean things up," I say. "That's why Vinnie and Rudy let me stay."

She looks at me and her eyes get older. Larry stands up and looks at Tom Vandy. I think he's going to be sick, but he isn't.

"Thank you, Johnny." Susie pulls the money out of her dresser and leads Larry out. The front door closes before Mrs. Terwilliger comes down the stairs. I'm cleaning Tom's blood off the rug with Susie's pillowcase when she starts screaming.

They find my fingerprints on Susie's pool cue and Tom's blood all over my shirt, but they don't find Larry and Susie. His car is at the train station in Medville, but they's gone. Still.

When they let me go in another three years, maybe Rudy will let me sweep out the pool hall again. Maybe Susie will come back and visit me then, too.

Just Passing Through

John Clark

I was on my way home from a particularly depressing shift at the teen group home, trying to shrug off problems that were beyond my ability to fix. Just before the curve by Denman Cemetery, the car ahead of me braked, its tail lights creating a series of eerie red eyes on the tombstones behind the black iron fence. I turned back from the momentary distraction to see a ragged figure immediately in front of me. "What the . . ." I said as I slammed on my brakes. Even as the screech of my tires ripped through the darkness, I knew there was no way to avoid hitting the old man.

My car was halfway across the road and I could smell the acrid stench of burned rubber. I didn't remember any impact, but how could I have missed him? Something wasn't right.

I pulled off to the side and waited until my legs stopped shaking. The flashlight in the glove compartment still worked and I used it to check the front end. There were no dents, no blood, nor any scratches on the paint. Had I been having a late-night hallucination?

I flipped off the light and closed the glove compartment. Good thing I only had another three miles to go. That was when I noticed something that raised the hair on my neck and sent a chill down my spine. I wasn't alone.

Even though there was nobody else in the car, I knew I wasn't alone. I could feel a heaviness in my head as if something was crowding my brain. "What in hell is this?" I muttered and tried to concentrate on driving. Downtown Simonton was sound asleep as I pulled up to the blinking light. My house was two miles west on Route 32. I flicked on the blinker and started to turn.

"Not tonight, Sonny. I have other plans for you."

The voice scared me so much it was good that whoever it belonged to was in control of my body. I fought to brake, but it was like my legs had turned to wood and my right foot was glued to the gas pedal. Even my arms seemed to be ignoring the terrible pounding in my chest.

We drove north at a leisurely pace, the interior of the car silent save for my ragged breath. By the time we passed Belfast and headed up Route 7, my adrenalin level was beginning to drop and I was trying to figure out what was happening.

"You've been borrowed, is what happened, Sonny."

This time I was calm or weak enough to realize that whatever was speaking had claimed my body. Was it possible that the ragged old man had some sort of supernatural power?

My head filled with a dry rustling chuckle. "Nope, I'm just an old veteran who likes to get out and visit his war buddies. I've been dead since 1917 and it's a mite hard to do my own driving, so I've learned to hitchhike."

Anger helped. I wasn't at all happy about being hijacked, especially by a ghost. "Where are we going?"

"Greenville. I've got cousins there who served in the Civil War and I haven't stopped by to chat since somewhere around the time Ike was president." Another dry wheezing laugh filled my head. "I know they're fine because that's how it is when you're dead, but still, family oughta count for something."

I chewed that over until we were climbing the hill between Brooks and Dixmont. Now that I was over the shock of being possessed and my anger had subsided, curiosity set in.

"How were you killed?"

"Mustard gas, nasty stuff. Good thing it was outlawed. It eats you up from the inside out and hurts worse than anything you can imagine. I was twenty-three when it got me. Came home in a box like a lot of other guys in my outfit. Had a grand funeral over in New Portland where I grew up, but when you're dead, all that ceremony don't amount to a hill of beans. I lay in the ground for some twenty years and then decided to see if I could buck the odds."

"And?"

"Well, Sonny, you're living proof that I did. It was some funny, that first time, rising through the ground like rainfall in reverse. I scared the crap out of a family of voles on the way up. Then I had to figure out what I wanted to do once I was above ground. I hadn't thought that through, just wanted to see if I could do it. The first time, I looked around and went back. I bet it was a couple years before this travel thing came to me. At first, cars were so scarce it was easier to walk, but after the big war, things got better and I've managed to go all over New England."

"What if you get caught?"

I winced as dry laughter thundered through my head, leaving a ringing ache in its wake.

"Think some more, Sonny. What can you do to someone who has been dead for eighty-five years? Kill them again? Heck, most of the folks I've hitched with have been so dense they never even realized what was happening. I bet you're the first live one I've latched onto in twenty years."

I turned onto I-95 and accelerated to avoid being rear-ended by a late-night trucker. We remained silent until I turned onto Rt. 7 again.

"I need gas."

The ghost backed off, letting me turn into the twenty-four-hour station. I thought briefly about asking the cashier to call the police, but realized my chances of getting anything like help at 4:45 on a Sunday morning were pretty slim. Slimmer still once I told them my body had been taken over by a ghost from 1917. Even if I didn't end up in the loony bin, there probably weren't any experts in Maine who knew how to remove ghosts. Besides, I was curious about how the old fellow was going to leave and what I'd remember when he did.

Dawn was breaking as I took the Sangerville Road. "What happens when you visit your friends?"

"It varies. I generally do the equivalent of knocking before I seep down. Some of them are glad to see me, but a few really bought into that eternal sleep business. The bunch in Greenville, though, they were pretty rowdy when they were alive and kicking. I've heard some really interesting stories from them. Stuff about liberating stills in the Tennessee hills and the like. Of course, they had their share of bad times too. Three brothers caught a direct hit from a sixteen-pound cannonball at Antietam. They say it wasn't pretty. Of course, when you're dead, you can look any way you want. Hell, I even stopped one old geezer in the middle of Wilton one night who thought I was Marilyn Monroe. He was some upset when he discovered what I really look like."

We continued our conversation through Guilford and into Monson.

"I sure miss working for a living. I had me a nice job in this town a few years before the war, apprenticed to a real smart Italian fellow who could cut slate like it was butter."

The wistfulness behind his words was the first real emotion I'd sensed since my odyssey had started.

"I guess you didn't have much chance to experience life if

you were killed at twenty-three."

"That's a fact. I saw far too much death, but aside from this one lady I met in one of the French towns we liberated, all I knew was schooling and hard work. I missed family weddings, telling stories by lamplight to nieces and nephews, going to the Simonton fair with a pretty girl on my arm. Heck, I never even got to vote for the damn fools who sent me off to get killed. Pull over for a moment. I want to see how much Greenville has changed since my last visit."

I stopped the car on the hill overlooking Moosehead Lake and got out to take in the view. The June morning was crisp and windless. From up here, I could see a number of early fishermen dotting the still waters below us. As I absent-mindedly tucked a stick of gum in my mouth, I thought back to the night before. Had my angst over being unable to fix my kids at the group home come anywhere near what this fellow had been through?

"I sorta wish we had those fancy outboards when I was alive. I bet they make fishing a lot easier. Of course, we had bigger fish back then, so maybe it was just as well." His voice trailed off.

I got back in the car and headed down into Greenville.

"Turn right, then left at the stop sign. The cemetery is half a mile down."

I wasn't sure what to expect when we reached our destination. As we came to the edge of the large rolling field dotted with gravestones of all sizes and stages of deterioration, I felt my foot move from the gas and hit the brake so hard I expected the airbag to deploy. Instead there was a slight tearing sensation in my chest that was followed by a feeling of lightness.

I shook my head and made sure there were no extra holes in it. As I turned to drive away, I swear I saw the faint outline of a hand waving from a mound in front of one of the older tombstones.

I pulled into the dairy bar just below the crest of the hill and got an odd look from the red-haired girl as I ordered a double banana split. I guess she thought it was a strange order for 10:30 a.m. on a Sunday. I didn't particularly care. The ghost seemed to have taken something with him when he left my body. I couldn't exactly describe how I felt. It was somewhere between detachment and acceptance, almost as though I had lived another, wiser existence.

I headed south, in search of sleep and a new way of looking at life. Every time I went by a cemetery, I slowed a bit, half hoping I might meet another spirit who was just passing through.

The Secret of the Pulluvan Drum

Susan Oleksiw

Anita reached deep into her cloth bag for the clutch of rupees she knew was there. She liked this new shop, with its odd collection of old Kerala things and new honky-tonk toys for tourists. She especially liked the owner, Macheri, a young woman picking out items to sell according to her tastes and no one else's. The old wooden boxes were falling apart and desperately needed oil, and the clay bowls and pots would probably disintegrate in the typical dry climate of North America, but the old earth colors were a joy to behold.

Anita had to keep herself from running her fingers over them or she'd buy every single one. Instead, she patted the ten hand-painted notecards she had selected, and fished around the bottom of her cloth bag for her money. What she pulled out was a broken rubber band and a torn envelope. The young woman behind the counter gasped.

"Ayoo! Shakunam aanu!" The young woman slapped her hands over her mouth and stared at the rubber band. "Oru naaga poole!"

"Omen? This?" Anita held up the rubber band, surprised at

the other woman's reaction. Macheri seemed shy but sensible when Anita had dropped by to welcome her, and tell her about life in the resort where Anita lived with her Auntie Meena in her aunt's hotel. "That would be a pretty tiny snake." Anita let the bands slip back into her bag. "Not really much of an omen, if you ask me." But she hadn't asked me, Anita thought, as she handed over her money. Macheri was young, in her early twenties, and obviously nervous in her new business venture. Her hand trembled as she took the bills while her eyes kept glancing at the cloth bag. Anita took her parcel, thanked Macheri with a few more words of welcome, and fervently hoped she'd settle into the business and prosper.

"Do you know the new shop at the top of Lighthouse Road?" Anita said to Ravi, the desk clerk, as she came through the doorway. Hotel Delite sat firmly on the rocky coast in South India, where Anita Ray's aunt catered to foreigners during the winter season, recovered during the monsoon, and Anita pretended to help. It was the least she could do, considering how ashamed Meena was of Anita's dabbling in photography and unmarried state. Ravi and the other staff members kept the hotel going and Auntie Meena relatively sane. Diners chatted out on the terrace as waiters clattered past with laden trays. "I stopped there today to buy postcards, just to see what it was like."

"You are welcoming the new ones to this lucrative neighborhood, isn't it?" Ravi looked up from the registration book that only he could decipher, since it was filled with his color-coded blocks and scribbles. "You are not scaring her away with tales of dead bodies? This is very kind."

"Would I do that?" Anita jumped up onto a tall stool.

"Does not Yama, the Lord of Death, wait for us all?"

"The woman who started it is a nervous wreck. I hope she gets used to talking to strangers. Look at these." Anita pulled out the notecards and spread them on the desk. A piece of paper fluttered to the floor, and Anita climbed down to pick it up. "Ayoo!" She held up the thousand-rupee note.

"Oh!" Ravi blinked and leaned closer.

"This is what she gave me for change!" Anita sighed and slipped the note into her cloth bag. "This is not a small mistake. I'd better return it right away." She headed back up the road, to the intersection, where stores were lit by small hanging lights. She saw before she reached it that the new shop was closed.

"I must have just missed her," Anita said to the man at the tea stall.

"No, no, she is leaving as soon as you are walking away." He pointed to a teacup, but Anita declined with a shake of her head.

"Do you know where she lives?"

The tea wallah called across the street to another shop, and after some backing and forthing, the two men agreed that Macheri lived near another intersection on the other side of Vilinzham. Anita thanked them and went in search of an autorickshaw, the small three-wheeled cab that sounded and ran like an enclosed motorcycle.

The driver pulled up in front of a narrow dirt lane, and agreed to wait. Anita scanned the area, decided that this was in fact where the directions from the last tea stall had meant her to go, and started down the path. The houses were only one or two rooms, with little yards around them and no compound walls or even sapling fences to keep animals from wandering. The neighborhood seemed a small, cohesive unit apart from the surrounding developments, the bustling shopping arcades and noisy traffic farther away. Anita threaded her way between the little houses, not one of which had a second floor. A few had lean-to kitchens with walls and roofs of woven mats.

Near the end of the lane she came to a house set on the edge of a sandy patch leading into a marsh. By the side of the house stood a brightly embroidered pandal, on four wooden posts, its colored threads sparkling in the candlelight. By the nearest post sat a large clay pot with a smooth, leather covering stitched over it. The pot sat on one end of a long stick; a single stout thread ran from one end, through the pot, to the other end, holding the pot in place. Anita recognized it at once as the pot drum played by members of the Pulluvan caste during certain rituals and pujas. Beyond that was Macheri sweeping the dirtyard. She started when she saw Anita, but lay down her broom and came to greet her.

"So I came to return the money," Anita said after explaining her visit. She reached into her bag and drew out the thousand-rupee note. Macheri extended her hand to take it, then clutched her trembling fist to her chest as she turned to the house. She stared at it so hard that Anita turned to look, but no one was there. "Are you all right?" Macheri's head jerked back, her neck so stiff with fear that she could barely move it.

Macheri nodded slowly, took the note. She held it in her hand for some moments before slipping it into her waist, pushing it down until it disappeared from view. She leaned toward Anita, shaking and shivering, as though waiting for her to speak. "Devi, our Goddess, did not come, not once." She glanced back at the pandal.

Perplexed, Anita followed her gaze. This was the setup for an exorcism, Anita suddenly realized. The pandal was empty now but Anita could see the grains of colored powders left over on the ground, swept into small piles to be carried away. She had seen this a few times before—the grotesque figure of a large serpent drawn on the dirt floor beneath the pandal in colored powder, white, yellow, red, green, and black—the colors on a serpent's neck. And the pot-drum was for the Pulluvan to play while he sang, his music leading the women undergoing the exorcism to fall into a trance and in that state destroy the serpent image. But if Devi did not come, if any one or all of the women did not fall into a trance, it meant that the Goddess was angry with someone in the household—a very bad sign. No wonder she was so distressed, Anita thought. She offered her sympathy to Macheri.

□ □ □

A few days later Anita spread her notecards out on the breakfast table and tried to decide which ones she would send to her parents in the States and which ones she'd keep for herself, just for their beauty. Her American father liked all things Indian and her Indian mother liked all things American, particularly washing machines, dishwashers, and other appliances.

"Are these from that new shop?" Auntie Meena leaned over her shoulder to better see them. "You are lucky to have gotten them. I am hearing the shop is closed now."

Anita turned around in her seat. "It can't be. It just opened."

"But it is. Just this morning I am hearing the news. The owner is dead." Auntie Meena flopped down in the seat opposite Anita and sighed. "Such is karma."

Karma? Anita recalled her meeting with Macheri, her uneasiness in her own home compared to her enthusiasm in her shop. No, Anita thought, this wasn't karma. Her thoughts must have flickered across her face because Meena blanched and grabbed Anita's arm.

"No, no, it is only the merest of accidents. Not murder, no, nothing like that." Meena closed her eyes, muttering to herself.

"I am certain you are right," Anita said.

But half an hour later Anita marched into the hotel office and unlocked the cabinet, taking out the cash box. She rummaged through the bills just as Auntie Meena came through the door.

"Anita? How much money is it you are needing?" The older woman leaned over the cash box, watching Anita's nimble fingers work their way through the notes. "You are welcome to whatever you want, but is it so much?"

"I'm looking for a thousand rupees." Anita continued her

search without meeting her aunt's eyes.

"But it's right there." Meena pointed to the bills.

"Ah, this one." Anita pulled out a thousand-rupee note and slipped it into her pocket. She locked the cash box and put it back into the cupboard. "Going and coming," she said to her aunt as she hurried out the door.

□ □ □

At the top of Lighthouse Road Anita banged on the wooden shutters. The other shopkeepers were already mostly open, rearranging their goods for sale, snapping a rag over the rows of biscuits and newspapers to drive away the dust. Behind the blue-washed shutters Anita heard a voice telling her to go away and sounds of work being carried on. She banged louder.

"I have money to give to Macheri," Anita said. "A thousand rupees." The shop grew silent. A moment later one of the shutters was pulled aside, and a young man leaned out.

"Money? You have money for Macheri? How is this?"

"I was here a few days ago and bought some postcards and left the change in the envelope she gave me, but only now have I checked, and Macheri gave me the wrong bills in change. A thousand-rupee note instead of a hundred-rupee note."

The young man's glance immediately went to Anita's hands, which were empty.

"Is Macheri here?"

"Macheri is dead." He pushed another shutter aside and leaned against the wall. His dour expression began to crumble, and Anita was shocked to see he was only a teenager. "I am cleaning out the shop. We are selling the goods to another store Kovalam side." He slid down the wall until he was sitting on a low stool, his head resting on his fist, his elbow propped up on his leg. He looked about to cry. His face reddened, highlighting the cluster of pimples along his chin.

"I am so sorry." It was all she had to say. A tear bulged over his thick black eyelashes. "Your sister?"

He shook his head, no. "Like my older sister. But cousin." He straightened up to look at her. "I am Raj."

"Was she unwell, Raj?" Anita pushed the other shutters out of the way and found a stool to sit on. Outside a few tourists wandered past, some looking for the chemist, others for an interesting place for a cup of coffee, still others on their way to the bus stop. "Some disease?"

"Yes, no." He buried his face in his hands.

"It's a mystery, is it?"

"No, it is no mystery how she is dying." Raj rubbed away the tears and kicked a box with his bare foot. "She is possessed by a devil but no puja is driving it away. The serpent is angry and so she dies."

"What serpent? What devil?" Anita had seen the pandal and the Pulluvan's pot-drum, but Macheri said the exorcism didn't work. What had happened afterwards?

"This is a nice shop, isn't it?" The boy suddenly looked up at the nearly empty shelves, the boxes of souvenirs stacked haphazardly in the small space. "She is doing this with her own jewelry. She is going to the bank and getting a loan for her gold bracelets and renting the shop and buying her goods. She is doing this. And her husband is agreeing and then he is not agreeing."

"Did you hear them argue?" Anita asked.

"Yes, they argue. And then he is agreeable again, and then they argue." He shook his head, confused over the changeableness of his cousin and her husband.

"Do you live near them, Raj?"

"We are all living together—cousin and her husband, parents, and older brother cousin and his wife. I stay with an aunt while I am in school in Trivandrum, but in the other months I am also there. My own parents are dead."

Anita studied his well-patched pants and imagined how cramped and poor the family must be. Macheri's foray into business would have raised the family significantly, if she had made a go of it. "Who decided she was possessed? Did her husband complain?"

"Not her husband. Older brother, Banu. He is unsettled. He is a bearer at the train station," Raj explained.

Which means he travels far for work every day and makes little. "What does Macheri's husband do?"

"Tullu? He works in the town for a builder," Raj said, his attention returning to the souvenirs still waiting to be packed away.

□ □ □

Anita had no trouble finding the small house a second time. A cooking fire smoldered at the rear and a few chickens scratched in the dirt before fluttering off toward the swamp. Anita paused at the end of the lane, listening for voices and the idle conversation that moves life along in a home during the day. Women's voices floated through the air but the words were too indistinct for Anita to make out. To her right, beyond the pandal, came men's voices. Anita called out.

Two young men stepped out of the swamp forest and came toward her, peering at her around the pandal. One carried a cluster of coconuts over his shoulder, a machete in his other hand. Once again she explained who she was and why she was there—patting the thousand-rupee note in her pocket.

"How foolish of her. My sister was foolish, Tullu." He pointed to the bereaved husband with his machete. "It is my sister who has died," he said to Anita. "I am Banu."

Anita introduced herself and explained she had been to the shop on Lighthouse Road. "We are sad to see it go. Even in its short opening we directed several of our guests there, from Hotel Delite."

"We are in mourning," Tullu said with almost no emotion. He seemed slight in build and energy next to his brother-in-law,

Banu, with his arms hanging slack at his sides, his black hair in little spikes pulled up by overhanging tree branches. Tullu's eyes flickered up to her, then away, as though too weak to focus. He must be stunned, thought Anita, perhaps even in shock. The silence deepened, only the sounds of chickens reminding them of where they were. Anita offered her condolences.

"Can you tell me how it happened? She had so many friends on the Road, even in so short a time."

Tullu's face softened, and Anita warmed to him. "Yes," he said, running his hand over his head, picking out the leaves and buds entangled in his hair. "She would draw them quickly. She was always a good daughter and a good wife."

"Was it an illness?"

"She was possessed," Banu said. Pain flickered across Tullu's face. "She would not listen. She went into this shop without consulting us, using money without consulting us. It was not like her. She was taken over by some evil."

"It was her money," Tullu said in a soft voice. "Her own bracelets. Did I not scrimp and save for them for years to give her on our wedding day?"

"Did she consult with her family? Her mother and brother?" Banu said. The bickering had the sound of a well-established family argument.

Tullu opened his mouth to respond, but instead turned to Anita. "She is dying in the serpent grove, just there." He nodded to an area behind Anita. "Come, I will show you."

Banu snorted and waved them away as he went into the small house, tossing the coconuts onto the floor and calling out as he did so.

□ □ □

Tullu was a man of few words. With no more than a wave of his hand, he led Anita along a little used path through the thick grove until they came to another lane, followed that until it widened enough for a cart, and then turned off onto a sandy yard in front of a row of small images. He walked without grace, stomping through the brush, leaning forward as though to propel himself. He grabbed hold of a tree at the edge of a grove and jerkily pointed at the ground.

"Here it is happening." Tullu stared at a spot in front of him, as if trying to penetrate the earth, expecting to see his wife emerge and rise from the dust.

"What exactly happened?" Anita knelt down and studied the stone serpent images, then the trees and shrubs behind them. This seemed an ordinary serpent grove, and perhaps even a kavu, the sacred grove that once delimited, cannot be entered by anyone—a home to animals and birds and plants until the earth comes to an end, or a relative sells the land to an outsider.

"We are having an exorcism. I am building the pandal and hiring the Pulluvan to sing and play, and perform the puja. All is going well. My mother and wife and sister-in-law, Banu's wife, Uccha, are drawing the serpent image in the colored powders and then sitting there. The music is most powerful—my sister-in-law and my mother are receiving Devi—they are one with the music. But Macheri, no. She is sitting as still and as quiet as a child in school."

"Did this happen more than once?" Anita asked but she knew the answer. This was the reason Macheri had been so distressed when Anita had seen her last.

"Five times we are beginning." Tullu paused to unwind a cloth from around his forehead, to keep off the sun, and wipe his face. "But the last time, we are doing more."

"What do you mean, doing more?"

"The Pulluvan is saying we are not finishing the rite, and we should all be going to the serpent grove, right here. Before we are leaving Macheri at home, and only Uccha and my mother are coming with us to the grove, but this time the Pulluvan is saying we must all go—even his wife, who sings too. Even Macheri."

"And did she go with you?"

"Yes, not willingly at first, but going."

"And this is where she died?"

Tullu waggled his head yes. "The three of them are coming to the grove and prostrating themselves in front of the serpent images. Macheri is slow to do this, but quick to finish. My mother-in-law and sister-in-law recover themselves and are so grateful to the Pulluvan. They finish their puja but Macheri is slow—she must pick up the water pots,, the Pulluvan says. We start back to the house, thinking she will catch up with us. But we hear a scream. It is Macheri. We rush to her—she is crying and crying. She is hysterical. She says she has been bitten by a snake. I am rushing into the underbrush looking and looking. And then I see the snake. Foolish woman, I tell her. There it is, only the wolf snake. It does not kill."

"Did you see the wolf snake?"

"Yes, yes, yes." He waved away Anita's question, but then his expression changed again. He grew sad and somber. "But she is very sick later, very sick. She cannot breathe. And I am thinking, can there be another snake? Was I wrong?" Anita winced at the pain of unbearable guilt in his eyes.

□ □ □

Macheri's mother was waiting for them when they returned to the house. With her hands pressed together in anjali, she bowed and welcomed Anita. Since the family was in mourning, they couldn't offer her any hospitality, but true to the practicality with which Hindu families address inconvenient restrictions, the mother had asked a neighbor to provide tiffin, coffee and biscuits.

A table was set at the edge of the lane facing the house and swamp. There Anita could be welcomed and visited with, but not polluted by the family death. It was a concept Anita had no choice but to tolerate. The neighbors had gone to considerable trouble and she knew they were lined up behind her, watching. She settled herself into the white molded plastic chair, drew the candle closer, and lifted the metal cup of coffee from its flat-bottomed bowl. The coffee was sweet with sugar and milk, and Anita offered appreciative comments.

Tullu squatted nearby, lost in his own thoughts. Banu was out back chopping wood for the fire, and a woman Anita assumed to be Uccha leaned against the far corner of the house, watching her.

"When I was here before," Anita said to Tullu, "I think I saw the Pulluvan's pot-drum over by the pandal."

Tullu followed the pointing hand, then nodded. "Yes, it was there between pujas, but now it is put away for safe keeping. It is over there." He indicated a small hut with no roof and walls of woven mats. The old latrine, she thought, looking around for the new one.

"I'm surprised he would leave his instrument here," Anita said. Pulluvans are not rich, she thought. None of them can afford to lose something so important to their livelihood. "Will he soon come back for this?"

"Of course." Tullu turned to his sister-in-law, Uccha, still half-concealed by the corner of the house, and repeated Anita's question. In a voice Anita couldn't hear well, she answered Tullu. "Yes," he said, turning to Anita. "He will come in one or two days' time."

"Where has he gone that he doesn't need his drum?" Perhaps with a few more questions, Anita could draw out Uccha, and have a real conversation with her. She was, after all, living in her husband's house rather than in her mother's, and that in itself was unusual.

Tullu repeated her question, but the answer was abrupt. Uccha muttered something, shrugged, and pulled away from the house, disappearing from view. "He has no performances to give in the next few days," Tullu relayed. Then, having done his duty, he returned to staring at the ground. His mother-in-law stared at Anita.

The only sounds were the squeaking of the chair under Anita's shifting weight, the murmurs of the villagers behind her, and the sound of an axe splitting wood.

Anita found her autorickshaw still waiting for her at the main road. She climbed in and settled back onto the seat. The driver started the little engine, then looked over his shoulder, expecting her to give him directions, but Anita was oblivious to his queries. Macheri was not that much younger than Anita, and seeing the other woman's life so circumscribed by both poverty and family brought Anita a sad anger and feeling of helplessness.

"Why would a family say one of its members is possessed when she isn't?" The question was directed to the ether and Anita frowned as she pondered this. "And why would a Pulluvan leave his drum behind, even if he can count on it being cared for, and come back and get it later?"

The auto driver shrugged and smiled. "Kovalam?"

"That's it!" Anita lunged forward. "That's it! Because he could! He left it because he could."

"Trivandrum?" the driver suggested.

"He knew he could leave it and it would be safe there." Anita clapped her hand over her mouth. "Of course."

"Varkala?" the driver suggested, now hoping for a huge fare and bigger tip from his crazy passenger.

"And why did he know he could?" Anita hunched over, trying to think.

"Bus station?" the driver suggested, wondering if he should just give up.

"Because he has a connection," Anita said, flopping back in her seat. "But which one?"

"Tea stall?" the driver asked sadly, now resigned to a short trip and no tip.

"Yes," Anita said, pointing at him, "a tea stall. Exactly right."

Surprised, but glad to at least get moving and thus make some money, the driver revved the engine and drove along the road to the first row of shops. At the end stood a small tea stall, and the auto driver pulled over. Anita hopped out. She ordered two coffees, and motioned for the driver to take one.

"I was sad to hear about Macheri," Anita said to the tea wallah. "Her new shop was popular with the foreigners."

"Ahhh!" The tea wallah dunked a dirty glass in equally dirty water, to rinse it out, and wiggled his fingers among the glasses to spread them around. "Very sad. She was a hard worker."

"Her family must have been proud of her."

"Ahh, yes. Well, yes." He seemed unsure of his answer.

"I would be jealous if my sister-in-law did something so brave." Anita sipped her coffee.

The tea wallah stopped rinsing glasses and seemed to think about her comment. "Yes, when there is more than one woman in a house, and not a sister, is there not jealousy?"

"Does the Pulluvan live in this area?"

The tea wallah shook his head. "Tullu is finding him. He is telling me his mother-in-law will be pleased he is finding only the best singer. If Tullu must do this, then he must have the best singer."

□ □ □

"Again?" The auto driver turned around to Anita and did not try to hide his confusion. It was close to midnight, a black sky with clouds covering the moon, and the Kovalam resort fast asleep. Anita's request to the driver to return by midnight had surprised him, and her request to return to the village where Macheri lived had stumped him.

"I want to go back to the village but I don't want anyone to know I have come again." Anita settled herself in the back seat. "Can you do that?"

"Of course." He waggled his head, but didn't smile. "Of course," he said again, grabbing the handlebars. He started the autorickshaw, and headed up the hill. Anita didn't recognize the route he took, but when the auto coasted to a halt on a dirt road, she thought she recognized some of the houses. "Along there is a path. It leads to a serpent grove and then on to the house."

"I remember that path." Anita climbed out. All was still and dark. The cooking fires were out, the lanterns out. Nothing moved, not even a goat or a chicken. The blackness had put all the creatures to sleep. "I'll be back." The driver agreed to wait, and Anita stepped into the darkness.

□ □ □

Anita moved cautiously along the path. This was the time for snakes—both venomous and non-venomous—and if Macheri had been killed by one, then there was a good chance one or more nested in the area. She moved past the serpent grove, all but holding her breath. When she came closer to Macheri's house, Anita crouched down and listened. Ahead of her was the dirt yard, the small house, the old latrine off to her right. She circled around to the right, knelt down, and crawled across the space, keeping the latrine between herself and the house. If anyone came out now, to smoke a cigarette, use the new latrine, or just gaze at the sky, he or she wouldn't see Anita.

The latrine floor had been covered over with a thick layer of dirt that seemed to have settled. Anita parted the leaves at the lowest section of mat and stuck her hand in. She felt around for a water pot, but was not surprised when she didn't find one. The water pot had served its purpose. Next she turned her attentions to the pot-drum. The pot-drum was only inches from her, its thin leather covering cold and dry beneath her fingers. It was a typical pot-drum—standing as tall as her knee, as round as a ball, with only a small flat bottom and equally small mouth. Gingerly, pulling away every few seconds because fear was stronger than curiosity sometimes, she felt along the mouth. It was covered with a thin skin that seemed to be tied on separately.

Confident that the entire mouth was covered, she tapped on the surface. Nothing. She tapped again. Still nothing. She moved her hand onto the pottery and tapped all the way along the surface until she had moved from bottom to top and back again. Then she listened. She was rewarded with the sound of something sliding against the inner surface and a soft, familiar hissing.

□ □ □

The following morning Anita arrived at Macheri's shop, and was relieved to find Raj finishing up the disposition of the store goods. A loaded handcart was just pulling away as Anita banged on the open shutters. Raj saw her over his shoulder, and smiled warmly. He dropped a pile of newspapers he'd been using to wrap things with and came toward her.

"You have met my family, isn't it?" The news pleased him and he motioned her inside.

"I wanted to give your family my sympathy," Anita said. "We shall miss your cousin." She felt a twinge at her deception, but pushed it aside. "It is sad that she should die just after the puja. But perhaps that means a good rebirth for her."

Raj shrugged and stuffed his hands into his pockets. "She was so fearful. Macheri told me every night this puja would not work. But no one would believe her." He lowered his voice and whispered, "She did not like the Pulluvan and his wife."

"Did she say she was not possessed?"

Raj nodded and slouched down on a stool, folding up like a measuring stick. "She blamed greed in others."

"In who?"

He shrugged. "Just others. That was all."

"Whose idea was it to get the Pulluvan to come and sing?"

"Ah, that was Banu." Raj was again a teenager, admiring the forceful decisions of his elders. "He sent Tullu for the Pulluvan."

"Then Banu knew him? They must trust each other, for the Pulluvan to go off and leave his pot-drum." This was an unusual step to take, and she wondered if Raj knew about it.

"This Pulluvan is known to us," Raj said. "That's why he left his pot-drum while he went visiting family."

"He has family nearby?" Anita couldn't conceal her surprise.

"Cousins, many cousins. Cousins to him and cousins to us."

Anita did her best to keep the excitement out of her voice. "Which part of your family is cousin to him?"

"Uccha. She is cousin to his wife's cousin." He went on to offer a careful recital of the relevant branch of the family tree.

"Uccha must be very unhappy at how these pujas turned out, yes? I mean, having her family involved in this."

"It is karma, she says. Macheri broke with the family practice and the family desires, so it is karma that has claimed her." He swung back toward the goods still waiting to be packaged, and heaved a sigh. "I return to Trivandrum tomorrow. To school. I liked helping out here."

□ □ □

By midmorning Anita was back at Macheri's house. Macheri's mother waved to her from the door as Anita approached, and she was careful not to cross the boundary onto their property.

"The Pulluvan's pot-drum? Yes, it is here." The old woman looked perplexed but pointed to the hut where it was being kept.

"That's good," Anita said. "I have sent word to your Pulluvan that we need him in our neighborhood."

"Ah, he is welcoming business," the old woman said. Uccha stood behind her, just inside the door, watching from the shadows.

"A maidservant's sister is in such difficulty, so we are having the exorcism tonight." Once launched on her tale of woe, Anita embellished happily on the plight of a hotel employee whose favorite younger sister was possessed to the point of stupefaction. It was a mesmerizing story, getting better and better as she went along, and Anita promised herself she'd tell it to others as soon as she got the chance. "So, you see, it is imperative he begin as soon as possible. And I am here to save him the trouble of another journey. I shall collect the pot-drum for him." And with that, she crossed the yard, reached over the mat wall, snatched the stick to which the pot-drum was attached and lifted it out of the hut.

"No, no!" Uccha rushed from the doorway, her arms outstretched.

"But I assure you, Uccha, he said it was all right." Anita held up the Pulluvan drum by its stick. "I am doing him a favor."

Uccha cringed, as though terrified. Her mother-in-law squinted at her, then stared at the pot. Anita held the pot up higher and began to swing it gently toward the two women. Uccha fell back, stumbling into the house, and slammed the door. The old woman banged on the door, calling on her daughter-in-law to open up.

"What is this noise?" Banu came from around the corner, Tullu behind him.

"What have you done?" the old woman screamed at Anita. With her gray hair flying, Macheri's mother began to run at Anita but swerved to the side, her eyes locked on the Pulluvan's drum. "What have you done to it?"

"Me?" Anita held the drum up higher, swung it, and watched as Tullu, the old woman, and now Banu followed it as though hypnotized. "I don't think it's me that's done anything."

With far greater care than she had shown so far, Anita laid the drum on the ground. "Listen," she said and squatted down close by. All three approached and knelt.

"Ayoo!" The old woman grabbed her son's arm. "It is Naagaraaja!"

"Nothing so grand as king of the snakes," Tullu said. His eyes hardened, grew blacker, and Anita winced at the sharp stab she always felt when a man's illusions fell.

"Look at the skin," Anita said. "It is a new covering over the old. Smaller, only for the mouth of the pot."

Tullu stood, and ordered Banu to do so too. "Banu, she is your wife. This Pulluvan is her cousin. This is his snake."

"You accuse her?" Banu's chest heaved and his fists clenched.

"She accuses herself. She is the only one to flee." Tullu reached down to run his hand over the drum. "My wife was generous. She would have shared her success."

The old woman lifted her arms, calling out the names of both men, before she set up an ear-piercing wail reciting the names of her daugher and daughter-in-law, each syllable wreathed in anguish. Her frail body swayed and trembled, as though it would shatter under the weight of her sorrow. Anita knelt down beside the old woman, and thought of the cheerful young Macheri, quirky and brave in her new shop, and all that she might have achieved for her family.

Self-Help

Norma Burrows

I have read that we have patterns of behavior that we are destined to repeat until we work them through. Once we identify the part we play in our pattern we can set about changing it. By modifying one's self, the cycle can be broken; the other players are forced to alter their positions. Ideally the end result will be rising to a higher plain of self-awareness. If the pattern of behavior is restricting your growth, there will be newfound freedom, leading eventually to self-actualization.

My personal pattern was developed more than thirty-five years ago. It may cycle through twice a week or once every four years. I know I am still in it as of this writing. I am paralyzed by bullies. I shrivel up inside and skulk away. At times I imagine a scenario where I have superhero courage and stand up to them, uttering marvelously witty phrases that leave them stunned in my wake. I am working on something more moderate for the next time it happens.

I have tried wearing a scarf that my daughter made for me. I feel emboldened by the knowledge that I am loved. This helps a little but when an aggressive coworker attacks me with, "Why are you always so difficult?" I walk away muttering, "Yeah, this is about me." Up to this point I am standing up for myself. The next thing I do upon reaching my desk is fall into a heap, crying like a baby. This is not helpful and is impeding my spiritual growth. I am left to ponder what I can do differently next time. I feel hopeless.

Patients have complained about the lack of security cameras in the hospital parking garage for years. Tonight this is playing in my favor. It has taken me weeks to figure out which car is hers and then for the exact right opportunity. I am dressed entirely in black, including my ski mask. I am waiting under the SUV parked next to her car, on the driver's side. She arrives and I silently roll out the side opposite her compact car. I look around to confirm that we are alone.

Then I sneak up behind her and grab her hair, wrenching back her neck. I quickly slash my hand brutally across her exposed throat with my red Sharpie marker. She collapses to the ground, hysterically sobbing. Now this is what I call empowering. I am soaring with the surge of adrenalin. Of course I could have used the switchblade in my other pocket, but that would have been bad karma.

Twenty-one Days

Leslie Wheeler

"You'll get over him," Dr. Naomi Shad-Somers said. "It just takes time."

Abby tossed the wet, wadded tissue into the trash and reached for another. "How much time?" she demanded, not really expecting an answer.

Dr. Shad-Somers leaned back in her chair and regarded Abby with all-knowing gray eyes. She steepled her long, narrow fingers. Light from the window glinted on the numerous thin, gold bands she wore. Abby knew nothing of Shad-Somers's personal life—whether she was married, divorced, widowed, with or without children—but if each ring represented a past relationship, as Abby sometimes speculated, the doctor had been around the block many times.

Quiet filled the room. As the silence stretched on, Abby began to find it oppressive. She'd never been good with silence. Growing up, motherless, with an attorney father whose every word was punctuated by a lengthy pause, Abby had gotten in the habit of finishing other people's sentences, answering her own questions. She shifted in her seat, stared at the oriental rug on the floor, then at the African masks on the wall. Both of her previous therapists had decorated their offices with African masks. Abby wondered if they represented some sort of shrink chic. The mouth of one mask was a gaping hole, as if it were about to say something. When Shad-Somers did finally speak, her words seemed to come from the mask: "Twenty-one days."

Abby turned back to her. With her mane of silver hair and loose, flowing clothing, the psychiatrist looked like a Grecian priestess—a tender of some Delphic Oracle.

"Why twenty-one?" Abby asked.

"Because that's how long it takes to break a habit."

"A habit! Like smoking? This is a *person* we're talking about. I'll never get over Gil. I don't want to."

The tower of Shad-Somers's fingers collapsed. "Forget him, Abby. He doesn't deserve you. Why would you want to be with someone who said such awful things to you?"

"But you said it was a healthy relationship, that he was perfect for me."

"I thought so until now."

"We had a fight. That doesn't mean we can't make up."

"You crossed a line last night. Both of you. You'll probably never be able to forgive him, or he, you. It's over, Abby. The sooner you accept that and move on, the better."

"But—"

"Here is what you must do. Avoid any form of contact with him for the next three weeks. No phone calls, no e-mails, no going places where you're likely to run into him, or where you and he used to hang out together. Put him out of your mind. If you find yourself thinking about him, force yourself to think about something else. Have you got that, Abby?

"Yes but—"

The psychiatrist glanced at her watch. "I'm afraid our fifty minutes are up. I think we should see each other more frequently—at least for awhile." She consulted her BlackBerry. "I can see you Monday at three."

"Okay." Stoop-shouldered with defeat, Abby got up to go. She'd started with Shad-Somers in the aftermath of another failed relationship. Back then, she'd been so distraught she'd seen the psychiatrist twice a week. Now, she felt she was back to square one.

"Remember, it's only twenty-one days." Shad-Somers's voice was like a gentle pat on the back.

Shrugging off the imaginary hand, Abby spun angrily around. "I can't do this!"

"Of course you can. We'll talk more on Monday."

As she was leaving, Abby glanced back at the psychiatrist. Head bent, fingers tapping on her BlackBerry, under the watchful eyes of the African masks, Shad-Somers recorded her notes from the session into the small, dark rectangle of memory.

□ □ □

"How'd it go?" Abby's friend and business partner, Moira, asked when she returned to the store.

Abby shook her head. "I don't know. She told me I'd get over him in twenty-one days."

"Twenty-one days?" Moira echoed.

"That's how long it takes to break a habit."

"Hmmm. Maybe I should try that." Moira frowned at her hard-bitten nails.

"Lots of luck." Moira had been trying to stop biting her nails for as long as Abby had known her. Now in their thirties, she and Moira had been roommates in college.

Moira looked at Abby with concern. "Will you be okay by yourself if I go out for lunch?"

Abby nodded. Alone in the shop, she glanced around. Ordinarily, she took pleasure in the merchandise, which included plastic rings with big rocks that lit up when you squeezed them, martini glasses with fake liquid and olives, inflatable pets, and other amusing toys for adults. Bon Vivant had been hers and Moira's brain child, conceived late one night when they were supposed to be studying for exams.

Moira said she wanted to do something fun after college, and Abby agreed. Putting their heads together, they came up with the idea of the store, combining Moira's knack for finding humorous gifts for her friends with Abby's business sense. Moira's wealthy grandfather provided the money for her share of the venture, while Abby used the insurance money from her father's untimely death to fund hers.

It was money well spent; the shop turned out to be a big success. Yet today, Abby felt no pride in their achievement. How could she when she and Gil had met at Bon Vivant?

That Saturday afternoon, a week before Christmas, Massachusetts Avenue in Cambridge had been thronged with holiday shoppers. The crowd that filled the tiny store reminded Abby of the subway at rush hour. She was frantically working the cash register, making change and swiping credit cards, when she looked up to see a youngish, nice-looking man holding a flashing ring. "Excuse me, but how do you make this stop?"

Abby was tempted to grab the ring, give it the necessary twist, and move on to the next customer. But something about the man's expression—his eyes half-embarrassed, half-amused behind wire-frame glasses, his cheeks flushed from the cold outside, and a shock of dark brown hair spilling onto his forehead—made her hesitate. Ignoring the long line of people waiting impatiently behind him, she said, "You're not the first person who's asked that question. Here, let me show you." She held out her hand for the ring, he gave it to her, and she made the light stop flashing.

"Thanks." He smiled shyly at her and she smiled back.

He didn't buy the ring or anything else then, but Abby didn't care because he returned to the shop almost daily, sometimes to make a purchase, sometimes merely to ask a question about an item. Shortly after Christmas, he asked her out.

The jingle of the shop doorbell pulled Abby out of her reverie. She turned expectantly, hoping against hope it was Gil. It was only Moira returning from her lunch break.

Leaving work that evening, Abby glimpsed the green neon bird perched over the entrance of the Parrot Lounge down Mass. Ave when an inner alarm went off. "Where do you think you're going?" Abby imagined Shad-Somers saying. "Isn't this the bar where you and Gil used to meet for drinks at the end of the day? Didn't I tell you to avoid such places?"

"What difference does it make? He won't be there," Abby answered back. She'd been seeing Shad-Somers long enough to have internalized her voice. The psychiatrist served as a kind of mental GPS, showing Abby the best route to follow, and steering her back on course when she went astray. But that didn't mean Abby accepted her advice without question. She wasn't her attorney father's daughter for nothing.

"It would be counterproductive for you to go in there now," Shad-Somers said.

"Oh, all right," Abby replied crossly. She turned around and kept walking until she reached her apartment, where she secretly hoped there would be a phone message or an e-mail from Gil.

Inside, no blinking light on her answering machine greeted her, nor was there an e-mail from him when she turned on the computer. Abby sank disconsolately onto the living room couch. As she did, she noticed a scrap of paper on the cushion. It bore the letters "il!" and was a remnant of last night's decorations. Abby had torn them down after their quarrel. Add an extra "l" to "il!" and it would describe how she felt: heartsick remembering the harsh words she and Gil had exchanged.

□ □ □

Divorced and in his forties, Gil was a good friend and sensitive lover. He was also bright, funny, and articulate, sharing with Abby the enthusiasm for science, and astronomy in particular, that made him such a wildly popular middle-school teacher. Ironically, Gil's dedication to his inner city students—one of the things Abby admired most about him—created problems in their seven-month-long relationship. Abby felt Gil made himself too available to his students, staying after school to help them with assignments, allowing them to call him at home, and even show up on his doorstep.

Yesterday had been Gil's birthday, and Abby had planned to surprise him with a special dinner. She left the store early to cook and decorate her apartment with crepe paper streamers, balloons, and a huge hand-lettered sign that said, "Happy Birthday, Gil!" He was due at 6:00 P.M., and when 6:30 rolled around, Abby assumed he'd gotten involved helping a student and lost track of time. She tried his cell phone but was transferred to voice mail. At 7:00 P.M., she tried again, and got voice mail. To hell with him, she thought irritably as she opened the bottle of champagne and poured herself a glass. By 7:30, the bottle was half-empty and Abby was steaming with alcohol-fueled anger. She was also starting to worry. What if something had happened to him? She called again only to get voice mail. At 8:00 P.M., after Abby had polished off the champagne, and was stewing with rage, laced with a liberal dose of anxiety, Gil finally called.

"Where on earth are you?"

"The Cambridge Hospital ER."

"What! Are you all right?" An icy hand of fear clutched at Abby's throat.

"Yes, but Carlos isn't."

"Who?"

"A former student. He came to the school while I was helping Washington with his science fair project."

"And?"

"He wanted to borrow my car."

"Omigod, Gil, you didn't let him, did you?"

"Maybe it wasn't such a great idea. He smashed up the car, and got into a fight with the kids in the car he hit. The police called me when they found out it was my car. I arrived just as an ambulance was about to take Carlos away. Fortunately, he wasn't hurt too bad. But I felt I should ride with him."

"Why didn't you call sooner? I've been worried about you."

"I meant to, but I just out and out forgot."

"Do you remember what day it is?"

"Sure, it's Wednesday and—"

"It's your birthday, for heaven's sakes! I cooked a special dinner, and now it's ruined."

"I'm sorry, Abby."

"When are you going to stop bending over backwards for hoodlum students like this Carlos?"

"He isn't a hoodlum. You have no idea what it's like when your dad's in jail and your mom's slaving to make ends meet. I'm trying to make a difference in the lives of kids like him."

"You're a teacher, not a case worker."

"With these kids, the two aren't mutually exclusive. But you don't understand that. How could you when you spend your days peddling pricey trinkets to people who have everything?"

"Thanks for sharing your true feelings about what I do," Abby shot back. "As for my not understanding things, I understand plenty. Like why your wife left you. I bet she couldn't bear watching a bunch of young thugs take advantage of you over and over again."

"At least I found someone to marry and stayed married for

ten years—a lot longer than any of your relationships has lasted."

Abby was stunned speechless. Before she could reply with something equally hurtful, Gil hung up.

The sound and fury of their fight still clung to Abby with the persistence of a bad dream. She felt a yawning emptiness now that Gil was gone. Why hadn't she kept her mouth shut about his students? Then, the whole poisonous exchange might never have occurred, and she wouldn't be sitting here alone. To escape the silence and memories of Gil crowding in around her, Abby fled her apartment and got into her car.

She drove aimlessly until, like a homing pigeon, her car brought her to Gil's apartment building. The light was on in his unit, and she was tempted to press the buzzer and let him know she was there. Shad-Somers's scolding voice stopped her: "You shouldn't have come here. Go home immediately."

"I'm not going inside; I'll just sit in my car," Abby said. "What's the harm in that?"

"Abby—"

"Leave me alone!"

Abby passed the time fantasizing about scenes of reconciliation—tearful apologies on both their parts followed by tender embraces. When the light went out, she drove home, her hopes deflated. Back at her apartment, she counted twenty-one days on the wall calendar. The numbered squares stretched before her like boxes from which the bright, new gifts had been removed. She would have to fill them somehow if she didn't hear from Gil, or break down and contact him herself.

"How is it going?" Shad-Somers asked on Monday, day five.

"Terrible, I can't stop thinking about him." Abby went on to confess her lapses on day one when she'd almost gone into the

Parrot Lounge and when she'd driven to Gil's apartment building.

"It will get easier as time goes on," the psychiatrist assured her. "Trust me."

Yet, over the next few days—six to eight—Abby didn't feel she was making any real progress. She was distracted and irritable at work, and poured out her unhappiness to Shad-Somers, and to Moira and her other friends who were willing to listen. Everything reminded her of him. It was as if Gil had broken up into thousands of pieces. He was there in this person's smile, that person's way of adjusting his glasses; in an empty bottle of Guiness Stout discarded on the sidewalk; in the moon they'd observed together in its various stages from crescent to full, so he could check the accuracy of the moon journals his students were keeping. All these parts of Gil lay in wait for her, popping out when she least expected them, causing her unbearable torment. On day nine she even thought she saw him from a distance.

Then, on day thirteen, she did see him. Usually Abby walked to the store from her apartment, but that day it was so rainy and windy, she decided to drive. She'd gone out to feed the meter on Mass. Ave when she noticed a couple hurrying up the street, huddled under an umbrella. Their backs were to her, but the umbrella—black with the solar system in gleaming gold—was painfully familiar. How many times had she and Gil shared that umbrella, which she'd bought for him at the Museum of Science? Now he was using it to shelter another woman. A jealous rage consumed Abby like a wildfire. Heedless of Shad-Somers's warning voice on her mental GPS, Abby rushed up Mass. Ave after them. At a bus stop several blocks away, Gil and his new love came to a halt. By the time Abby reached them, a small crowd had gathered behind the couple, but she was able to insinuate herself between them and the others.

The bus barreled toward them like a runaway train. A shove from her would pitch Gil and girlfriend off the curb into its path. As she stepped forward, Abby heard Shad-Somers calling to her from faraway. A strong gust of wind caught the umbrella and carried it aloft. Gil turned to retrieve the umbrella—except it wasn't Gil.

Ducking into the entrance of a beauty salon a block down, Abby telephoned Shad-Somers on her cell. "I need to see you as soon as possible. I almost did something terrible."

□ □ □

"At least you realized your mistake in time," Shad-Somers said carefully. "Still . . ." She paused, and in that moment of hesitation, Abby saw a flicker of fear in the psychiatrist's eyes.

"What?" Abby prodded.

"You're obviously having a hard time with this. I think it would be wise if I gave you some medication to take the edge off." Shad-Somers picked up a pen and prescription pad.

"I don't want any medication. I can deal with this on my own. It was a one-time thing. It's not like I've become Glenn Close in *Fatal Attraction*."

"No, of course not. But if you ever find yourself even thinking about doing anything like you nearly did today, I want you to call me immediately."

"I will."

"Good. Now there's something else I want you to do for me: try washing him out of your hair."

"Huh?"

"It's a line from a musical—before your time," Shad-Somers said, reminding Abby they belonged to different generations. She guessed the psychiatrist was somewhere in her fifties, but she wasn't sure; despite her silver hair, Shad-Somers seemed ageless.

"Seriously, Abby," the psychiatrist went on, "you should take more care of yourself. You'll feel better if you do."

"What d'you mean?"

Shad-Somers sighed deeply. "Have a look in the bathroom mirror on your way out."

Abby did, and was shocked by the way she'd let herself go. Her long hair hung in oily strands—literally a dirty blond. Now, she understood why Moira had been muttering about hair and hygiene lately. Abby also noticed the dark circles under her eyes and the yellowish pallor of her face. She resembled a plant shut away from the light too long. Not only that, her rumpled khaki pants and shirt were spotted with mud from her race up Mass. Ave. Maybe she *was* becoming Glenn Close.

Abby went home and showered and washed her hair. During her lunch break on day fourteen, she stopped in at one of the trendy boutiques along Mass. Ave, and bought the hottest outfit she could find: a bright floral tunic over white leggings and turquoise cowboy boots. When she returned to the store, Moira dropped the stuffed Spiderman cat toy she'd been playing with to exclaim: "You look fantastic!"

Moira wasn't the only one who approved of the "new" Abby. Female customers asked where she bought her clothes, and men began giving her the eye. On day sixteen, an attractive thirty-something male came into the shop, and spent so much time talking to Abby she knew he was interested in her. He returned on day seventeen, and on day eighteen, he asked her out. Shades of Gil, she thought with a pang. Yet her anguish wasn't as sharp as before. Maybe because she was approaching the homestretch of the habit-breaking period. Her date with the new guy would take place on day twenty-one.

The only trouble was he suggested beginning the evening with a drink at the Parrot Lounge. "Absolutely not," Abby imagined Shad-Somers saying. "You need to wait until *after* the twenty-first day before you go there. Insist on another place." Abby and the psychiatrist had their usual mental tug-of-war until Abby came up with a compromise in the form of a "dry run." She would go to the Parrot Lounge by herself the night before. That way, she'd know whether she was ready to return with a date.

After work, on the evening of the twentieth day, Abby headed down Mass. Ave to the bar. In the distance, the neon bird beckoned like a green traffic light, telling her it was safe to cross the threshold, that she was doing the right thing. But as she got close, the neon suddenly went out. Without brilliant light pulsing through it, the bird became an ugly, washed-out piece of glass and metal. Maybe this was a bad omen, and she should turn around. The next moment, she scolded herself for being so superstitious. It was purely a coincidence the sign had gone out when it did.

Besides, she'd be seeing Shad-Somers on day twenty-two. Wouldn't it be cool to report that she'd walked into the Parrot Lounge *before* the specified time was over without being overwhelmed by pain and regrets? "I knew you could do this, Abby. I'm so proud of you," the psychiatrist would say, flashing Abby one of her rare smiles.

Abby strode boldly into the bar, then almost immediately stopped short. Gil sat at a booth in the rear. This time she was certain it was Gil because he faced her.

At the sight of him, Abby was overcome by a yearning so intense it pulled her toward him like a magnet. He looked up from his beer mug and saw her. He rose shakily and took a tentative step toward her, a stricken look on his face. An arm angled around the back of the booth like a tentacle. Be-ringed fingers clutched at Gil's jacket. "What is it, darling? Where are you going?" Even before the speaker's face appeared at the edge of the booth, Abby knew. She'd recognize that low, well-modulated voice anywhere.

Shad-Somers's mouth opened in an "o" of surprise. Her normally sympathetic face hardened with anger. "You weren't supposed to—"

Abby didn't wait to hear any more. Heart thudding, stomach churning, she fled the bar. On the sidewalk she nearly plowed into a woman with a baby in a stroller, but managed to swerve out of the way at the last moment. Behind her, she heard Gil call, "Abby, wait! I can explain."

Yeah, sure, she thought furiously. She went on running. Gil continued to call her name. He sounded as if he were gaining on her. Abby glanced over her shoulder to gauge the distance between them. She realized then that not only was Gil chasing her, but Shad-Somers was pursuing him. Her arms were outstretched. Her silver mane flew away from her face. "Gil, come back!" she cried.

Damn them both! To Abby's right was a cluster of shops and restaurants, while to her left lay four lanes of speeding traffic that made crossing Mass. Ave almost as dangerous as crossing an interstate. The light turned red, and the cars jerked to a halt. Abby darted into the street. She got as far as the island when an orange warning hand replaced the white figure of a pedestrian. Abby figured she had a nanosecond or less to cross before the cars zoomed over the line and smashed into her. She sprinted across the street, reaching the other side just as the vehicles began their forward surge.

Abby fell against a lamppost, struggling to catch her breath for the next leg of her flight. Gil and Shad-Somers were trapped on the island, surrounded by an angry swarm of cars. The psychiatrist clung to Gil, while he tried to shake her off. Suddenly he freed himself from her grasp, but with such force that his momentum carried him off the narrow divider and into the path of oncoming traffic. Howling with horror, Shad-Somers dove after him. Abby shut her eyes, but couldn't help hearing the screech of brakes, then the sickening thud of metal against flesh and bone.

□ □ □

In the ER waiting room at Mt. Auburn Hospital, Abby stared straight ahead as if her main purpose in life were to bear witness to the restless squirming of the young girl who sat opposite Abby, hair bound in tight braids. She felt rather than saw Gil take her hand and squeeze it, the warmth and pressure bringing her out of the trance she'd fallen into. "Why my therapist of all people?" Abby asked

"I didn't mean to get involved with her. She approached me at the Parrot the night after our fight."

"What were you doing at the Parrot?"

"I was too ashamed to call or send an e-mail, so I went there, hoping you'd show up and I could apologize in person."

"I would have come if I hadn't taken her advice to avoid our old hang-outs."

"She told you that?"

"Yes. She convinced me our quarrel had ended things, and I needed to get over you. She said it would take twenty-one days."

Gil stared at her, dumbfounded. "That's exactly what she told me."

Abby shook her head with disbelief. "But why?" She paused long enough to answer her own question. She remembered how Shad-Somers had listened eagerly while she'd sung Gil's praises. "He sounds wonderful. I'm really happy for you, Abby," the psychiatrist had said. She'd even asked to see his picture, and Abby had obliged, little guessing that Shad-Somers was becoming smitten with Gil herself.

"She fell for you, based on what I told her," Abby said. "Then when we fought, she saw her chance. What I still don't understand, though, is why you two went to the Parrot tonight."

Gil pushed his hair off his forehead, a futile gesture because it promptly flopped back. "Maybe she really believed in the twenty-one-days thing. She thought I'd be over you, that it was safe to go there. Plus she never dreamed you'd show up after she told you not to."

"What she did was unforgivable," Abby said.

They fell silent, and in that silence, Abby imagined Shad-

Somers joining the conversation. "I shouldn't have betrayed you with Gil. But two wrongs don't make a right, Abby."

"What do you—" Abby was cut short by the approach of a doctor. Even before he spoke Abby knew Shad-Somers was dead.

But the psychiatrist went on speaking to Abby: "You led me into the street, hoping I'd be killed."

"No, no—stop!" Abby's scream bounced off the waiting room walls. Gil drew her to him. Abby pulled away. Shad-Somers's voice was gone, replaced by another inner voice—her own. "Did you? Did you? Did you?" it repeated like a stubborn parrot.

Therapy

Janice Law

I wouldn't be doing this if I weren't bored. There's no point in it, none. Everything's decided and I'm not going anywhere, that's for sure, but since boredom's a killer, since this is like the worst study hall ever, like Ms. Clancy droning on and on, like an eternity of volleyball with six-foot Suzi Altmeyer across the net, I'll give it a try. So, First Attempt:

I fell in love. How's that? With a man I met at my uncle's house—I don't think you knew that, did you, Dr. Langston? We're at my uncle's house on the water, family all round, food enough for fifty, catered naturally, and red wine by the bucket—plenty for us kids to sneak a bottle and pass it around behind the cabana, so that Joey, that's Joe Junior, barfed up in the rhododendrons, and second cousin Anthony kissed my older sister and tried to put his hands down my bikini bottom.

You had to be there to get the picture. There were decorator place settings and centerpieces, bug-fighting torches, luminaries, lights in the trees, sparklers on the grass. Typical Uncle Joe production, designed to show the rest of the family that he's made it bigger than anyone else. Boring! But Louie was there. He'd sold my uncle the power boat, a fast, expensive model with a design of skulls on a red ground up the side. You've seen those zooming around in the Sound? Drug Runner boats, that's what they are.

My uncle owns this big shoreline restaurant that makes lots of money. So he could afford a band, too—not a great grooving band like say, Fannypack, but not a geezer group, either—and Louie, my Louie, who sold the boat—but I don't need to tell you about Louie; you know all about Louie and probably have some ideas about him—Louie asked me to dance and I fell in love with him. How's that?

The thinness of the narrative shows a detachment from the actual facts of the case. This distancing indicates . . . bla, bla, bla.

Dr. Langston wants details. He wants all the dirty bits, like what we did in Louie's car after the party, or what Louie said when he called me up on his cellphone at midnight. Well, duh! Use your imagination. Or ask Louie. I'm sure he remembers. Maybe it was a novelty to him, I mean someone my age, him being older, old. I might as well say old now. It wasn't a novelty to me. What do you make of that, Dr. Langston?

Still, there's no getting around the fact that boredom is the enemy, therefore, as my algebra teacher, Mr. Simmons, used to say, therefore, Second Attempt:

I was fourteen years old and three quarters when I met Louie, who was six feet tall and handsome with black hair and brown eyes. Not too fat. Grown up and interested in me. Like he would listen to what I had to say, which boys don't, you know, and other adults didn't. I had things to say, which might surprise you even though you're paid to listen. If you weren't paid, you probably wouldn't. Listen, I mean. But our present topics don't interest me as much as all the things that Louie and I talked about, like my dreams and my future—my future with him—dreams that didn't sure include my present secure facility.

I'm wandering and losing structure. That happens here; boredom softens the brain, and Mrs. Kennelley would take points off this composition. Fortunately, you're not as grammatically fussy, are you, Dr. Langston?

Let's see where I was . . . I was fourteen years old and three quarters . . . oh, yes. First phone call. Louie calls me up and goes, "Hey, Cathy, what'd you think of the band," and I go, "I've heard better but they were okay to dance to," and he goes, "It depends who you're dancing with." This is encouraging, like he knows what to say and doesn't just talk about himself—at least, not at first.

Plus I liked the fact that Louie knew what he wanted and how he was going to get it. Boys don't always know, do they? Or girls, either, I guess. But I knew right away that he was the one, the one I'd love. Madly.

I don't think I want to go on with this.

Classic resistance as evinced by the desire to remain within the parameters of the fantasy life, etc.

I've been forgetting about parole, about official forgiveness or, at least, leniency. Dr. Langston is careful to remind me. Still, best case, I'm looking at years, years and years longer than it would have taken me to finish high school, which would have been three years, minus two months. After that would have been college, four more years, an eternity, a life sentence. I can't imagine so much time. I can't imagine being bored and scared forever, which I am here and with good reason. So I have to encourage Dr. Langston, who says he wants what's best for me and who will speak on my behalf if I tell him the kinds of things he wants to hear, in the way he wants to hear it.

Mucho problems there! First off, he's surprised at the way I write. He expected me to be illiterate, not literally but, you know, duh! Clearly he didn't have Mrs. Kennelley for English. A theme a week and structure, structure, structure. I liked that. Words are the stuff of ideas, and sentences and paragraphs are the structure. You want to keep your ideas in order so they don't go flying off in all directions like the skulls on the sides of your rich uncle's fast boat, the fastest boat in the family, a boat that can race out of the marina, out forever, with just me and Louie, away, away. That's the sort of idea that came to me often. So, here I am with the Third Attempt:

Dr. Langston thinks it was all about sex. *The immature mind gets overwhelmed,* he says. I'm not sure he's ever been overwhelmed or he wouldn't talk about it so casually. But I fell in love with Louie, that's the thing no one wants to hear. They think because you're a kid you're (a) stupid or (b) emotionally retarded, like you don't know what you feel and have to have some adult, some expert, explain it all to you.

Here it is straight: I wanted to get away. I was like this grown-up person trapped in ninth grade. Can you imagine that, Dr. Langston? I doubt you can in your big, quiet office with the thick carpet and nice chairs and a pretty receptionist to answer the phone for you and screen your calls and only take the ones that sound interesting. Do you know the luxury of getting phone calls? Of making them? Who do you think I'd like to call? And what do you think I'd say?

There I was, anyway, grown up and waiting for my real life to begin, and there was Louie, who was perfect, just perfect for someone who was grown up. Do you suppose he recognized me, Dr. Langston, recognized that I was grown up and good to go? Or was I just a kid to him, was he into youth, into pretending he was still just a young guy without responsibilities, instead of husband to Pat and father to those two brats, Staci and Noel? I don't know; I keep changing my mind.

Louie had, and probably still has, a classic Corvette convertible that we used to drive up to Newport where we'd park and eat and he'd buy me clothes my mother would have considered unsuitable. That was one of her favorite words with me, *unsuitable*, as in that dress is unsuitable or that boy is unsuitable.

It's kind of odd that she never found my uncle Joe *unsuitable*, when he was the most unsuitable adult I knew. But she didn't want to hear about Uncle Joe, being as how my dad and she had borrowed money from him and not paid it back. I know that for a fact, not family gossip. Fact, which my uncle told me one day when I was thirteen and a half and sitting with him—well, not exactly sitting—in the cabana in their yard.

He said Mom wouldn't be interested in anything I had to say, and I said, "Oh, yes, she would," and he said, "No, she wouldn't," because of how she and Dad owed him money, which I sort of understood and sort of didn't. Now and again, I used to bring up the idea anyway, and Uncle Joe would laugh and say something about the money, but he'd buy me something expensive to keep me quiet just the same.

But I was writing about being out with Louie, who was very different from Uncle Joe, who'd influenced me—is that a suitable and appropriate word—in my pre-grown-up mode. Louie bought me a tattoo one day at the shore. I'd wanted one that said Louie, but he wouldn't let me. What do you think, Dr. Langston, was that a little, bitty warning that he didn't see our love as permanent? I think so, but I wasn't as realistic and hard then as I am now. Boredom makes you realistic, I guess.

"Names look vulgar," Louie said. "Get a flower. Get a rose, or better yet, get an orchid. I'll treat you to an orchid, because you're like a tropical flower." The dialogue kinda makes me gag now, and I could write better myself, but at the time I said yes, and that's why

I have this stupid orchid, which I used to love, inked on my ankle. I had to wear high socks whenever Mom was around, so she wouldn't notice and ask questions, like where had I gotten that and were the needles clean. I know she'd have called the shop and reported them to the Board of Health or the archdiocese or her favorite congressman. Whoever. But she never reported Uncle Joe. So I got grown up in a hurry. And you'll maybe understand that I hated having to sneak around like a regular kid when I wasn't one anymore.

After I got the orchid tattoo, Louie and me went to the beach—oops, another mark off from Mrs. Kennelley—Louie and *I*, if you please. But in my present circumstances, *me* is safer. All the guys here are suspicious of me, because I'm small and suburban and I don't look particularly tough. I'm having enough interpersonal problems with my criminal peer group without the burden of perfect grammar.

But for you, Dr. Langston, Louie and I went to the beach and lay in the sun a long time. I like the sun and so does Louie. I had on a new thong bikini with sea shells in the right places. Very hot, but no good for swimming, which I like, too. I'd give just about anything for a swim right now. Maybe my orchid tattoo? Could I swap that?

Digressions, but salient and suggestive reflections. More work along these lines will be productive . . .

Salient reflections! Where does the guy get his vocabulary? But he's big on the therapeutic work, *theraputric* more likely, of writing. Mrs. Kennelley never told us about that. She told us about participles and gerunds and subordinate clauses. I wonder whether there are insubordinate clauses, which would be, I think, something like me.

There's another thing: Langston doesn't have a sense of

humor. None. *Nada.* Unlike Louie, who knew how to laugh. Even Uncle Joe could see the funny side of things, although his was a basically nasty sense of humor. He used to call our little sessions in the cabana interest, as in interest on my parents' debt. I don't think Dr. Langston would find that funny.

Anyway, the doc's all focused on my relationship with Louie; mostly, I think, because my rich Uncle Joe is paying the bill. How do I know that? I keep my ears open and I looked through the papers on his desk one day while I was still outside. There's a word with a whole new meaning for me. Outside. To which I want to return, so Fourth Attempt:

I'm really Greek, you know. I know, I know, off the topic, Dr. Langston, and factually insupportable. Another phrase I've picked up from our correspondence. Oh sure, Morelli is a good Italian name. It's right there on Uncle Joe's restaurant, one of the best and fanciest in town: Morelli's. Nice script with curlicues that strike me as somewhat salacious. Do you like that? Good use of two of the last vocab words I learned from Mrs. Kennelley. Bet she'd be surprised to know how I'm using my vocabulary building.

But Greeks, back to the Greeks. You'll never understand me unless you understand Greeks. Not Greeks like Pete Sampras, who I've seen on TV and you probably have, too. I remember that you kept a tennis racket in your office and a signed photo of Andre Agassi, which reminded me of the celeb photos in my uncle's restaurant and almost put me off you for good. I don't suppose you noticed that or cared to.

Mark Philippoussis is another modern Greek, but I only mention him because Louie and I spotted him one afternoon in Newport. I believe Louie said he had done his knee or maybe it was his shoulder. Done as in done in, so by then he was only a semi-celebrity, although Uncle Joe would have put him up anyway and maybe you would have, too.

But Philippoussis is not my sort of Greek. Or not that I know of, because the kind of Greeks I'm talking about are more than just name deep. They don't always recognize themselves, either, like I didn't, not until after I'd met Louie and other things happened.

Perhaps I'm not being clear. Mrs. Kennelley was big on clarity. "Remember to think of the reader as a bit stupid," she'd say. "You've got to spell everything out in your writing." I guess she didn't have a real high opinion of the reading public, probably including you, Dr. Langston, so I'll start at the beginning and ask if you've read the Greek myths? I have because I was in this private school with a traditional academic curriculum, including the classics.

My mom picked the school. If she'd known anything about the place, besides that it was expensive and prestigious, she'd have found the courses unsuitable for sure, and I would never have realized I was Greek. There is some good in parental ignorance.

What do we get in the myths? Oh, boy! There's Jocasta hanging herself and Oedipus gouging his eyes out, and Medea killing her kids, for starters. And Phaedra falling in love with someone unsuitable and lying about him and getting him killed, then killing herself, and Daphne turning into a bush and ruining her life because of some dirty-minded old god, and Hera doing terrible things on a weekly basis to her husband's lovers. Not to omit people getting their tongues cut out—yuck—and others roasting their near relatives and serving them up as cannibal surprise. Those are the Greeks I'm talking about, the all-or-nothing guys who fell in love and killed—or died—for passion.

Somehow I'm a Greek. What do you think about that, Dr. Langston?

Circuitous but revealing, though still lacking any sense of responsibility, indicating a juvenile moral sense . . .

I'm not even going to try to tell you what I think of that! Is this man stupid or what? Mrs. Kennelley was absolutely right. There's some people you got to write everything out for—in triplicate. So, though you shouldn't commit yourself when you're mad, here goes the Fifth Attempt:

He got nervous. Louie, I mean. Someone who knew his wife, Pat, had seen us out—wherever. And she, Pat, had asked him what was going on and made a scene. So this one day he says to me—but before I tell you about that, you've got to realize we were in the car, the Lexus, this time, a black, serious car for a serious, grown-up discussion, after he'd picked me up two blocks from school just like always. He was committed to that!

He says to me, "I think we have to cool things off for a while. Pat's upset."

I shrugged. I hadn't thought Pat mattered, and it took me a minute to run over the things I wanted to say and to edit them down to the best and wisest.

"She'll tell your mother," he says. "Unless we stop seeing each other."

"Do you care?" I says. I still didn't see the urgency.

"Of course, I care. At your age, this" —Listen to him! Not us, but—"*this* could get messy. I could go to jail. You don't want that, do you?"

Even you can see where this was going, can't you, Dr. Langston? I don't think it is necessary for me to report any more of the conversation. The important thing is that within the twenty minutes of getting into Louie's black Lexus, I'd realized I was Greek.

You want details? You want to know how I felt? My world had ended; I'd died right there in the front seat, and all my love had turned to rage. The only thing I could think of was how Pat was going to pay for killing me. And maybe how Louie would, too.

How, how, how? I bet you'll want to know, so I'll tell you,

and you'll be surprised. I called up Uncle Joe, who has, besides the cigarette boat and the fancy restaurant and the cabana with its wet bar and big, soft couch, a gun collection. I said I had something to talk over with him, something that would interest him, emphasis on *interest*, as in the famous, secret interest payments. You bet he was willing to pick me up after school. So the next day, I didn't see the Lexus, but Uncle Joe's big-as-a-house Cadillac SUV instead.

I said I'd missed him. He gave me a look, but the thing was, he really wanted to believe me. It was as simple as that. How did I get the keys to the gun closet—which, because of dopey Joe, Jr., is kept locked tight every minute along with the liquor? Uncle Joe carries them in his pants pocket. It wasn't hard at all. I had this big purse with me, and when I went inside to use the john, I went to the cabinet and picked up a pistol that was black and shiny and ugly. It was already loaded. I put it in my purse and I slipped the keys back into Uncle Joe's pocket when we were saying goodbye.

As soon as I got back home, I called a cab and had it drop me off a block from Louie's house. I took out the pistol, making sure the safety was off, and walked right through the neighborhood with the gun in my hand. Crazy, right? I didn't care anymore. When I rang the bell, Pat opened the door.

"What are you doing here, you little tramp?"

Would I have shot her otherwise? I don't know, but I think I would. I was a Greek, after all, and I hated her. I raised the pistol and pulled the trigger, twice, because I wanted to kill her. I really meant to, and I was shocked and disappointed when I looked down to see her lying there still alive and bleeding.

Louie came rushing into the hall. "What's happened? What's happened? What have you done?" he yells at me like I just walked in off the street, like he never loved me, like all that's really important to him is his wife, who he's been cheating on for four and a half months. He's kneeling on the floor crying and holding on to her, saying things like, "Pat, Pat, I'm so sorry. Don't die, Pat, Jesus, Pat, don't die!" On and on, so that I see he was no different from Uncle Joe after all.

I should have shot him, too. I should have. I'd be happier today.

The big question is should I send this attempt to Dr. Langston? I'm not sure. In my experience, adults aren't fond of the truth, and I can't see attempt number five getting me parole, leniency—or even a positive psychiatric report. These doubts lead to a bad day, which gets worse when Sissy Carmichael of the cornrows and biceps punches me in the face for no reason whatsoever, except that she weighs 175 pounds and I weigh 101. At that moment, I was afraid I'll never get out, never, ever, and I began to have bad thoughts about razor blades and bed sheets that probably would interest Dr. Langston a good deal.

That night, I'm lying on my cot, considering the best way to store up an overdose, when I remember the Greeks again. I'd forgotten Odysseus! *The great tactician, all craft and guile, lord of all the tricks of war,* deep thinking, sly, a liar. He was a killer, too. Remember Penelope's suitors and the poor handmaids, who didn't have much choice, did they, surrounded by people like my uncle Joe?

Anyway, it came to me that Odysseus would have known how to handle Dr. Langston and parole boards and even Uncle Joe, who's paying some of my legal bills. Inspired by Big O's example, I got right up to begin the Sixth Attempt.

I was so upset when Louie said we had to break it off. He was worried about me; he said our wonderful love had been a bad mistake. He had tears in his eyes. "It's all my fault. You'll grow up and understand," he said, but I didn't grow up soon enough. How could I when my heart was broken?

Instead, I stole a gun from Uncle Joe's house while I was

over hanging out with Joe, Jr., and Anthony and a couple of our cousins. I wasn't sleeping good by then. I was nearly out of my mind, because I couldn't bear not to see Louie. I hardly know how I got to his house. I had the pistol out and I guess the safety must have been off. I hadn't even known that it was loaded; I just wanted to scare him.

When the door opened, Pat screamed and the gun went off.

It was awful; all that blood and her screaming. She's such a nice woman; I never meant to hurt her. I wish there was something, anything, I could do to make up for her getting shot.

So, what do you think? Too much, too little? Mrs. Kennelley always said how we had to consider our audience. My audience is Dr. Langston and the parole board, so perhaps something more, which I can add tomorrow. Maybe about how I see Louie differently now—which is certainly true. Something about how I'm over him and getting grown up, and how I'll be a good girl forever if I get out.

This version is definitely the best. It sounds sincere, I think, and it's the kind of thing they're expecting. So maybe I will be released. Odysseus got out of tighter spots than this. I'll get paroled—or maybe even pardoned—and I'll be out of here.

Then Louie had better watch out. I can maybe forgive Pat, but not him. Never. I trusted him, and he deceived me even worse than Uncle Joe. I'll make Louie pay, all right; I just have to be grown up and careful how I do it. I've got to keep thinking of Odysseus instead of Phaedra! But one way or the other, I'm going to settle with Louie.

Dumb Beasts

Clea Simon

I really didn't want to go over when Mrs. M called. Sheila, as I think of her. With most people I'm on a first-name basis immediately. They've invited me into their homes, into some of their most intimate relationships, after all. It only makes sense. But not her. We were introduced formally the first time I came over, but although I immediately reached out, saying, "It's Beth. Please, call me Beth," she never reciprocated.

Her husband's another sort entirely. I think it was his idea to call me the first time. At any rate, he was the one who cared, who wanted everyone to get along. She might've complained about the noise, though. I wouldn't have put that past her.

It was a compatibility issue, that first time. The dog had been hers originally, a yappy little Yorkshire terrier, spoiled and insecure. More of a fashion accessory than a companion, I figured, them both being blondes and all. The Yorkie had been understandably unsettled when they had moved into his townhouse. The presence of his pets—a cat, a parrot, an aquarium full of fish—didn't help the Yorkie's mood, and, to be fair, the cat—an elderly Persian—hadn't made it any easier. But I think they would have worked it out.

Animals do. She was the problem. Couldn't stand the barking, the hissing, the squawking. I tried to tell her it was all part of the change, everybody finding their new place in the social order. She was having none of it. I thought that what really got her was Bridget's betrayal. Bridget—that's the Yorkie—took to Paul right away. I try to keep my feelings out of it. I'm not here for the people anyway. It's all about the animals. That's why I came over when she called.

Paul was away again. Traveling. I don't know what he did. Whatever it was, it kept him on the road, but it sure was profitable. I figured the animals missed him. They do, you know, and not just in that obsessive-grooming, separation-anxiety neurotic way. They become used to us, as we do to them.

"Dumb animals," she said. She didn't get it, never had, if Bridget's rapid defection was any clue. Didn't realize that "dumb" in that context means unable to speak, not stupid. Not that she tried to listen. She was colder than those fish, if you ask me. But then, she didn't want my opinion so I held my tongue. She wasn't really the client.

They were, and I find I do best if I keep my mind clear of human thoughts. Complications. I don't get those as clearly. I think they're not as clear to their owners, half the time. All those convoluted thoughts and dreams, all that longing. All that rage. Animals are straightforward. I want. I have. I am. It's not just my natural gift. I really prefer to work with them.

Still, I couldn't avoid picking up on something when Sheila—Mrs. M—let me in. First of all, she opened the door herself. The last time I'd been here—a molting issue—there'd been a houseboy. Man servant. Whatever you call the help these days. But also, she was bothered, agitated about something. Even I could sense that.

"It's the racket," she said. "I can't hear myself think." So much for dumb, I thought, but I was glad I'd come. It was probably loneliness. I wondered if she'd taken Bridget out for more than the necessary. If she'd played with Lucille—that's the Persian—at all.

"How long is Mr. M away for this time?" I don't call him Paul, not to her. She gave me a look. Was I that transparent? "It's just that he seems to exercise the animals quite a lot. Maybe there's some pent-up energy here."

"I do plenty." She drew herself up, all five-foot-nothing of her. "I'd do more if I had the time." She'd read my mind. "Besides, that's what Alain is for."

As I said, it's none of my business. I smiled as bland a smile as I could conjure up and asked to see the animals. She let me in and I climbed the stairs. Lucille tended to spend her days in Paul's office.

Tucked into the back of the townhouse, it overlooked an alley. The room on the other side had all the sun, but that was Mrs. M's "atelier." She did something with design before they had married. Still, Paul had made a cozy space in that back room, with built-in bookshelves and a window seat that opened to hold odds and ends. The aquarium in the corner acted like another window, colorful and full of life. But Lucille had claimed the wide window seat as her own, rather than go for the fish, and I always suspected Paul left that window cracked for her. So she could smell the wide world through the screen. Lucille was a peaceful sort, as long as her position wasn't questioned. And maybe there were rats in the alley, or at least pigeons.

But even though the midmorning sun was making a rare appearance, highlighting the velvet cushion placed just so, Lucille was nowhere in sight.

"I don't know what's gotten into that cat. Maybe it's age."

"She's not that old." I responded quickly and she gave me that look again. You don't have to be sensitive to pick some things up. Mrs. M had wanted to get rid of Lucille from the start. Even after I'd told her that Bridget had fallen hard for the silver feline, and that Lucille had accepted the dog as her charge and loyal subject.

"Well, maybe she's sick." She motioned me over to Paul's desk. I peered underneath. Two green eyes blinked up at me. "You don't think it's *fleas*, do you?"

"No, Mrs. M." I got down on my hands and knees, cat level, and looked back up at her. From here, she was gigantic. "She never goes out."

Mrs. M snorted, if such a ladylike nose could produce such a sound. For a moment, I was afraid she was about to take a seat beside us.

"If I could have a little time with her alone?" I know that look. Those suspicions. But I'm bonded and insured for my other job as a pet sitter. And my specialty really did pay well enough that I wouldn't have been tempted, even if I were the sort to steal.

She lingered, her pretty eyes narrowed. There was something wrong, something I didn't like coming off her today. Almost a scent. But like I said, people aren't my specialty. That feeling—distrust, dislike, whatever you want to call it—could have been coming from me.

At any rate, she left, and I got comfortable on the thick wool rug, just a few feet from Lucille, letting us both get used to each other.

"I didn't do anything wrong." The thought came to me entire, not in words exactly but as a sense of hurt. Injustice. Someone had been punished unfairly. "I didn't do anything wrong."

I looked at the gray Persian before me and contemplated stroking her. Sometimes the physical contact is calming, making a stronger bond and easier connection. Sometimes . . .

I put my hand out, palm up and fingers extended for her to sniff. She closed her eyes. "So *loud.*"

"Shh." She looked up at me then and sniffed my fingers, inviting me to stroke her long, silky fur.

"What was loud, Lucille? Did someone yell at you?"

"Call me Pussums. He always did." I felt her relax as I rubbed the base of one broad, velvet ear. "And it wasn't a yell. It was a clap."

Now we were getting somewhere. I could imagine Mrs. M slamming those neat, manicured hands together, not caring how sharp the sound to the sensitive feline ears. "Was it Mrs. M?" Lucille looked up at me, silent, and I realized I had no idea what they called her. If they thought of her at all. "Was it the lady?"

"So *loud.*" Lucille had withdrawn back into herself. "I won't sit there again."

I sighed, promising both myself and the Persian that I'd come back before I left, give her silver fur a good brushing. But I wasn't going to get any more from her now. I worked my way to my feet.

"Wa-awk! Honey." Rufus, the parrot, noticed me standing, his greeting an eerie echo of Paul's voice. "Honey?" I didn't know if he called the bird that, or his wife, but Rufus had it down. "Honey?" Maybe Paul had been trying to get Rufus to learn a trick.

"Hey, Rufus. What's up? You want me to do something?" The green bird whistled softly. "Wa-awk." That was it. I don't get much from birds.

"Mrs. M?" Usually Bridget had the run of the house, but as I stood on the landing I heard no sign of her. Not the scuffle of claws on hardwood. Certainly not the barking she'd complained of.

"Oh, I'm down here." I descended to the first floor. She was in the kitchen, browsing the open refrigerator. It must have been the help's day off.

"You wanted me to see Bridget?" She took out an individual container of yogurt and closed the door behind her, like a safe.

"She's in the work room." She meant the basement, and she must have seen the look on my face. "The noise. It's intolerable."

She pointed to a door, and I let myself down. Sure enough,

as soon as I flipped the light switch, Bridget started yapping, bouncing up and down with an urgency I'd not seen in the tiny toy.

"Must go out! Must go out! Now, now, now!" It came through so clear I found it hard to believe Mrs. M didn't hear it. But she stood there, at the top of the stairs.

"Has she had her walk?" I looked around for her leash.

"She did her business. I took her down to the shop, too." Mrs. M had a storefront gallery space for her designs and those of her friends. I thought of it as a clubhouse, but it was a good five blocks away. "Just an hour ago." She said it like she didn't expect me to believe her.

"Must go out! Must go out!"

"She seems restless." My head was hurting. The little dog was loud, and there was an urgency to her yelps.

"Must go out! Now! Now! Now!"

"As you wish." She raised a hand, clearing herself of any involvement and stepped back from the door. As more light came down, I saw the leash, hanging from a brass hook. But before I could snap it onto Bridget's collar, the little dog took off. Scrambling up the stairs, she didn't stop by the front door but made straight for the upper floor. Her claws scraped and scrabbled for their footing and I almost caught up. In this mood, with Lucille already in a funk . . . Behind us, I heard the clip-clip-clip of Mrs. M's heels.

"Must go out! Must go out!" None of this was making sense. The little dog ducked into Paul's office. Ran up to the window. Lucille was back on her pillow, staring into the alley, her tail hanging limp. Bridget barked up at her. "Must go out!"

"Honey? Honey?" Rufus began flying around his cage, strong green wings beating against the sides. "Honey!"

"Must go out!" The little dog leaped up to the window seat, knocking the silver cat aside as she threw herself against the screen. "Must go out! Must go out! Master!"

No! That's what I heard as the silver Persian reared back and hissed. "*Stay!*" Bridget sat back, stunned.

"Wawk! Honey? Honey, *don't!*"

Behind me, I heard a gasp. Mrs. M stood frozen, her face as white as Lucille's undercoat. Then she turned and clattered down the stairs. The animals stared at her departing back, the blonde head bobbing downward. "Wa-awk!"

I scooped Lucille up in my arms. She was shaking, her back tense, fur raised.

"Pussums." I held her close, nuzzling her soft coat until I could feel the trembling subside. "We have to talk."

□ □ □

By the end of the day, the cops had the whole story. Mrs. M hadn't wanted to give it up, but the evidence did it for her. Which was good, because I really didn't want to explain why I had called. Or how I'd happened to unearth the pearl-handled Remington tucked into the window seat. Why she'd taken it back in, after dispatching her husband, I couldn't figure. An animal would have had the sense to bury it, to throw it after him into the dumpster. They found Alain, once they knew. He was traveling in Paul's name, leaving a paper trail that would have had him disappear somewhere in L.A. She was more of a California type anyway.

I was sad, of course. Paul had really loved those animals. But I wasn't surprised. Not really. I guess I'm better at people than I'd thought.

I never did talk to those fish.

Shot by Mistake

Kathleen Chencharik

At the Regalstone, Massachusetts, Police Department, Desk Sergeant Wayne Jennings glanced up from his paperwork. He nudged Officer Dale Roland and said, "Oh, no, here she comes again."

"If it's Monday, it must be Esther," Dale said, following Wayne's gaze. He glanced outside and saw old Miss Esther Forbes, cane in hand, limping along the handicap ramp.

"Wonder what the complaint of the week will be," Wayne said.

"Who could forget the obsessive-compulsive crook who, instead of cleaning her out, cleaned up her apartment," Dale said. "She didn't believe me when I told her it was the housekeeper at the elderly housing complex. And the housekeeper refuses to clean if Esther is at home."

"Can't say I blame her," Wayne said. "My all-time favorite was the alien invasion complete with little green men."

"You mean little green woman, don't you?" Dale corrected.

Wayne nodded. "Poor old Mrs. Kettle," he said, thinking back. "She forgot to remove the facial mask that turned her face green when she went to borrow a cup of sugar from Esther. I don't think they've spoken since."

Wayne and Dale burst out laughing. Wayne pulled a tissue from the box on the counter and blew his nose. Then they both grew silent when they heard the sound of Esther's cane, tap, tap, tapping along the tile floor.

"Cane's new," Dale whispered, knowing Miss Forbes was a bit hard of hearing.

"Bet it's a malpractice case this week."

"Practice? With a cane?" Esther's laughter reverberated throughout the empty hallway as she stopped in front of the desk. She brushed back a strand of gray hair and adjusted her glasses. "I don't need practice for a cane. Crutches maybe, but that's neither here nor there. I came to report a crime."

Dale flipped through the pages of his notebook. "What kind of crime, Miss Forbes?"

"A robbery and shooting."

"Who got robbed and who got shot?" Wayne asked.

"I did." Esther limped over to two chairs set against the wall. She placed her pocketbook on one and took a seat in the other. "Come out here and see for yourselves."

Dale and Wayne came out from behind the desk. They squatted in front of her as she slowly unwrapped a bandage from her lower left leg, exposing a tiny red mark on her shin.

"Doesn't look like a gunshot wound to me," Dale said as he stood up. "Have you seen a doctor?"

"What do doctors know? He didn't believe me either."

"What was stolen?" Wayne asked.

"My brand new state-of-the-art 110 camera." Tears began to well in her eyes.

Dale raised a bushy eyebrow and looked at Wayne. "Do they still make those?"

Wayne shrugged his shoulders, went to the desk and returned with the box of tissues. As he offered one to Esther he said, "I thought everything was digital today."

"Well, that may be," she said, pulling out a tissue and dabbing the corner of her eyes. "But it was brand new to me."

"Tell us what happened," Wayne said.

Esther reached for another tissue, took the whole box instead, then continued. "I had just bought the camera at the town-wide yard sale yesterday. You can ask Olivia Dodson. She sold it to me. Film was included so I stopped by the Buckners' place on my way home to take a few shots of their gardens. They have the best ones in town and they attract lots of wild birds. I had just taken my last shot of a gorgeous red cardinal. The next thing I knew a man came out of nowhere, and I ended up being shot."

"Did you see who it was?" Dale asked.

"At first I thought it was Johnny Cash."

"Isn't he dead?" Dale whispered to Wayne.

"Last I knew," Wayne whispered back.

"So the man looked like Johnny Cash," Dale said, writing in his notebook.

"Well, he was dressed all in black but I can't say for sure he looked like him. He had a pair of nylons pulled down over his head. As a matter of fact they might have been mine. I'm missing a pair."

"What happened next?" Dale asked.

"He demanded my camera. I refused. He pulled out a gun and I started screaming. Nobody came out. Maybe they were all at the yard sale. Anyway, the man covered his ears until I stopped screaming, then lunged for my camera. I got so scared I threw it at him. The camera hit his hand and the gun went off. Lucky I wasn't killed. Then he picked up the camera and high-tailed it off into the woods toward the river."

Wayne looked at Dale. "Did you get it all?"

Dale nodded.

Miss Forbes tucked her bandage into her pocketbook, the box of tissues underneath her arm, then rose from her chair. "If I don't hear from you in a week, you'll be hearing from me." She placed her cane over her shoulder like an infantryman would a rifle, opened the front door and marched down the slate steps to the parking lot.

"Do you believe that?" Dale asked.

"That she was robbed and shot? It has a ring of truth."

"No. That she just stole our last box of tissues."

"Shall I go arrest her and bring her back?"

"No!" Dale shouted a bit louder than he intended. "Let's consider it a gift."

"Good. Because we're straight out with the usual summertime break-ins. We don't have enough men as it is. How are we going to check out her story before she comes back?"

"What about Constable John St. John?" Dale suggested. "He's always looking for something more to do than sit at the polls and post warrants."

"Great idea. Give him a call. Have him check out her story and make sure it doesn't take him longer than a week."

"Copy that," Dale said as he picked up the phone.

Constable John St. John whistled as he picked up his dog Hoover, a small white Bichon, and placed him into a padded milk crate behind the seat of Old Blue, his Free Spirit bicycle. John had named his dog for the great job he did keeping the floor of the children's room at the library free of crumbs.

"We're on duty, Hoover," John said, donning his blue ball cap as he walked his bike down to the end of the driveway. He stopped and glanced out at the Mills River, his only neighbor across the quiet country road. Sunlight filtering through the trees sparkled on the dark water. John gave Hoover a pat on the head. He mounted his bike, turned right, and pedaled toward Olivia's house, a mere three miles away.

As they got under way, Hoover gave a short yip of approval. He put his front paws on the top of the crate, and balancing on his hind legs, he let the wind whip back his curly white ears, exposing the pink skin beneath.

John spotted Olivia moving about in her large front yard. Hoover let out a bark. Olivia glanced up and waved. John signaled with his right arm, then swerved into her dirt driveway. He got off his bike, dropped the kickstand and let Hoover loose. The little white dog raced as fast as he could to greet Olivia, knowing a treat would be in the offing.

"Here you go, Hoover," Olivia said as she reached into a pocket of her jeans, pulled out a dog biscuit and handed it to him.

"I'm surprised he doesn't weigh a ton the way everyone feeds him," John said walking onto the grass to join them.

"But John, who can resist those cute little coal black eyes. And that face." Olivia bent down and scratched Hoover's ear. "You are so-o-o-o adorable."

"Well, thank you, ma'am," John said, scuffing the tip of his sneaker across the lawn.

Olivia looked up and scowled. "Not you, John, your dog." Then she straightened up and smiled. "So where are you two off to today?"

"Actually, this is our destination."

"Huh?"

"I need to ask you a few questions about your yard sale."

Olivia glanced at the word *Constable* above the bill of his ball cap. "Oh? I didn't think I needed a permit. It was a townwide yard sale sponsored by the Friends of the Library."

"I know that. I just need to know whether or not Esther

Forbes was here yesterday."

"Are you kidding? She never misses anything. I bet she hit every yard sale in town."

"Did she buy anything from you?"

Olivia scratched her head. "As a matter of fact she bought an old camera of mine."

"What kind?"

"A Kodak Ektralite 110. I'd had it for years. I'm sure it wasn't worth much, but more than that old skinflint paid me. She got a real bargain, too. I had it tagged for ten dollars. I even threw in my last cartridge of 110 film and loaded it for her. She offered me a buck. I took it just to get rid of her."

John pictured the transaction in his mind's eye and chuckled.

"Esther put in a complaint the camera doesn't work?" Olivia asked.

"No, she claims it was stolen. I'm just here to check out her story."

"Another tall tale?"

"Could be." John turned toward his bike. "Guess I'll head out."

"Kitty home?" Olivia asked, walking alongside him.

"She's working at the bookstore today."

"Tell her to stop by for coffee sometime in the near future, will ya? I miss her."

"That makes two of us. Between the bookstore, writing for the *Regalstone Newsletter*, and taking a class on film developing, she barely has time to have coffee with me." John stopped at his bike. He removed his ball cap, reached into the back pocket of his jeans and pulled out a red-checkered rag. "Gonna be a hot one," he said, wiping sweat from his brow.

Olivia nodded. She tried hard not to laugh when she saw a

tuft of white hair standing at attention on top of his balding head. "Looks like you could use a haircut," she said, biting her lower lip.

"Going to the barber tomorrow," John said, stuffing the rag back into his pocket and replacing his ball cap. He whistled for Hoover, then said, "Oh, before I go, did you hear anything that sounded like a gunshot yesterday?"

"Are you kidding? The way sound travels along the river I hear everything. Yesterday was no exception. It could have been a gunshot. But since there's no hunting on Sunday, and it isn't even hunting season, I just figured it was fireworks. The Fourth of July is only a few days away and even though fireworks are illegal in this state, people still use them. Especially the Buckner teens. They shoot them off before, during and after."

Hoover came at a run. John picked him up and put him in the crate. "You think that's where the sound came from?"

"Pretty sure. It happens this time every year."

"Thanks, Olivia," John said as he mounted his bike.

"You're welcome. And don't forget to have Kitty give me a call."

"Will do." John pedaled out to the road, turned left, and followed the river back home.

□ □ □

The next morning, John returned home from the barbershop and was greeted by Hoover and the aroma of coffee perking atop the gas stove.

"Which hair did they cut?" Kitty asked from the kitchen table. She lowered the *Regalstone Newsletter* she'd been reading and took a sip from her mug of coffee.

"Ha, ha," John said, taking a seat opposite his wife of thirty-five years. "Everyone's a comedian this morning. When I told my barber I wanted him to cut my hair even shorter, he said, 'John, if I cut your hair any shorter, I'd need a license to do brain surgery.' "

Kitty burst out laughing, and nearly lost her coffee. "That's a good one," she managed to say between laughs.

"Do you have any plans today?" he asked once she stopped laughing.

"Nope, I've got a clean slate. Why?"

"I'm going to kayak down river to the Buckners' place. Care to join me?" He got up, grabbed a mug off the stand on the counter and poured himself a cup of coffee.

"You bet. It's been way too long since we've been kayaking together."

"That's because you're always too busy."

Kitty looked at him and curled her upper lip. "Why are you going to the Buckners'? They aren't home."

"Are you sure?" he asked in surprise, returning to his seat.

"Positive. Karen told me they'd be gone for the week. They were supposed to leave last Saturday for Rhode Island. Then on the Fourth of July they were joining family in Newport for a clam boil."

"That's funny. Olivia thought she heard the Buckner teens setting off fireworks on Sunday."

"When did you see Olivia?"

"Yesterday. By the way she wants you to call her."

"Gee thanks for telling me."

"No problem. I'll explain on our way to the Buckners'."

"Maybe they had a change of plans," Kitty said. "You want breakfast?"

"No, thanks. I grabbed a donut on my way home."

"Tonight's my last film-developing class," Kitty said, glancing at her husband.

"Thank goodness. Did you learn anything?"

"I learned," she said, batting her baby blues at him, "that if I had my own darkroom I could save money. Best of all, I could fend off the omnipotent digital age for awhile longer."

"Darkroom, huh?" John tipped back in his chair.

"Yes. A room that is dark. A room that would allow me to spend more time at home." Kitty got up from the table.

John looked up at her askance. "I'm not sure I'd like that."

Kitty cuffed the back of his head.

"Hey. Watch it," John said. "You'll mess up my hair. Besides, I'm only kidding."

"I knew that," she said and bent down to kiss his bald spot.

"Trust me, hon. Ain't nothin' gonna mess that up."

John finished his coffee and got up. "Come on, Hoover, let's get the kayaks." Hoover's white tail waved like a flag as he followed his master outside.

"I'm right behind you!" Kitty called after them. She polished off her coffee, placed the empty mugs into the sink, grabbed her nondigital Konica camera, and locked the door behind her.

They carried the kayaks across the road, and carefully made their way down the sloping river bank. John helped Kitty into her yellow kayak, then handed Hoover to her. With Hoover between her knees, Kitty paddled out to the middle of the river and waited.

Soon, John's red kayak pulled alongside and the transfer of Hoover was made from one to the other.

Kitty looked through her camera's viewfinder. She took a shot of a great blue heron in mid-flight, and two snapping turtles on a log in the water as her kayak glided past. Even Hoover knew better than to bark when he saw a camera in Kitty's hand. After taking a few more pictures, she noticed she had some paddling to do to catch up with her husband. She spotted a different shade of green along the riverbank and saw it was a trash bag inside a boat tied to a dock. The boat was nearly hidden from view by purple loosestrife and weeds. "Did you see that boat back there?" Kitty asked when she finally caught up to John.

"What boat?"

"I guess that answers my question. If it weren't for the bulging green trash bag, I might have missed it, too."

"There are cabins out-of-towners own and use during the summer," John said. "But if there was a trash bag, it could be Chip's boat. He makes a few extra bucks picking up empty cans and bottles. Anyway, the Buckners' place is around the next bend."

Kitty passed John, paddling fast and furious. Hoover barked in protest at no longer being first. He didn't stop until John caught up and rounded the bend ahead of Kitty.

By the time Kitty spotted John, he was pulling his kayak onto land. Hoover jumped out and disappeared into the woods. As her kayak drifted in, John grabbed the front end of it and said, "Maybe you should wait here while I check out the house."

"No way. Pull me in. Besides, if Karen is home she owes me a recipe for the next newsletter."

John rolled his green eyes. He pulled her in, helped her out, then they trudged through the woods, slapping at mosquitoes. Soon they reached the clearing where the Buckner house stood. It was surrounded by colorful flower gardens. Birdhouses dotted the tree line and bird feeders hung everywhere.

"I'll go knock," John said as he walked around to the front of the house.

"I'll see if there are any cars in the garage," Kitty said.

"You mean check out the garden by the garage."

"Whatever."

John knocked on the front door. No answer. The door swung slowly inward as if guided by invisible hands. "Roger? Karen? You home?" Still no answer. He noticed the lock had been broken.

Kitty looked through the window of the garage, then walked through the garden, enjoying the fragrance of the summer flowers. She saw Hoover, rounding the corner of the garage and heading her way. He carried a black rectangular object in his jaws. Although the top half of his body was still white, his face and bottom half were covered in dark brown mud. He sat at her feet and wagged his tail.

"John!" she called. "What kind of camera did you say Esther had?"

"A 110. Why?" he asked, leaving everything as it was and joining Kitty and Hoover in the garden.

"Because I think Hoover found it."

"Good boy," John said. He reached into his back pocket, pulled out a rag, and gently removed the camera from Hoover's mouth. From his front pocket, he took a small plastic bag he kept on hand to pick up after Hoover. He placed the camera inside, then sealed it.

John glanced at Kitty. "There's no one here, but the house has been broken into. Did you check the garage?"

Kitty nodded. "The family car is gone. Everything else looks fine. Maybe Esther scared off the intruder."

"Could be. Whoever was here is long gone now. Let's go back home. I'll take the camera to the police department. They can check for prints, then send someone out to secure the place until the Buckners return."

□ □ □

John brought the camera to the police department, then waited for the results. Dale returned to the front desk.

"Anything?" John asked.

Dale shook his head. "Guess Esther can have her camera back. The water and mud destroyed any prints."

"I can drop it off. I go right by."

A Cheshire cat grin lit up Dale's face. "Be my guest," he said, handing it to John.

John went outside. I said I'd drop it off, he thought, as he hurried down the steps. But I didn't say when.

□ □ □

John helped Kitty clear the table after supper. "Did you say tonight was your last film-developing class?"

"I did," Kitty said. "Why?"

"How would you like to do Esther a big favor and develop the film in her camera?"

"Something tells me it would be more of a favor for you. You think there's something on the film?"

"Maybe."

"I'd want something in return."

"Such as?"

"My own darkroom."

□ □ □

John heard the sound of Kitty's car pull into the driveway later that evening.

"Start making that darkroom," she shouted, bursting through the front door, waving an envelope in her hand.

"You found something?" John shuffled through the pictures, then handed them back to her. "Great job developing them, but I see nothing there worthy of a darkroom."

"That's right, John," Kitty said, sorting through and pulling a picture out. "You look but you don't see. And that's the difference between us."

"What's that supposed to mean?"

Kitty handed him the picture of a cardinal on a bird feeder outside the Buckners' house.

"Yeah. It's a pretty red bird," John said, glancing down at the picture. "And I've heard that a bird in the hand is—"

"Look closer," she said, tapping the picture. "See the window next to the feeder? Can't you see a person looking out?"

John squinted. "Well, I'll be. If you can make this picture bigger, you may get your darkroom after all."

□ □ □

Rain cooled the heat of July. John turned on the wipers of his F150 Ford truck as he drove to the police department on Monday morning. Old Miss Esther Forbes, her cane replaced by an umbrella, was almost to the door. John hurried up the steps, opened the door for her, then followed her inside.

Wayne was sitting behind the front desk.

"Well," Esther said, adjusting her glasses. "It's been a week. Guess you didn't find my camera or the man who shot me."

"Actually, we found both," Wayne said. "But because of the holiday, it took a little longer than expected."

"Really?" A smile lit up her face, looking like a wave in a sea of wrinkles.

"Here's your camera," John said. "We even had your film developed."

"I didn't ask you to," Esther said, the wave receding. "And I'm not paying for it."

"No need to," Wayne said. "As a matter of fact, we'll be paying you."

Esther thumped her ear with her hand. "Something's wrong with my hearing," she said, shifting her gaze from Wayne to John.

"It's true," John said. "One of the pictures identified a man who'd been breaking into houses all over Worcester County."

"You mean I got a picture of Johnny Cash?"

John raised a white eyebrow and looked at Wayne.

Wayne shrugged. "Guess Dale left that part out." He turned back to Esther. "Anyway, we have him behind bars."

Esther looked shocked. "The man's a drinker?"

"No. Dale has him in custody in the holding cell."

"Cell?" Esther shouted. "No. I don't own one. It was only the camera. And it's not a custody case. It was a robbery and a shooting. What's wrong with you people?"

John tapped Esther on the shoulder. When she turned her head, he spoke loudly into her ear. "They arrested the man who shot you."

"Well why didn't you say so? Who is it?"

"His name is Shawn Mistake. He was renting a cabin. When I got in touch with the owner, he identified him as the renter."

"Oh, no," Esther said, shaking her head. "You'll never convince me I was shot by mistake!"

Flowers for Amelia

Kate Flora

Amelia and I have been friends since I was five and her family moved into the new house next door. I was the only child of older parents, timid and cautious and rule-bound. I had internalized my mother's soft-voiced admonitions and was careful not to scuff my shoes or get my clothes dirty. The day we met I was wearing my favorite dress, watermelon pink with a crinoline and a white collar, tied with a big bow in the back, serving tea under the flowering dogwood tree to my three favorite dolls—Lady Caroline, Miss Pink, and Mrs. Carl Smith.

I had been allowed, for this special occasion, to use the blue-and-white doll's tea service from when my mother was a girl that was real china, the one that usually stayed, untouched, on the middle shelf of my bookcase. I was just pouring tea into the first cup when she came roaring into the yard like a small, red-haired tornado and sent the tea table flying.

Amelia was six, a whole year older, the youngest of five and the only girl. Trying to hold her own against all those older brothers had made her bold and fearless. A wild-haired, overalled tomboy, Amelia was never still and rarely quiet. She came crashing into our yard while the movers were still carrying in their furniture, surveyed me and my scattered guests with her odd Husky-blue eyes, then planted her grubby hands on her hips, and said, "Oh, goody. You're a girl."

Without asking if it was okay, she grabbed my hand and hauled me next door to meet her parents. On that first day, Amelia didn't give me time for second thoughts or observing the forms. From the moment I took her outstretched hand and did the unthinkable—left Lady Jane and the others lying scattered in the dirt and went out of our yard without permission—I began what would become a life-long pattern of following Amelia and her suggestions.

I was startled and breathless then, and within an hour, utterly enchanted. I've pretty much been that way since, whenever Amelia chooses to come darting into my life, and that was over half a century ago.

When I look back over the years—something we tend to do when we realize that we've got less ahead of us than behind—Amelia is responsible for nearly all the times I deviated from the narrow course I was set upon by my parents. She bummed the cigarette from Cary Randall that we smoked behind her garage in seventh grade. She stole the razor I first used to shave my legs from one of her brothers, and I did it during a sleepover at her house. I did a pretty awful job that left me bleeding from a dozen wounds and looking like I'd been dancing among razor wire, but despite the gore, I felt defiantly proud. It was a defining moment in my awkward journey toward womanhood.

Amelia took me to buy my first bra, too, weeks after she'd given me one of her old ones and my mother still hadn't taken me shopping. I'm sure she meant to get around to it; only my poor mother was so reserved she could hardly utter the word "bra" without blushing. She ordered hers from a catalogue so she wouldn't have to face a salesgirl. Finally impatient, Amelia got her own mother, the pretty but spacey Annette, to drop us off at W.T. Grants. Of course, I couldn't blame Annette for being spacey. No one could endure the incessant chaos of the Thomas household without learning to tune things out. But Annette Thomas tuned out randomly rather than selectively, so we took a chance that day, letting her drive away. She might not remember to come back.

Amelia wasn't worried. "Hey," she said, "if she doesn't come back, we'll hitch a ride home." The very thought gave me shivers.

Together, blushing and giggling in the dressing room, we each bought a couple of bras and several pairs of bikini panties. Our colored bras and bikini panties seemed so risqué at the time. Today, in this era of thongs and Wonder Bras, they'd be modest by anyone's standards. But back then, women carried the whole burden of propriety. If anything happened sexually, we were to blame, even if we were innocent victims. Of course, I wasn't thinking about any of that then. I was just guiltily giddy about grown-up underwear, and relieved about how things would be at school.

Without Amelia's intervention, I would have bounced unrestrained through junior high with no protection from those creepy blemished boys and their grabbing hands. Back in our day, junior-high boys were free to sexually harass girls. The teachers all knew but nobody did a thing about it. At least a bra was something. And Amelia taught me to carry a book against my chest.

When my mother came into my room and found my new underwear lying on the bed, she'd sighed and shaken her head, sighed again and then quietly admitted the purchase was probably a good thing. "I hadn't realized you were so grown up." She and my father always seemed baffled by the challenge of having a daughter after more than twenty years of sedate married life. Though she was only a year older, Amelia often filled the role that my mother should have. My mother handled housekeeping, manners, and propriety.

Amelia dealt with bras, periods, shaving, and boys.

Boys, especially. Having four older brothers had made her a supreme manipulator and given her a keen understanding of the male psyche. It also made her too competitive, with a desperate need to win even when winning didn't matter or she didn't even want what she won. It was so hardwired she couldn't help it. Amidst all those big, loud boys, she had to fight just to hold her own. As we grew older and better at articulating our feelings, she stopped trying to win against me. Not that that happened very often, since I almost always did what Amelia wanted.

She did steal my first boyfriend, Teddy, though. It's supposed to be one of those things that leads to secret animosity and life-long grudges, but that's not how it was for us. Men were drawn to Amelia like moths to flame. They couldn't help it. In a way, she was a kind of flame. Not just her hair, though that always stayed bright and red and didn't darken with time, and she truly did have a temper that matched. They were drawn to Amelia because of her animation, the sense she always gave that life was full of possibility and she was perched on the cusp of an adventure.

Amelia was as alive at twenty, and thirty, and forty, as that day at six when she charged into my yard and dragged me from sedate tea parties into a fuller, crazier life. Being within her orbit seemed more exciting than any place else a person could be. So how could anyone expect a man to resist?

The boyfriend thing wasn't a very big deal anyway. It didn't take me long to realize that a guy who was attracted to Amelia probably wasn't going to be right for me. The one time I stole a guy from her, he wasn't hard to steal because being with her was making him nuts, a poor trapped fly buzzing in crazy circles. That was my Jim. I married him and we've had decades of placid bliss while Amelia has torn through three marriages and a couple explosive affairs—including one in which the wronged wife threatened her with a gun and Amelia had to knock her senseless to get the gun away.

Along the way, her own broken hearts and occasional pangs of guilt about hearts she's broken have fueled enough hours of phone conversations to keep Ma Bell solvent for a good long time.

She was the maid of honor at my wedding; I've stood up with her three times, the second two keeping my fingers crossed that this time it would take. But marriage requires patience and flexibility, and the ability to stay in one place long enough to work things out, while Amelia skitters around like mercury. She can barely read a magazine article without getting up to pace. She'd rather be hiking, kayaking, windsurfing, or skiing. When night falls, she likes to be arguing in a smoky bar, doing hot yoga, or speaking passionately at a public meeting.

I have sometimes thought, in my more cynical moments, that the rest of us, the *ordinary people* who get tired and need rest or quiet, ought to bleed her and drink her blood. But whatever my criticisms of her disordered personal life might be, she has always been the best of friends. Amelia was my first visitor after my daughter Anna was born, peeping around the door of my hospital room to be sure she was in the right place, then coming in with a picnic basket full of wonderful and wicked food. Champagne and fresh squeezed orange juice for mimosas. Two cups of heavenly espresso now that coffee was no longer forbidden in the interest of little brains and fingers and toes. Paté and gherkins. Crisp crackers and creamy triple crème blue. Real crystal flutes of decadent chocolate mousse and real silver spoons.

We clinked our glasses and Amelia said, "Here's to daughters. May yours rule the world." And I cried from gratitude, and hormones, and pure love.

It was Amelia who bullied the oncologist and the surgeon when I found a suspicious lump in my breast. While Jim sat beside me, paralyzed by the possibility that I might die, Amelia researched and read and questioned and created an entire treatment plan while I was still at square one trying to grasp what had hit me.

Amelia is my big sister and my best friend, rolled into one. She's always been there at the other end of the phone or a long or short drive. We can pick up where we left off without awkwardness or preliminaries. We finish each other's sentences. Sometimes we're more like an old married couple than Jim and I are.

Amelia has always been there, and now life is going to dim that fire and there isn't anything that she or I can do to stop it.

When Amelia called, her voice was small and scared and not like her. Not roaring out of the receiver, but a whisper. I knew it was bad news before she said anything. She told me she'd been diagnosed with pancreatic cancer. "The doctor says they could operate, but the likelihood of success is small. He told me to put my affairs in order."

At that, briefly, the old Amelia was back. "He was such a prissy old wart that I didn't ask him what order. Best to worse? Most recent to earliest? Best looking to most plain? Longest to shortest? I just nodded. Actually, for once I was speechless. You've been here, so you know. What's a person supposed to do or say when some authority figure in a white lab coat decrees that you're gonna die a mean, nasty death pretty soon and there's nothing they can do?"

I was sitting on my sun porch when she called. It was warm and pleasant, the inside plants all blooming and giving off gentle scents. I had some vaguely Eastern music on for the meditation I thought I might do. Outside, my gardens, newly emerged after the winter's cold, were hopeful tufts of varied greens. For a moment, I thought, *If I hang up now, I can pretend I never got this call. My life will still be intact. I can pretend that Amelia is the same.* But in all our lives—all those years of being there for each other—I had never before heard Amelia scared. And I could tell just from those few words that she was absolutely terrified.

"I'm on my way," I said. "Hold on. I'll be there as soon as I can."

I lived in Boston; Amelia lived in New York. I called Jim at his office and told him where I was going and why, said I might not be back for his company dinner the next day, and got his sincere, "Give her my love." Then I threw some things in a bag and jumped in my car.

Amelia was in her sitting room, looking elegant and ravaged. She wore a purple velvet tunic over lighter purple satin pants, a heavily embroidered purple and magenta scarf around her neck like a priest's vestment. Her long, graying red hair curled and flowed magnificently, alive and springy and undaunted. She looked like an ancient, battle-worn queen preparing to board her Viking ship and sail away in a burst of flame.

"There's a bottle of wine in the fridge," she said. "Can you open it?"

"Should you be . . ." I began. Then realized I was an idiot. What I'd been about to ask was the equivalent of, 'Shouldn't you be avoiding pleasure for the sake of your health when you've been told death is inevitable?'

"Is it very bad?" I asked.

We drank the wine and she told me just how bad it was. Badder than bad, she said, like being gnawed alive by rats from the inside out. And Amelia was anything but a coward. From time to time, I saw the rats bite. Saw her jaw set and quiver and her face go absolutely white. This wasn't newly received news. I was the "little sister." She'd kept it from me as long as she could.

"And of course," she said, pouring more wine into her glass, "it's getting worse all the time. They're giving me morphine now. That's the best they can do. They keep giving me more and more of it. Soon I won't be Amelia anymore. I'll be a zoned-out, brain-dead zombie. But . . ."

She lowered her voice and leaned toward me, as though her

house was full of spies. “They will be very careful not to give me too much, because then . . . Oh horrors . . . I might die before the rats have eaten their fill.”

She leaned back in her chair, using her arms to find the position that hurt the least. “Medicine is such a joke.”

She drained her glass and held it out for more. “How long have we been friends?”

“You’re fifty-nine, and you were six when we met. So, fifty-three years.”

“That’s a long time, isn’t it.”

“Not long enough,” I said.

I was mad, but not at her. I was mad that now we’d never get to be the willful, eccentric old ladies we’d always planned on being. Wearing red hats and purple and other gaudy colors, and smoking dope with impunity. Listening to The Stones at full volume. Now I’d have to be on the porch of the home alone, rocking in my lonely white chair, waiting for her voice to suggest some mischief or make a telling comment about the staff, or to remind me of one of the crazy things we’d done.

It just wasn’t fair. I blinked to hold back my tears.

“Will you stay overnight?” she said.

“As long as you want.”

“Overnight would be lovely. And will you make dinner? Something really decadent?”

“Do you remember when Anna was born? A feast like that?”

“Yes.” Her voice was weak. “A feast like that.”

I made a list of what she wanted. As I rose to go to the store, she stopped me. “Before you go . . . will you go out to the garden and pick me a bouquet of Lily of the Valley? I’d like it in one of those blue glasses from the kitchen.”

I wondered, with her elegant garb and her love of luxury,

why she'd picked something so plain. "I could get you roses. Or stargazer lilies. Or a whole bouquet of scented flowers. Wouldn't you like that better?"

"I'd like . . ." She adjusted her position, trying to be comfortable, wearing the strain of it like a tight white mask. She'd put off telling me until she couldn't wait any longer. "I'd just like Lily of the Valley from my garden."

I picked a lavish bunch of Lily of the Valley and put them in the blue glass, setting it on the table beside her chair. Then I drove to the store.

When I returned, she was asleep. I went quietly into the kitchen and started fixing food. On the kitchen table a book was open, one of her gardening books. As I marked her place and picked it up to move it, I saw that it was a book about poisonous and medicinal plants. I opened it again to the place I'd marked. Amelia had been reading about Lily of the Valley. After a few hours, the book warned, even the water the flowers have been sitting in is poisonous.

Precautions should be taken so that vessels used for food and drink are not also used as vases without a thorough cleaning. Teapots were mentioned, and canning jars.

And glasses.

I removed the bookmark and put the book back on the shelf with her other gardening books. Then I finished making dinner. When it was ready, I placed the bouquet of flowers in the center of the table and woke Amelia.

She seemed stronger and almost defiantly happy as we had our lobster, asparagus, hot bread, and champagne. By the time I cleared plates smeared with the last streaks of decadent chocolate, she was fading.

"I have a woman who comes in to help out in the morning," she said, her voice small, as though talking exhausted her. "Before I go to bed, I always leave a glass of water beside the sink for her to mix my medicine. I can't drink anything that's too cold, you see, so we've worked out this system. Then she mixes it and brings it in."

She looked at the flowers and then at me, and nodded. "You'll be leaving early, won't you?"

I'd thought I was supposed to be there with her until the end. But she had another plan, and I always do what Amelia wants.

Obediently, I said, "Jim has a business dinner, and I promised . . ."

"I'm so glad you came," she said. "Come sit beside me until I fall asleep, will you?"

We talked in murmurs as she faded in and out of sleep. Small snatches of memory. Pregnancy scares. Her abortion. The one man she'd truly loved, the one she couldn't hold. Once, she asked about Lady Jane. Did I still have her or had I given her to Anna?

Later, she ordered me to get a pen and paper, and gave instructions for her funeral. "I have most of it written out. In the desk drawer. Be sure I'm buried in my purple, with the scarf. It looks so regal."

"What shoes, Amelia?"

"In my closet. In a box. Purple boots. Be sure they use the purple boots. And wasteful or not, I want my gold necklace and my amethyst earrings. I want you to have the opals. That's all in my will, of course."

She took another dose of medicine. It must have finally kicked in then, because she fell into a deep sleep. I kissed her forehead and stayed in my chair, watching her sleep.

Early in the morning, I put on her kitchen gloves, strained the Lily of the Valley water into a clean glass, and left it by the sink. Then I put the flowers in fresh water and set them in the center of the table.

I drove home in silence. No radio. No audio book. Just the soundtrack of my life as it intersected with Amelia's. Imagination is a powerful thing. An hour into the drive, I distinctly heard the clink of a spoon on glass. Later, I felt a tug, something like a labor pain, and then an emptiness.

When I got home and checked my machine, a sorrowful voice regretted to inform me that Amelia had passed.

Contributors' Notes

Stephen Allan's stories have appeared in *Spinetingler Magazine, Flashing in the Gutters,* and the *Thuglit* anthology, *Hardcore Hardboiled.* He has an MFA in Creative Writing and the paperwork to prove it. You can read his random thoughts at noirwriter.blogspot.com. Steve lives in Maine with his wife and two children. He owes all his success to them.

Norma Burrows was born and raised in New England. She currently lives in the seacoast area of New Hampshire with her family. She has a story in *Seasmoke*, a crime anthology, and is a member of Sisters in Crime. Visit her at normaburrows.com

Kathleen Chencharik has published poetry, articles, and short stories in numerous publications. She was ecstatic when hand-written notes such as "Too Hokey" appeared on rejections from *Woman's World* mini mystery. Her first story for *AHMM* Mysterious Photo Contest received honorable mention, with many more to follow. Now, thanks to Level Best Books, her first mystery story has been booked and printed.

John Clark, a long-time member of the Maine library community, is a regular contributor to *Behavioral and Social Sciences Librarian, Wolf Moon Journal,* and *The Sebasticook Valley Weekly.* When not writing, he gardens, collects New Age music and enters sweepstakes. He lives in Hartland, ME, with his wife, Dr. Beth Clark, a professor at Husson College.

C. M. Falcone has published fiction in *The Larcom Review* and is currently working on her first mystery novel. In addition to her writing, she is also an RN and works in a Neonatal Intensive Care Unit. She lives in Guilford, CT, with her family.

Kat Fast dabbles in watercolor and crafts besides writing. She hasn't held an honest job since the 1980s, preferring to give seminars on business writing and also contracting to convert truly ugly documentation into works of beauty. When you contact Kat about the novel tucked in her drawer, type your message: she's a professional handwriting analyst. Kat, her husband, dog, and two cats live in Weston, MA.

Kate Flora, former attorney, is the author of eleven books. Thea Kozak returns in 2008 in *Stalking Death* and her Joe Burgess series continues with *The Angel of Knowlton Park. Finding Amy: A True Story of Murder in Maine*, co-written with a police officer, was a 2007 Edgar nominee, and her story "Mr. McGregor's Garden" was a Derringer nominee. She is researching a new true crime and plotting a light-hearted series. Flora's stories have appeared in *Sisters on the Case* and in *Per Se*, an anthology of fiction. She teaches writing for Grub Street in Boston.

Judith Green is a sixth-generation resident of a village in Maine's western mountains, happy to have three other generations living nearby. Formerly director of adult education for her eleven-town school district, she continues to volunteer in adult literacy, and has twenty-five high-interest/low-level books for adult new readers in print. Her Maine high-school English teacher/sleuth hopes to star soon in a novel set in England.

Woody Hanstein has been a trial lawyer for over twenty-five years. He also teaches at the University of Maine at Farmington and coaches that college's rugby team. He is the author of five mysteries: *Not Proven, Cold Snap, State's Witness, Mistrial,* and *Sucker's Bet.* He is also a co-publisher of www.dailybulldog.com, a highly acclaimed online daily newspaper that covers the foothills of western Maine.

Vaughn Hardacker, a member of the New England Chapter of the MWA, has had stories published in several magazines. His story, "It's My Job," was published in *Mouth Full of Bullets* June 2007 edition and is included in an anthology of the Best of MFOB's first year. He lives in New Hampshire.

Steve Liskow left teaching English to resume writing. He has also acted, directed, designed, or produced ninety theatrical productions and a training video on teaching Shakespeare, and teaches a playwriting workshop. "Running on Empty" appeared in *Still Waters* last year. A member of Sisters in Crime and MWA, he is working on a PI series and a stand-alone novel.

Ruth M. McCarty became an editor and partner in Level Best Books in 2006. Her short mysteries have appeared in *Undertow, Riptide, Windchill, Seasmoke,* and *Still Waters*, all anthologies by Level Best Books. Ruth has received honorable mentions in *Alfred Hitchcock Mystery Magazine* and *N.E.W.N.* for her flash fiction. Please visit her website at www.ruthmmccarty.com

Susan Oleksiw is the author of five mysteries featuring Chief of Police Joe Silva (*Murder in Mellingham, Double Take, Family Album, Friends and Enemies,* and *A Murderous Innocence*), and numerous stories featuring Anita Ray, a Hindu-American photographer living in India. Her *Reader's Guide to the Classic British Mystery* is considered a classic, and she co-edited *The Oxford Companion to Crime and Mystery Writing*. She is co-founder of

Level Best Books, and co-founded The Larcom Press, publisher of *The Larcom Review* and several mysteries. www.susanoleksiw.com

Margaret Press publishes true crime (*A Scream on the Water*) and mystery fiction. Her essay "Salem as Crime Scene" appeared in the award-winning anthology *Salem: Place, Myth and Memory*. "Feral" (*Windchill*) and "Wednesday's Child" (*Still Waters*) launched a collection of concurrent stories viewing one murder from different points of view. "Family Plot" expands that collection with a sequel of sorts. Press can be reached at www.margaretpress.com and www.whokilledscottrogo.com.

Libby Mussman is a true New Englander, raising her two sons in the town where she was born. After living in Massachusetts long enough to no longer be a newcomer, she moved to Maine. Grandchildren are her delight. "The Name Game" is her first publication.

A. J. (Ang) Pompano has been writing short fiction for more than twenty years. His kayaking sleuth, Quincy Lazzaro, was introduced in "The Copy Cat Didn't Have Nine Lives," published in *Still Waters: Crime Stories by New England Writers.* A past winner of the Helen McCloy/Mystery Writers of America Scholarship, Ang has written many academic pieces including one on teaching detective fiction. He lives in Connecticut with his wife, Annette, and his dog, Quincy.

Pat Remick won the 2007 Al Blanchard Award for "Mercy 101," published in *Still Waters*, and has a novel-in-progress—"Murder Most Municipal." The veteran newspaper, wire service, newsletter, Web and television journalist has co-authored two nonfiction books, including *21 Things Every Future Engineer Should*

Know. She lives in Portsmouth, NH, with co-author/husband, Frank Cook, and their two sons. www.PatRemick.com

Joseph Ricker grew up in Sanford, ME. After graduating from high school he attended Marion Military Institute. After living in Oxford, MS, for several years he moved to Portland, ME, and is currently working on an MFA in Creative Writing through Goddard College. "Ice Shack" is his first fiction publication.

Stephen D. Rogers has published over five hundred stories and poems in more than two hundred publications. His website, www.stephendrogers.com, includes a list of new and upcoming titles as well as other timely information.

J. E. Seymour lives in a small town in seacoast NH and has had short stories published in *Windchill, Thriller UK Magazine, Shots Crime and Mystery Magazine, A Cruel World, Shred of Evidence, Mouth Full of Bullets*, and *Mysterical-E.*

Clea Simon is the author of three nonfiction books and the Theda Krakow mysteries, *Mew is for Murder, Cattery Row, Cries and Whiskers*, and the upcoming *Probable Claws* (Poisoned Pen Press). A frequent contributor to such publications as the *Boston Globe*, *Boston Phoenix*, and *San Francisco Chronicle*, she lives in Cambridge, MA, with her husband, Jon, and their cat, Musetta.

Janice Law has written the Edgar-nominated Anna Peters mystery series and nine novels published by Houghton Mifflin, Walker Books, and St. Martin's. They have gone into UK, Danish, and Japanese versions. She regularly publishes short stories in *Ellery Queen* and *Alfred Hitchcock Mystery Magazine,* and has had stories selected for the *Best American Mystery Stories* series (1998) and the

Fourth Annual *The World's Best Mystery and Crime Stories*, among other anthologies. Her most recent publications are *The Night Bus, The Lost Diaries of Iris Weed,* and *Voices;* the latter two were nominated for the Connecticut Center for the Book Fiction Prize in 2003 and 2004. In addition to fiction, she has published three history books and numerous articles. She teaches English at the University of Connecticut. www.janicelaw.com

John Urban grew up in Springfield, MA, and now lives in Wellesley. His Steve Decatur short story "Halfway Rock" appeared in *Seasmoke*. He is working on a novel featuring Steve Decatur, which is set along the waters of Buzzards Bay and Rhode Island Sound. "Courtesy Call" is dedicated to two close friends, police officers Amico Barone and Denis Sheehan.

Mo Walsh was a bingo caller for seven years and has the scars to prove it. She now writes weekly newspaper features and is co-coordinater of the South Shore Writers Club. Mo's stories have appeared in *Mary Higgins Clark Mystery Magazine*, *Woman's World*, *Windchill,* and *Still Waters*. She lives in Weymouth, MA, with one husband, three sons, an old beagle, and five novels in progress.

Leslie Wheeler is the author of two Miranda Lewis "living history" mysteries: *Murder at Plimoth Plantation* and *Murder at Gettysburg*. For her short fiction, she often uses Cambridge, MA, where she lives with her teenage son and a feisty feline, as the setting. "Twenty-One Days" is her fourth story to appear in a Level Best Books anthology. When not writing, Leslie reads many, many great stories as chair of the Al Blanchard Award Committee. A board member of Sisters in Crime, she currently serves as Speakers Bureau Coordinator. www.lesliewheeler.com.

Mike Wiecek lives outside Boston, at home with the kids. He has traveled widely in Asia and worked many different jobs, mostly in finance. His stories have won a Shamus and two Derringers; he was a finalist for the PWA's Best First PI Novel. His novel *Exit Strategy* was short-listed for the ITW Thriller Award. www.mwiecek.com.

Deadfall

Crime Stories by New England Writers

edited by
Kate Flora, Ruth McCarty
& Susan Oleksiw

Please send me ______ copies @ $15 per copy _________

postage & handling ($2 per book) ___________

Total $________________

Please make your check payable to Level Best Books.

If you wish to pay by credit card, you may order through our website at www.levelbestbooks.com.

Send book(s) to:

Name ________________________________

Address ________________________________

City/Town ______________________________